"I cannot live without you,"
the Duke said softly.

For a moment they looked into each other's eyes. The Duke felt Verena tremble and knew that her heart was beating as violently as his. Then his arms tightened and very slowly, as if he must savour the moment, his lips sought hers.

His kiss was as soft as the touch of a butterfly's wing, and yet she felt as if he lifted her high in the sky towards the sun. The world was forgotten.

"I love you!" the Duke exclaimed hoarsely. "God, how I love you!"

Books by Barbara Cartland

- THE ADVENTURER
- AGAIN THIS RAPTURE
- ARMOUR AGAINST LOVE
- THE AUDACIOUS ADVENTURESS
- BARBARA CARTLAND'S BOOK OF BEAUTY AND HEALTH
- THE BITTER WINDS OF LOVE
- BLUE HEATHER
- BROKEN BARRIERS
- THE CAPTIVE HEART
- THE COIN OF LOVE
- THE COMPLACENT WIFE
- COUNT THE STARS
- CUPID RIDES PILLION
- DANCE ON MY HEART
- DESIRE OF THE HEART
- DESPERATE DEFIANCE
- THE DREAM WITHIN
- A DUEL OF HEARTS
- ELIZABETH EMPRESS OF AUSTRIA
- ELIZABETH IN LOVE
- THE ENCHANTED MOMENT
- THE ENCHANTED WALTZ
- THE ENCHANTING EVIL
- ESCAPE FROM PASSION
- FOR ALL ETERNITY
- A GHOST IN MONTE CARLO
- THE GOLDEN GONDOLA
- A HALO FOR THE DEVIL
- A HAZARD OF HEARTS
- A HEART IS BROKEN
- THE HEART OF THE CLAN
- THE HIDDEN EVIL
- THE HIDDEN HEART
- THE HORIZONS OF LOVE
- IN THE ARMS OF LOVE
- THE IRRESISTIBLE BUCK
- JOSEPHINE EMPRESS OF FRANCE
- THE KISS OF PARIS
- THE KISS OF THE DEVIL
- A KISS OF SILK
- THE KNAVE OF HEARTS
- THE LEAPING FLAME
- A LIGHT TO THE HEART
- LIGHTS OF LOVE
- THE LITTLE PRETENDER
- LOST ENCHANTMENT
- LOST LOVE
- LOVE AND LINDA
- LOVE AT FORTY
- LOVE FORBIDDEN
- LOVE HOLDS THE CARDS
- LOVE IN HIDING
- LOVE IN PITY
- LOVE IS AN EAGLE
- LOVE IS CONTRABAND
- LOVE IS DANGEROUS
- LOVE IS MINE
- LOVE IS THE ENEMY
- LOVE ME FOREVER
- LOVE ON THE RUN
- LOVE TO THE RESCUE
- LOVE UNDER FIRE
- THE MAGIC OF HONEY
- MESSENGER OF LOVE
- METTERNICH: THE PASSIONATE DIPLOMAT
- MONEY, MAGIC AND MARRIAGE
- NO HEART IS FREE
- THE ODIOUS DUKE
- OPEN WINGS
- OUT OF REACH
- PASSIONATE PILGRIM
- THE PRETTY HORSEBREAKERS
- THE PRICE IS LOVE
- A RAINBOW TO HEAVEN
- THE RELUCTANT BRIDE
- THE RUNAWAY HEART
- THE SCANDALOUS LIFE OF KING CAROL
- THE SECRET FEAR
- THE SMUGGLED HEART
- A SONG OF LOVE
- STARS IN MY HEART
- STOLEN HALO
- SWEET ADVENTURE
- SWEET ENCHANTRESS
- SWEET PUNISHMENT
- THEFT OF A HEART
- THE THIEF OF LOVE
- THIS TIME IT'S LOVE
- TOUCH A STAR
- TOWARDS THE STARS
- THE UNKNOWN HEART
- THE UNPREDICTABLE BRIDE
- A VIRGIN IN MAYFAIR
- A VIRGIN IN PARIS
- WE DANCED ALL NIGHT
- WHERE IS LOVE?
- THE WINGS OF ECSTASY
- THE WINGS OF LOVE
- WINGS ON MY HEART
- WOMAN, THE ENIGMA

BARBARA CARTLAND

59
THE ODIOUS DUKE

A JOVE BOOK

THE ODIOUS DUKE

A Jove book / published by arrangement with
the author

PRINTING HISTORY
Pyramid edition / November 1973
Sixth Pyramid printing / August 1977
Jove edition / January 1982

All rights reserved.
Copyright © 1973 by Barbara Cartland.
This book may not be reproduced in whole or in part,
by mimeograph or any other means, without permission.
For information address: Jove Publications, Inc.,
200 Madison Avenue, New York, New York 10016.

ISBN: 0-515-06123-9

PRINTED IN THE UNITED STATES OF AMERICA

Author's Note

Readers interested in history will like to know that Highwaymen on the roads in the 17th or 18th Century constituted a very real threat to the Banks.

For instance, in 1815 a $15,000 consignment of Bullion for the Bank at Chipping North was stolen by Highwaymen with the result that the Bank had to close down.

In this story, which takes place in 1824, all references to Wellington's armies in the Peninsula and at Waterloo are authentic. To this day the 14th Light Dragoons use King Joseph's silver *pot de chambre* at Mess functions and drink toasts from it in champagne, after which the pot is placed ceremoniously upon the drinker's head.

1

The Duke of Selchester tooled his team of four prime, perfectly matched chestnuts with consummate skill round the corner from Alford Street into Park Lane.

He then had only a short distance to travel before he pulled into the gravel sweep before the imposing pillared entrance of Selchester House and drew his horses to a standstill with a style that was unmistakable.

As he did so he took his watch from his waistcoat pocket and exclaimed:

"We have beaten the record, Fowler, by five minutes and thirty-five seconds!"

"I were sure Your Grace could do it!" his groom replied. "A remarkable piece of driving, if Your Grace will permit me to say so!"

"Thank you, Fowler."

The Duke stepped gracefully down from his Phaeton. His servants watching him were all admiringly conscious that in his many-tiered driving coat, with his high hat at an angle on his dark hair, his hessian boots shining from the application of champagne they received every day, he was very much a Corinthian.

"A Non-pareil" was the expression used to describe him by the younger members of White's Club, who followed slavishly the manner in which he tied his cravats, the cut of the coats fashioned on him by Weston, and the innumerable little individual quirks of fashion which he introduced from time to time.

None of his imitators, however, could quite emulate the Duke in the manner in which he carried himself and the way in which he could set down an impertinence or the shadow of a presumption by the mere look in his eyes and an infinitesimal lift of his eyebrows.

Well over six feet with a superb carriage, the Duke, as he passed through the doorway of Selchester House, seemed to tower above his array of liveried flunkeys despite the fact that none of them was employed unless they topped six feet.

He handed his hat to one, his gloves to another, and allowed the Butler, an elderly man with a face like an Archbishop, to remove his driving coat, thus revealing one of his famous plain whip-cord riding jackets which fitted without a wrinkle across his broad shoulders and over which his tailor had spent many sleepless nights before bringing it to the perfection demanded by its owner.

Only Mr. Weston—cutter and fitter to the Quality—was aware that, although the Duke seemed so thoroughly at ease in his clothes, he was in fact a difficult Gentleman to dress.

It was certainly not the fault of his figure, which, with his great breadth of shoulder tapering to narrow hips, was a tailor's dream. It was rather the fact that the Duke had the rippling muscles of an athlete—for His

Grace was extremely proficient at boxing and fencing besides spending many hours in the saddle—which made it hard to achieve the effect of effortless languor which the fashion demanded.

The Duke now, though he had been driving at an inordinate speed for nearly three hours, was not in the least fatigued. Alert and with an air of satisfaction he walked across the marble Hall with its huge family portraits and inlaid French furniture bought by his Grandfather for a song during the French Revolution, towards the Garden Salon.

Two flunkeys in the Selchester Livery of blue and yellow flung open double mahogany doors and His Grace passed through them into a delightful room running the whole breadth of the house.

It had no less than five windows opening onto the large garden which lay behind the enormous grey stone mansion enriched by turrets which had been built by the Duke's Grandfather.

The garden, bathed in spring sunshine, was ablaze with daffodils and corcuses. The formal walks, like the paved terrace, were edged with hyacinths and tulips which, all of identically the same height and growth, gave by their uniformity, the impression of being like soldiers on parade.

It was the King when he was Regent who had teased the Duke a few years earlier by calling him "His Most Noble Perfection" and the joke had become a fact rather than a jest.

Almost unconsciously the Duke had begun to expect perfection around him so that everyone in his household strove not only to serve him to the best of their ability, but almost to perform miracles because he expected it of them.

He had been sure, His Grace thought now with complacency, that his horses could beat the record from

Epsom to London set by Lord Fletcher—a notable Whip—three years earlier.

He looked forward to telling the "Four Horse Club" of his achievement, and he knew that it would infuriate a number of his contemporaries who had themselves tried over and over again to achieve a new record and failed.

The Duke sat down at his desk to look at a large pile of invitation cards which had been set there by his secretary, and several unopened letters on which the handwriting or a faint fragrance proclaimed them as being of an intimate nature.

The Duke glanced at them without any particular interest. Then as with an air of boredom he picked up one of the letters and an emerald-studded letter-opener shaped like a dagger, his secretary, Mr. Graystone, came into the room and stood bowing respectfully.

A grey-haired man of middle age, it was on his shoulders that the smooth running of His Grace's residences rested. Chief among them were Selchester Castle in Kent, Selchester House in London, a hunting lodge in Leicestershire, and an enormous Mansion in Northumberland.

The engagement of the senior staff, the payment of wages, both those of the households and of the estates, were all under his jurisdiction.

He had, it was true, the services of attorneys and accountants, Major Domos and junior secretaries to help him, but his was the hand which kept the whole complicated Ducal state in motion.

Yet never for a moment did Mr. Graystone approach his Master with anything but humble servility—a commendable attitude which the Duke accepted without question.

" 'Evening, Graystone," the Duke said. "Have you anything of import for me? And pray do not bore me with the problems from the country; for I am in no mood for them at the moment."

"No indeed, Your Grace. There are no problems. I only came to inform Your Grace that all the arrangements that you requested have been made for your departure tomorrow. The horses have been sent ahead and all three of your hosts have signified their delight at being honoured by Your Grace's presence. I have, however, purposely left unspecified the actual time of your arrival at each residence."

"Quite right!" the Duke approved. "I dislike being constrained!"

"Is there anything else Your Grace will require?"

"No, thank you, Graystone. I am grateful for your attention."

The kind word of condescension seemed to lighten the worried expression in Mr. Graystone's eyes.

"Your Grace is most gracious," he said and bowing went from the room.

The Duke sat for a moment, the letter-opener in one hand, a letter which exuded the cloying fragrance of gardenias in the other. Then on an impulse he threw both down on the desk and rising to his feet walked languidly upstairs to change for dinner.

There were two Valets awaiting his appearance—an elderly man who had served his father and who had known him as a child, and a younger man who had only been in the Ducal service for ten years.

They removed His Grace's boots, helped him out of his clothes and when he had taken his bath in front of the fire in his bed-chamber, enveloped him in a big lavender-scented turkish towel with which he dried himself.

The Duke accepted such ritual as too familiar for him to notice it. He was assisted into his close-fitting evening pantaloons; the elder Valet shaved him with an expert hand that had never been known to falter; a shirt of the finest lawn, frilled and goffered by women from his Estate in his own country laundry, was buttoned across his muscular chest by the younger Valet.

Then all three men considered the serious question as to what style of cravat the Duke should wear around his neck to hold high the points of his starched collar.

"His Majesty is very partial to the Mathematical, Your Grace," the elder Valet suggested.

"And a sad mess he makes of it!" the Duke retorted. "The King's neck is far too thick and his chin too heavy for anything but a simple neck-cloth!"

"We can be thankful that it will be many years before the same could be said of Your Grace," the Valet replied with an admiring smile.

"I have a feeling, Jenkins, that I shall never give my horseflesh a sore back!" the Duke remarked.

"No indeed, Your Grace, that is very certain; for Your Grace's physique is remarkable! I was saying to Mr. Weston only last week, Your Grace, that there's not an ounce of spare flesh on Your Grace's body."

"I think that tonight I will wear the Waterfall," the Duke said reflectively.

"I was just about to proffer that very suggestion for Your Grace's consideration," his Valet said enthusiastically. "Only someone with a high neck like Your Grace's and indeed a Gentleman with Your Grace's presence could attempt the very intricate folds which are, I am told, the despair of Lord Fleetwood's Valet!

"In fact, Your Grace, after casting two dozen neckcloths away, 'tis said that both His Lordship and his man burst into tears!"

"It would not surprise me," the Duke said laconically. "If ever there was a ham-fisted creature, either with the ribbons or with a cravat, it is Fleetwood!"

"Quite so, Your Grace, and I hear Your Grace broke

the record today. May I offer my most humble congratulations on a feat which would have given extreme satisfaction to Your Grace's father had he been alive."

"A Top-sayer himself, was he not, Jenkins?"

"Indeed, his late Grace was unrivalled in his day, and yet I sometimes think that Your Grace has the edge on him."

"I wish I could believe that," the Duke said good-humouredly.

Having shrugged himself with some difficulty into his evening-coat which was cut so tightly that he required the assistance of both Valets before it was finally adjusted to his satisfaction, he then proceeded slowly down the carved gilt stairway.

A flunkey scurried to open the door and His Grace entered the Ante-Room adjoining the long Dining-Room, which with its marble pillars and gold-leafed cornice, was considered one of the finest achievements of its architect.

"In the Ante-Room two footmen offered His Grace a glass of wine. One carried the silver tray on which rested crystal glasses engraved with the Ducal cipher; the other poured from a heavy cut-glass decanter, its lip also encircled with silver.

The Duke accepted a glass of matured Madeira and was sipping it appreciatively when the Butler announced:

"Captain Henry Sheraton, Your Grace."

A Gentleman with a pleasing countenance, as elegantly dressed as His Grace but without quite his distinction and air of consequence, came into the room.

"Good evening, Harry!" the Duke said. "You are late! I began to think you might have forgotten our arrangement for this evening."

"Not so bird-witted! Been looking forward for the

last three days to seeing the new Cyprians the Abbess has procured from France! Apologies if you kept waiting."

"I was but roasting you," the Duke anwered. "I have returned from Epson only in the last hour. I broke the record!"

"You did! Congratulations!" Harry Sheraton exclaimed. "Was hoping you would do it this time. Bumptious fellow Lumley been boasting all over White's would achieve it with those roans he bought at Tattersall's last month. Ask me; not all they are puffed up to be! But nothing will convince Lumley that they are not prime horseflesh!"

"I would not accept Lumley's opinion if I were buying an army mule!" the Duke exclaimed.

"Nor I!" his friend replied. "God, Theron, do you remember those blasted cattle we had to cope with in Portugal? Never forget way they and the horses stampeded in that colossal thunderstorm before the Battle of Salamanca!"

"The lightning reflected on the musket barrels almost blinded me," the Duke replied. "It also made me decide that I could never look at a damned mule again! Do you recall how many of the officers were smothered in the folds of their tents when the horses and mules got caught in the ropes? I can now see Major Dulbiac saving his wife's life by depositing her under the nearest gun carriage!"

"God, yes!" Harry Sheraton laughed. "Remember Wellington's fury when he had to send troops mulehunting? Thought it might delay the advance!"

"He would have been much more furious if there had been no animals to move the guns!" the Duke remarked drily.

"Know what, Theron?" Harry Sheraton said more

seriously. "Often wish to God war was not ended! Sick to death of being a 'Hyde Park Soldier'!"

"So you know that is what they call you in the Clubs?" the Duke said with a twinkle in his eyes.

"Blast their impertinence! Wonder how those fops would enjoy turning out at moment's notice to quell riot in Hyde Park; disperse a mob hooting and throwing stones at Houses of Parliament; or catch some blasted fellow with ingenuity of a rat in avoiding the gallows!"

"A soldier's life is a hard one!" the Duke said mockingly.

"Damned hard when has to do that sort of thing!" Harry Sheraton agreed. "Hear talk of special force for just such jobs. What that chap's name always spouting about it in House of Commons?"

"Sir Robert Peel," the Duke replied.

"That fellow! Sooner he introduces a Police-force or whatever they to be called, better pleased I shall be! Another flap-doodle on today—why I was late."

"What is it about this time?" the Duke asked.

Captain Sheraton did not answer for a moment; he was intent on taking a glass of Madeira from the silver salver and raising it to his lips.

"Damme, Theron, if you do not offer your guests better Madeira than anyone else in whole country! Who is your wine-merchant? Could do with a few bottles of this nectar."

"You cannot buy it, dear boy," the Duke answered. "I put it away in the cellars six years ago and it is only now that my Wine Steward has permitted me to drink it."

"Will have another glass," Harry Sheraton said. "Hope you have several pipes of it."

"Enough to keep you drinking it for a year or so at any rate," the Duke smiled. "But you were telling me what made you late."

"Colonel called sudden conference of officers to inform us that the Prime Minister taking serious view of Bullion robberies"

"What are those?" the Duke asked.

"Do you never read newspapers?" Harry Sheraton asked. "Headlines about them for weeks!"

"Oh, I remember now," the Duke exclaimed. "You mean the ambushing of coaches carrying Bullion from the Bank of England to County Banks?"

"That's the cannon ball!" Harry Sheraton exclaimed. "Think the whole operation damn well planned, if you ask me. Must be a brain behind the robberies! Not work of ordinary highwaymen."

"I am afraid I did not pay much attention to the reports."

"Powers-that-be getting thick head over it. Two big robberies last week! Both cases guards shot dead, coachmen trussed up and left on the floor of coach. Last couple—poor devils—there for five hours before anyone found them! When questioned their information of little use."

"They must have seen who tied them up," the Duke remarked languidly, without showing much interest.

"Wore masks, coachmen hit over head with bludgeon, rendered unconscious within seconds! In flurry of pulling in horses and hearing the shots too flustered to be reliable eye-witnesses."

"Well, what are the intrepid Military going to do about it?" the Duke enquired.

"Commanders can think of nothing except to double guard on Bank of England! No clod-head would attempt to raid that stronghold!" Harry Sheraton said in disgust. "Would have thought from way Colonel was spouting a revolution had broken out!"

"If it does I will put on my uniform and come and

help you," the Duke commented with a smile as the door opened and the Butler announced dinner.

The Dining-table had no cloth in the fashion introduced by the King, and on its polished surface were gold ornaments which had been in the family since the reign of Charles II.

Trails of green orchids were arranged around them and encircled the base of the big gold candelabra which each held six candles.

The two Gentlemen settled down to a long and exceptional meal, the Duke's Chef being considered the best in the *Beau Ton*. The wine was superlative and only when the third remove left the table did Harry Sheraton lie back in his chair, wave away a Sèvres dish containing peaches soaked in brandy and sprinkled with roasted almonds, and remark:

"Regret, Theron, can no longer do justice to these culinary specialties. Heaven knows that if I ate in your House every day should soon be stout as our most beloved Monarch."

"I think Chef is on his mettle tonight," the Duke replied. "I sent a message to the kitchen two nights ago to say that I had not found the dinner to my satisfaction."

"Good God!" Harry Sheraton ejaculated. "If you find fault with food like this, must be no satisfying you."

The servants had left the room and the Duke answered with a little smile:

"I was but keeping the man up to scratch; if one is too easily pleased people get lazy!"

"Of course, forgot—'His Most Noble Perfection'," Harry Sheraton laughed.

"Damn it all, do not talk that sort of fustian at me!" the Duke exclaimed, "or I swear I will not invite you here again!"

"Stuff!" his friend replied. "Know well as I do that I

am touch of spice in your epicurean life which brings savour you get from no one else.

"Have known you too long, Theron, to be subservient! Not saying that you not remarkably impressive chap. But have seen you in far too many undignified situations to be stupefied into state of admiring idiocy like majority of your friends, staff and envious acquaintances!"

"Your compliments overwhelm me!" the Duke drawled. "At the same time, Harry, you are right! I would hate to lose you!"

"Want another war," Harry Sheraton sighed. "Do you good, Theron, rough it as you were doing ten years ago on the Peninsula. Ever forget the excitement of routing Frenchies after Battle of Vittoria and capturing King Joseph's baggage-train?"

"No indeed," the Duke laughed. "Wyndham's Dragoons acquired from it the King's lordly silver *pot de chambre*."

"Could never forget!" Harry Sheraton exclaimed. "Christened 'The Emperor', all drank champagne out of it!"

"When I got through the medley of horses, mules, bullocks and donkeys, pet monkeys and parrots," the Duke went on, "I found the tenth Huzzars had split open the Treasure Chests and the ground was littered with doubloons, dollars, watches, jewels and trinkets."

"So many females among the French camp-followers that our troops called it 'a mobile brothel'," Harry Sheraton reminisced. "But Wellington's booty was what counted—a hundred and fity-one cannons, two million cartridges. Those the days, my boy!"

He raised his glass to the memory before he exclaimed:

"God, but we are getting old! Next year 1825, will be ten years since Waterloo!"

"Yes indeed," the Duke replied, "and that means, Harry, that I shall be three and thirty next month—as my Uncle Adolphus pointed out to me a few days ago in no uncertain terms."

"Wager His Lordship came round with family tree in his pocket," Harry Sheraton said knowingly.

"He did indeed," His Grace replied. "He went through the whole genealogy of the Royds from the one who served under Ethelred the Unready to the Royd who cuckolded Henry the Eighth with one of his wives—I forget which, and the Royd who beat Casanova to the bed of some Princess or other!"

"Which led your Uncle Adolphus up to one demand," Harry Sheraton mocked.

"Exactly!" the Duke agreed. "That I should get married immediately! Otherwise Cousin Jasper will inherit."

"Never able to understand how Jasper comes into it," Harry Sheraton remarked. "More yellow-livered outsider have ever met! Pardon, Theron, if plain speaking distresses you."

"It does nothing of the sort," the Duke said, "and I said far worse to Jasper himself three months ago when he approached me for the hundredth time—or was it the thousandth?—for a 'small loan'."

"The smallness being, of course, relative!"

"You are right. This time it was for fifteen thousand pounds. He thought he must be improving as the time before it had been for twenty thousand!"

"What did you do?"

"I gave him ten and told him if he ever came whining for more I would personally kick him into the street, even though it would damage my hessians!"

"Heard he was gaming high, and knew only question of time before he would be at you again!"

"This is the last time!" the Duke said firmly. "But he

is a cheese-monger of the worst description, and Uncle Adolphus is convinced that he is borrowing on the possibility of stepping into my shoes."

"How happens has any claim at all?" Harry Sheraton asked.

"It is quite easy," the Duke replied. "My Grandfather had five sons. The eldest had one child, Sylvester, who was killed at the Battle of the Nile; the second son—my father—produced me; the third, Uncle Cornelius, who died last year, had eight daughters!"

"Poor devil!" Harry Sheraton ejaculated.

"Then came George Frederick," the Duke continued, "an extremely unpleasant man who died some years ago and had one son—our friend Jasper—and lastly Uncle Adolphus who has never married."

"So Jasper's father as nauseating as he is?"

"According to Uncle Adolphus, George Frederick was smuggled into the family in a bed-pan! Personally, I do not believe a word of it, but he was very unlike the rest of his brothers. He had no sense of propriety; he was a mad gambler and had a partiality for the lowest type of strumpet!

"Anyway, his wife—an innkeeper's daughter—went to an early grave and Jasper was dragged up amongst women one would not trust with a dog, let alone a child. At times I am almost sorry for him!"

"To let in your attic!" Harry Sheraton ejaculated. "Done more for your importunate relative than anyone could credit! What has he given you in return—word of honour he has broken too many times to enumerate; manner of blackguarding you behind your back that has nearly got him into a dozen duels with your friends?"

"There is no need for anyone to be in a miff over Jasper," the Duke said, "but I think that Uncle Adolphus is right—Jasper must not under any circumstances inherit—and therefore, Harry, I am to be married."

"Congratulations!" his friend ejaculated. "Announcement sudden, but not unexpected. Who is the bride? Do I know her?"

"I have not decided on her as yet," the Duke replied.

"Not decided!" Harry Sheraton began incredulously and then burst out laughing. "You are roasting me!"

"No indeed," the Duke answered. "I have given full consideration to Uncle Adolphus's impassioned pleas combined with those of my sister, Evelyn. She came with him and was even more insistent than my Uncle that Jasper should cease his pretensions of being the heir presumptive. Apparently he insulted her at some Assembly or another! Anyway, she has compiled for me a list of eligibles for the position of my Duchess."

"Good God, Theron, not serious? Not contemplating marrying some chit for whom you have no affection whatsoever?"

"That is of no consequence!" the Duke replied.

"Doing it a bit brown!" Harry Sheraton retorted. "Not saying need go in for heart throbs with an orchestra wailing under full moon, or should throw dramatics like that wearisome chap Byron, whose poems bore me to distraction, but must be some female with whom you have a slight . . ."

"There is no one," the Duke interrupted. "As you well know, Harry, I have not paid much attention to unfledged girls."

"Suppose that true," Harry Sheraton agreed ruefully, "but you have stood up with few of them for a dance at Almack's. Must have encountered one or two staying in the houses you visited."

"If I did, I have no remembrance of them," the Duke admitted, "and after all it is of little consequence. All I require is a well-bred wife who will provide me with an heir.

"She must have dignity, she must not cause any gossip. Otherwise, as long as we deal well in public, what happens in private is no one's business."

"Suggesting that your wife can go her own way, as you intend to go yours?"

"Within reason," the Duke replied. "I am not likely to keep her incarcerated in the Norman tower at Selchester or lock her into a chastity belt while I go a-roaming. She can have another interest, I imagine, without it being the *on dit* of St. James's."

"What this paragon to look like? Decide that?" Harry Sheraton asked mockingly.

"Yes indeed, she must be tall, fair, blue-eyed, with good features. Blondes look best in the family jewels. Duchesses must be tall, and you know as well as I do that those blue-eyed, fair females are always somewhat insipid and not given to flights of emotion as much as the darker breed."

"Imagine with required qualifications clearly set out you able to purchase one, or half a dozen if you wish, at Partheon Bazaar!"

"I am serious!" the Duke said. "I know exactly what I require and I promise you, Harry, I shall find myself a wife who will play the part of my Duchess in exactly the manner that I expect of her."

"What really saying," Harry Sheraton said, "is that you know damn well wretched girl will fall in love with you, twist her round your little finger, conform in every way to your desires—grateful for occasional pat on head as if a pet pug you had added to your household."

"That is not very funny, Harry," the Duke said loftily.

"May not be humorous but the truth," Harry Sheraton retorted. "God above, Theron, cannot go into marriage in such cold-blooded manner. Surely there is somewhere a female with whom you can fancy yourself trifle enamoured; some wench who makes your heart beat a little quicker; or at least delights your eye!"

The Duke did not speak and Harry Sheraton continued:

"Anything better than this calculated demand for a foolish unsuspecting creature who will doubtless in few years be grateful if you so much as nod in her direction."

"My dear Harry, I am, as I have already said, nearly three and thirty," the Duke replied, "and I have never been enamoured of any woman I could marry, and I see no possibility of my ever becoming so.

"As you know full well, I have had many *affairs de cœur*, but they have always been with married women who were well up to snuff. I cannot imagine anything that will bore me more than the chattering of an unsophisticated chit just out of the school-room!"

The Duke sighed wearily at the thought before he continued:

"But for the sake of the family, because I have to produce an heir, then I shall marry someone who will fit in with the pattern of what I require in the woman who bears my name."

"What about Penelope?" Harry Sheraton asked.

There was a moment's silence before the Duke exclaimed:

"Fancy your remembering Penelope!"

"In love with her. Remember what you felt then?"

"Of course I do. I remember too how swiftly Penelope, so sweet and maidenly, jilted a youth without a handle to his name and whose expectations were remote, when Lord Hornblotton, already a peer of the realm, asked if he could pay his addresses to her!"

There was almost a bitterness in the Duke's voice and Harry Sheraton, looking at him sharply, said:

"Are you telling me, Theron, after all these years

still wearing the willow for that title-seeking woman you met your first year in the Regiment?"

The Duke shook his head.

"You are trying hard to make me a romantic, Harry, but it will not stick! No indeed, I have seen Penelope since she married. I met her, let me see, two or three years ago: she had run to fat and it was difficult to recognise the thin, ethereal girl who had once captured my fancy. I believe Penelope has five children by now, maybe more!"

"You loved her!"

"I was infatuated—as any raw youth is likely to be infatuated the first time he puts on his regimental tunic and knows that his appearance makes him appear a hero in the eyes of some green girl. But I am grateful to Penelope! She taught me a very important lesson."

"What lesson?"

"That women, whoever they may be, will always go to the highest bidder!" the Duke replied. "For the 'Fashionable Impure' it is of course entirely a question of money, and for the social chicks it is the highest title that matters.

"Penelope showed me that a Baronet will beat a Knight, a Viscount will beat a Baron and a Marquis an Earl. But at the very top of the hierarchy, Harry, there is a Duke! A Duke is ace-high and therefore unbeatable!"

"Suppose by that you are telling me none of those fair-haired, blue-eyed nitwits to whom you condescend will refuse you?"

"Of course not! That was the lesson Penelope taught me. It is not a question of whom a girl loves, but what her suitor can offer.

"And that is where Harry, I can now take the trick every time! I am a Duke and that rank makes me automatically the favourite in the matrimonial stakes! I must pass the post ahead of all other competitors!"

"Curse it, you are too plausible!" Harry Sheraton remarked, "and too puffed up with your consequence. Only wish that just one of those social butterflies would turn you down flat! Do you world of good!"

"Your wish is very unlikely to be granted," the Duke sneered.

"Know it," his friend said with a groan. "Not only a Duke, Theron, also have damned handsome phiz, fine figure of a man! Excellent sportsman—grant you that—a Corinthian; a Non-pareil; and so disgustingly wealthy—do not believe you know yourself what you are worth; No, Theron, first past the winning-post! Hope it brings you happiness!"

"It will!" the Duke answered, "for the simple reason that I am not expecting to find my happiness in marriage. I shall be gratified, of course, if my wife has some slight affection for me, but my enjoyment will still rest, you may be sure, with those delightful creatures that one can purchase so easily and who each bring us a fleeting, if brittle amusement, however jaded we think we are with their charms!"

"If we intend to inspect new batch just arrived from France, let us set about it," Harry Sheraton said. "Promise you, Theron, you have depressed me! Cannot bear to think about your plans for the future. Given me a disgust for the whole idea of marriage!"

"Poor Harry," the Duke commiserated. "You are romantic, that is what you are! I am practical—severely and sensibly practical! I know what I want, I shall get it, and my life will proceed on my own carefully calculated lines which you admit yourself makes for comfort if for nothing else!"

"Really determined to carry on with this crazed idea?" Harry Sheraton asked in a serious tone.

He rose to his feet as he spoke and stood looking at the Duke at the end of the table. There was no one who could appear more elegant, more at ease, than His Grace as he leant back against a high-backed armchair, a glass of port in his hand.

"As a matter of fact," the Duke said with a twist of his lips, "it is quite an adventure!"

"Humbugging yourself!" Harry Sheraton snapped. "Know perfectly well this is a travesty of what marriage was intended to be. Can only prophesy, Theron, that if you are not careful it will prove disastrous."

"Romantic and now the prophet of doom!" the Duke jeered. "Despite all your warnings—and curse it you are as gloomy as a Good Friday sermon!—I leave tomorrow morning. I shall visit first the Upminsters in Bedfordshire. My sister assures me they have a most commendable, fair-haired, blue-eyed daughter who was greatly admired at Almack's last season."

"You have met her?" Harry Sheraton asked.

"I have a sort of vague remembrance at the back of my mind that I did," the Duke answered. "But you know, Harry, that the moment I speak to one of these girls I can see only one expression on their face."

"What is that?" Harry Sheraton asked, almost as if he could not help himself.

"An expression of greed, and a glint in their eyes as they think how attractive they will look in their coronets and a peeress's robes. When they speak to me I can almost see them murmuring to themselves beneath their breath—'The Selchester Diamonds'!"

"God, what a cynic!"

"And when I return them to their Mama's side," the Duke went on, "I see the smirk on her face! Oh, the Dowagers try to appear nonchalant and unmoved that their little chicken has been fluffing her feathers in front of my Ducal eyes, but they have a smile like a Chesire cat who has been at the cream. I know the one thing they want is to lap me up!"

"Make me sick!" Harry Sheraton ejaculated.

The Duke, laughing, exclaimed:

"Forgive me, Harry, but to tease you is irresistible! We are the same age, but I swear that you still believe in dragons and Knights in armour setting out to rescue a frail virgin with whom he will fall immoderately in love. My dear fellow, that is not life!"

"If life is what you have been describing to me," Harry Sheraton said firmly, "all I can tell you, I will thank God on my knees every night am a commoner!"

The Duke laughed again.

"Over-brewing the ale, Harry! You are related to half the aristocracy on your mother's side and you are pretty warm in the pocket! You are a catch, my boy! Not one of the giggling creatures lining the walls at Almack's would refuse your addresses! In fact, if I am not mistaken, they would snatch at an opportunity of accepting you."

"For God's sake, shut up!" Harry Sheraton cried. "Making me blue-devilled, Theron! If we do not cheer ourselves up with those little 'bits o' muslin' from across Channel, swear I shall run myself through with my own sword!"

"Poor Harry!" the Duke ejaculated. "I really have upset you! Let us repair to the Haymarket. There is nothing like the sport of spotting a new Venus with whom to grace one's bed to sweep away the dismals!"

The Duke rose as he spoke and the two men moved towards the Dining-Room door. As they reached it Harry Sheraton gave a sudden cry.

"Heavens, Theron, said you were leaving tomorrow! Forgotten the date?"

"The date?" the Duke queried.

"Eighteenth! Arranged for Bombardier Hawkins to meet Farrington's Jed Blake!"

"Good God, so we did!" the Duke ejaculated. "I had forgotten!"

"Both wagered couple of monkeys on the result. Could not miss watching our man making mince-meat of Farrington's!"

"I should think not," the Duke agreed. "I will leave the following day!"

"In other words," Harry Sheraton said, determined to have the last word, "a boxer takes precedence over a prospective bride!"

"But naturally!" the Duke drawled.

2

The Duke's plans, owing he thought afterwards to Harry Sheraton's gloomy predictions, went awry from the very beginning!

Having seen Bombardier Hawkins pummel Lord Farrington's man into a blood pulp, he spent a most convivial evening with his friends, who had also backed the Bombardier, celebrating what was to them a lucrative and satisfying victory.

Lord Farrington had for a long time irritated the members of White's by his boastful assertions that he and he alone was capable of picking out an unknown bruiser and putting him into a mill in which he would be a winner.

His Lordship had in fact on several occasions supported his contention by finding men who were so immensely strong and heavy that they won the fight by sheer weight of flesh.

But on this occasion the Duke and Harry Sheraton

had foreseen the type of fighter that His Lordship was likely to produce and had confronted him unexpectedly with the Bombardier.

The latter had been kept away from London at Harry Sheraton's Estate in Suffolk and trained until he was in tip-top condition; and the mere sight of him in the ring was enough to send the odds soaring in his favour.

A magnificent specimen of manhood, with huge muscular development, enormous shoulders and with it a nimble pair of legs, he floored Jed Blake in the first five minutes and finished the fight in under twenty.

"Farrington lost a packet!" Harry Sheraton exclaimed with glee as he and the Duke drove back to London from Wimbledon Common, where the mill had taken place.

"Serve him right, he has crowed like a cock on a dunghill for long enough," the Duke replied. "He will not be so top-lofty in future, not when we are about, at any rate!"

"You spotted Hawkins! Remember?" Harry Sheraton said. "When you visited me in barracks six months ago. Saw him as we walked across the Square and remarked: 'That chap ought to strip well!' "

"Did I?" the Duke queried. "I had forgotten."

"You were right! Once again proved your superiority over the enemy!" Harry Sheraton mocked. "Somewhat insignificant foe, nevertheless the one who needed to be defeated!"

"Still gunning for me, Harry?" the Duke asked, quizzing him with a glint of amusement in his eyes.

"Thinking over what you said last night," Harry Sheraton replied. "Only ask you once again, Theron, not to do anything so nonsensical! Call whole plan off—not be difficult."

"If there is one thing for which I have dislike," the

Duke drawled, "it is the well-meaning efforts of those who try to interfere in my life. I regret now, Harry, that I revealed my intentions. I should not have told you what I was about until my approaching nuptials were announced in the Gazette. I would then have been spared this endless sermonising which I find intolerably wearisome."

"All right! All right!" Harry Sheraton exclaimed. "Will cease prosing, but promise you, Theron, nothing but ill-luck will come of it!"

It was these words that the Duke was to remember quite frequently in the days to come.

However, the following morning he rose with a clear head, feeling beneath a fashionable air of languid passiveness a faint stirring of interest because he was setting in motion a plan he had thought out down to the last details.

This was the way he had deployed his troops on the Peninsula, following the example set by Wellington, who always averred that nothing was too insignificant or too small to command his personal attention.

As the Duke ate his breakfast—partaking heartily of several lamb chops, a well-roasted spring chicken and a dish of kidneys enriched with cream—he sent for Mr. Graystone to ask him for the last-minute details concerning not only his journey but also those of whose hospitality he intended to avail himself.

"I know Lord Upminster," the Duke said when Mr. Graystone appeared. "A verbose Nobleman who I am certain will wish to confound me with the wonders of his country Estate. Did he not win some prize or other?"

"His Lordship's cattle, Your Grace, were highly thought of at the Show which took place last year and which was honoured by the presence of his Majesty."

"I thought it was something like that," the Duke said. "And Wilmington? What are his interests?"

"Racing, Your Grace. His Lordship won the Derby three years ago and has a horse that is fancied for the Gold Cup this year."

"Then we will have plenty to discuss," the Duke said. "Do you think his animal will beat Clarion?"

"I am convinced that Your Grace's horse will be the winner," Mr. Graystone said quietly. "And so, may I add, Your Grace, is every member of your staff."

The Duke smiled.

"It is early days, but Clarion certainly seems to be shaping well. There is no doubt about it, Graystone, Lawrence is a good trainer."

"He certainly is, Your Grace. No one could doubt that, considering Your Grace's recent successes on the turf."

"No indeed," the Duke agreed. "And Mallory? What are the Earl of Mallory's interests? I have met him, of course, but I cannot recall anything outstanding about His Lordship. A somewhat anaemic individual and I shall be surprised if he has a decent piece of horseflesh in his stables!"

"You are right, Your Grace. The Earl of Mallory is interested only in building. He has enlarged his house, torn down the Elizabethan wings, erected others, and is now completing a Chapel adjacent to the Mansion which, they say, will be one of the most outstanding pieces of architecture in the whole of Yorkshire."

"That will be interesting at any rate," His Grace said. "Thank you, Graystone. You are sending Carter with me I suppose?"

"Naturally, Your Grace, seeing that it is inevitable that your Grace must spend several nights on the road! Mr. Carter will deal with everything concerning accommodation at the Inns.

"I have given him full instructions, Your Grace, and a groom has been sent ahead to see that every possible comfort is prepared for Your Grace's arrival."

"Excellent!"

The Duke walked from the Dining-room, accepted his hat, gloves and whip from the attendant flunkeys, and stepped into the spring sunlight.

The cavalcade outside was attracting attention from a number of wide-eyed small boys, a ragged crossing-sweeper, several draymen, and an Italian with a hurdy-gurdy and a small red-capped monkey on his shoulder.

It was not surprising that they stared in admiration at the magnificent team of four black horses which pulled the Duke's Travelling Carriage. There was a coachman and a footman on the box, both wearing blue and yellow livery which was as well-known in London as the Royal crimson and gold.

There was another footman up behind the Carriage and two outriders both mounted on fine examples of horseflesh from the Duke's stables.

Behind them, prepared to ride at the rear of the Carriage, was the Duke's Head-Groom astride an animal which in its very magnificence seemed to make all the other bloodstock pale into insignificance.

The Duke's favourite stallion—Salamanca—was also jet-black with a white nose and three white fetlocks. He was the Duke's favourite mount, and when His Grace rode him it was difficult to imagine that any other man and beast could appear so perfectly complementary, one of the other.

Drawn up behind Salamanca was the Baggage Chaise containing Mr. Carter, who was Mr. Graystone's senior clerk, and the Duke's valet—Jenkins.

This vehicle boasted only two horses, but as it was specially built for speed it was seldom left behind on a journey. And there was indeed great rivalry between the two Coachmen as to who would reach the destination first.

The Duke, who always insisted on inspecting his bloodstock before they set out on any major expedition, looked them over now and said sharply:

"The luggage can go ahead. Where do we change horses?"

"At Baldock, Your Grace."

Mr. Graystone gave a slight nod to the Butler who in his turn made an almost imperceptible gesture to the Coachman of the Baggage Chaise.

Moving smoothly, the horses' silver bridles glinting in the sunshine, their coats polished as brightly as the Duke's hessians, the Baggage Chaise glided across the gravel sweep leading to the stone-flanked entrance which led into Park Lane.

The Coachman and footmen removed their hats as they passed the Duke, who nodded to them briefly.

As soon as the Baggage Chaise had moved its place was taken by the Duke's Highflyer Phaeton drawn by four blood-chestnuts. Its high yellow wheels and small black-painted body made it appear almost like an enormous wasp, as the chestnuts, tossing their heads and fretting to be off, moved behind the Travelling Carriage.

"Your Grace has a pleasant day for the drive," Mr. Graystone remarked respectfully.

"It is certainly not a day to be cooped up inside a carriage," the Duke said. "I shall change vehicles at Eaton Socon. I think you told me that Lord Upminster's house is only three miles from there."

"That is right, Your Grace."

"I will arrive in style but I will journey with speed!" the Duke remarked. "The Carriage can leave now."

He was well aware that his Head Coachman who drove the Travelling Carriage was raring to be off. Already incensed that the Baggage Chaise had gone ahead, he was frightened that this small advantage might enable the junior Coachman, with whom he engaged in a persistent rivalry, might reach Baldock before him.

He had on various occasions suffered this indignity because the smaller chaise could pass other vehicles on the road more easily and was very much more manœuvrable in towns or villages.

As soon as the Duke gave him permission the Head Coachman set his team in motion with a determined air which told those who watched their departure that the animals would be put into their stride at the very earliest opportunity.

At the same time there was no question of the horses being sprung or pushed too hard, for if the Head Coachman had a fault, it was that he was inclined to over-cosset his bloodstock.

The Duke was just about to step into his Phaeton when a footman approached the house wearing the resplendent livery of the Hungarian Embassy. The man appeared to be in such a hurry that he was almost running to reach His Grace.

Slipping behind the Duke, the Butler intercepted the flunkey before, with inconceivable vulgarity, he could thrust the note he held into the Ducal hands.

There was a pause when the note, having been taken from the messenger, was held by the Butler while one of the footmen fetched a silver salver from inside the marble Hall.

When it arrived the Butler placed the note on the salver and proffered it to the Duke with an apologetic air of one who expects to be waved aside.

But the Duke, instead of leaving the matter in Mr. Graystone's capable hands as his staff had anticipated, took the note from the silver salver and opened it.

It only contained a few lines, but those watching His Grace thought they saw a glint of interest in the lazy expression of his eyes.

"Tell the man I will myself convey an answer," the Duke said to the Butler, who relayed the message to the Embassy footman with an air of one who condescends.

"Good-bye, Graystone," the Duke said, and without further ado climbed into his Highflyer and took the reins from his groom's hands.

There was no mistaking the expert manner in which he drove his horses across the gravel sweep and into Park Lane. His coachmen were all exceptional drivers, but the Duke had a style and a flair which made everyone of his staff, from Mr. Graystone down to the youngest flunkey, stare after him appreciatively and wish they could emulate even a quarter of His Grace's expertise in everything he undertook.

The Duke, to his groom's surprise, instead of turning right on leaving Selchester House and proceeding up Park Lane towards the road leading North, turned left and after travelling but a short distance cornered his chestnuts into Curzon Street.

There, amongst other important houses of the nobility, was one impressive mansion which flew the Hungarian flag.

The Duke pulled up his team and gave the reins to his groom with the injunction: "Walk the horses, Fowler."

A moment later he entered a door headed with the imposing coat of arms of the Hapsburgs.

There seemed to be an inordinate amount of red carpet up which His Grace was led to the first floor. Through the open doors of several large Salons he could see huge crystal chandeliers, a profusion of gilt furniture and marble statues as he proceeded along a corridor which led to the back of the house.

The servant knocked discreetly on one of the closed doors, and a woman's voice bade him enter. The Duke was ushered into a large room bathed in sunshine. It was furnished as a sitting-room, but there was also a draped Empire-shaped bed in the style of those made popular by the Empress Josephine against one wall.

Seated in front of a decoratively painted mirror, having her hair arranged by the most famous coiffeur of the *Beau Ton*, was the Princess Zazeli Muzisescu.

She glanced round indifferently as the door opened, then when she saw who stood there, sprang to her feet with a cry of joy.

For a moment the Duke was stationary in the doorway, a smile on his lips. Then as the Princess threw wide her arms, he moved towards her, a glint of amusement in his eyes as he saw how she was garbed.

Zazeli Muzisescu was one of the famous beauties of the whole of Europe. Half Hungarian, half French by birth, she had married a Hungarian diplomat whose meteoric rise in his profession was entirely due to his wife's machinations on his behalf.

Nicknamed by her detractors in England as "Dusk to Dawn," in France as *"Toujours prête,"* in Italy simply as *"Presto,"* Zazeli with her beauty, her passionate nature and her unerring instinct in collecting the most important men in every country as her lovers, had an almost unique place in the social world.

She made no pretence or apology for her behaviour, and being a member of the oldest and most revered family in Hungary, and in fact a cousin of the Emperor, it was impossible for anyone to snub her socially.

At the same time her husband's diplomatic position gave her an immunity from the scandalised set-downs of the straight-laced and disapproving dowagers.

Zazeli was beautiful in a manner that was peculiarly her own. She had long, dark-red hair which fell to her waist; high cheekbones, and slanting, passionate eyes which always seemed to be smouldering with the fire of desire.

Her features were classical, her mouth provocative, and she had an almost perfect figure which was an allurement in itself.

Now, quite oblivious of the hairdresser, who was bowing himself tactfully from the room, she ran towards the Duke, who saw in the sunshine that she was wearing only a huge emerald necklace and a négligé of emerald green chiffon which was completely transparent.

There were huge rings on the long fingers of each of her white hands—Zazeli was never without them.

As she flung herself tempestuously into the Duke's arms he could feel the warmth of her exquisite body and knew before she looked up at him with smouldering eyes that she was just as desirable as she had ever been.

He had not seen Zazeli for three years, since they had enjoyed a brief but dynamic interlude in Paris which had made the gossips shake their heads and go out of their way to warn the Duke he was playing with fire.

His Grace was quite unperturbed by their croakings. He enjoyed Zazeli, but, however much people might fear such a possibility, there was no likelihood of his losing his head even in the face of such extreme provocation and temptation.

Nevertheless he was amused by her behaviour, and the fact that she was in some ways a forbidden pleasure made him quite determined that if Zazeli desired his company he had no intention of refusing it to her.

"*Mon brave! Mon cher!* It is enchanting to see you!" Zazeli cried, lifting her lips to his and inviting his kiss with an abandon that in other women would have seemed shameless.

The Duke kissed her, then held her at arm's length.

"Let me look at you," he said. "You have not changed, except perhaps you are more beautiful than I remembered."

"*Vous êtes charmant*," she smiled. "It is how I remember you, *mon cher ami*, always saying the right thing. *Ma foi!* I believe you are taller than ever! That delightful air of distinction is still there! You are very handsome, *mon Duc*, and I have missed you! How I have missed you! Have you missed me?"

"But of course I have missed you," the Duke replied. "Who else but you could do such outrageous things? Or indeed appear so alluring at ten o'clock in the morning!"

"I did not expect you so soon," she answered. "Had I known I would have not been so over-dressed."

She glanced at him under her long eyelashes and they both laughed.

"Your husband?" the Duke enquired. "Is he with you?"

"He arrives today," Zazeli replied. "I travelled with the Ambassador, it is always much more comfortable."

The Duke laughed again.

"And so we have one day at least," Zazeli said, "not that Viktor would interfere, but there are many official engagements to which I must accompany him."

The Duke moved a little further into the room to perch on the arm of the sofa. He looked as handsome as Zazeli had declared him to be with the sun shining on his thick dark hair, his grey eyes twinkling, his lips twisted in a smile which most women found irresistible.

There was also a little gleam behind his eyes which dispelled the cold indifference which often made his fine features seem hard and a little grim. He watch Zazeli and the gleam became accentuated.

The necklace encircling her long white neck glittered in the sunlight; it revealed also the lovely curves of her tip-tilted breasts; her tiny waist; the almost Grecian perfection of her narrow hips.

"It is unfortunate," the Duke said slowly, "and I only wish you had let me know you were arriving, but I am at this very moment leaving London."

"C'est impossible!" Zazeli exclaimed, her eyes clouding over, her lips pouting like a child who has been deprived of a toy on which it has set its heart.

It was part of her charm and fascination that Zazeli could mirror in her face every emotion with the passing of a second.

Now, at the Duke's words, from being radiant and excited, she became woebegone and distressed. So much so that he said:

"I shall not be away from London for long. What is the length of your stay?"

"A week—ten days—a fortnight, who can tell?" Zazeli asked. "Viktor attends a Conference at the Court of St. James'. *Alors*, if the negotiations are over quickly, perhaps I shall be gone before you return."

Her voice was so forlorn that the Duke smiled.

"I am sure there are a great many people who will console you in my absence. But I am indeed deeply apologetic that you should have come to London at such an inopportune moment. I have made my plans, Zazeli, and I cannot unmake them at a moment's notice."

"Not even for me?"

The Duke's eyes were on her lips.

"Not even for you!"

"Mon Dieu, but you are cruel! So cruel, so hardhearted! It is that icy control of yours which I have

tried so hard to break. Once I thought I had succeeded, but now once more it possesses you. Where is the fire, the burning fire, that we kindled between us and which burst into flame—at least for a little while—in Paris?"

Zazeli came nearer to the Duke so that he was aware of the tantalising, exotic scent she used. It was a fragrance made specially for her, and those who had once been Zazeli's lover never forgot the manner in which it lingered in her hair, in the smooth whiteness of her skin and even in the touch of her lips.

She stood in front of the Duke, her body touching his knees, her face almost level with his. Very slowly she reached out her arms, rounded and soft, towards his neck.

"Où est le feu?" she whispered. "Can it really have gone out—so that I can no longer—kindle it again?"

Her lips touched his at the last word and now her arms entwined round his neck held him captive. There was something almost snake-like in the manner in which her body moved sinuously against him.

With experienced hands the Duke pulled the green négligé from Zazeli's white shoulders and let it slither away to the floor. Then picking her up in his arms, he carried her across the room to the draped bed in the corner.

Two hours later the Duke tooled his horses up Park Lane past Tyburn and out towards the North. There was still a faint fragrance of Zazeli on his hands and on his clothes. He was well aware that his plans had gone astray but he knew that he could make up a good deal of the time lost once they reached the open road.

The chestnuts he was driving were a team he had purchased the previous year and which had cost him over two thousand guineas.

There had been hot competition for them amongst

the Corinthians, but the Duke was determined to be their owner and had continued to bid long after most of his friends had said the price was beyond their pockets.

Now the Duke congratulated himself on not having been deterred by their costliness. The horses, as if they knew their master's hurry, responded magnificently to his touch on the ribbons and the Phaeton sped along in the sunshine.

The Duke overtook every vehicle on the Great North Road in a manner which made his groom exclaim:

"Indeed, Your Grace drives to an inch! There's no one who could gainsay that!"

"Do no' let me frighten you, Fowler," the Duke said with a smile.

"You won't do that, Your Grace! But there's many on the roads today that aren't fit to be behind anything but a donkey, and that's the truth!"

It was a remark which was to prove itself regrettably true when the Duke reached the outskirts of Baldock.

Here, on the hill running down into the town, they could see long before they reached it that an accident had taken place. But when they were within a hundred yards Fowler ejaculated:

"'Tis Your Grace's Travelling Carriage!"

"I can see that," the Duke said sharply.

It was indeed the Carriage pulled up on the left-hand side of the road, the footmen at the horses' heads, while the Coachman in his tiered riding-cape was having an extremely noisy altercation with a burly, red-faced man who clearly had been the driver of the Stage-coach which had come to rest in the opposite ditch.

The Stage-coach, it was quite obvious to the Duke at first glance, had taken the corner too sharply and encountering the Travelling Carriage, had been unable to pull left in time to prevent a collision.

Slow-brained from an over-indulgence in strong ale

at the last stop, the Coachman had snatched at the reins. The horses had swerved desperately but the heavy, over-loaded vehicle had just touched the wheel of the Carriage before being precipitated over the bank into the ditch.

That it had not overturned was due to a thick hedge on the other side which kept it more or less upright.

However, the outside passengers had been tumbled into the road and those inside were threatened with suffocation as they fell screaming on top of each other.

The highway was littered with baggage, fruit and food scattered from luncheon-baskets, the guard's blunderbuss, the Coachman's hat, trunks that had burst open and disgorged their contents; and a number of passengers were standing disconsolately amongst the debris. Women were being assisted from inside the coach, weeping more with fright than from any vital injury.

The Duke drew his Phaeton to a standstill, handed the reins to Fowler and stepped into the road.

The noise of the altercation between his own Coachman and the driver of the Stage-coach was almost deafening. It combined with the whinnies of the frightened horses, who were still plunging about in the ditch, one of which had a leg over the shaft and was doing its best to kick itself free.

The Duke, striding up to the irate Coachman, said tersely:

"Go to your horses' heads, you fool!"

The man after one startled look at the tall, commanding figure speaking to him, instinctively obeyed the voice of authority, ceased his blasphemous abuse and turned to do what he was told.

In what seemed a remarkably short space of time, the Duke replaced chaos with order.

The Stage-coach horses were freed from the traces

and dragged onto the road; the coach was towed out of the ditch and by extraordinary good fortune was found to be undamaged.

The Duke's manner of speaking to the passengers calmed their fears and prevented them from refusing to continue their journey, as most, if not all of them, had been determined to do from the moment the accident happened.

With the help of the Duke's staff, luggage was once more packed on top of the coach, the passengers restored to their seats, and their food collected from the roadway.

Almost before the travellers realised what had happened the Coachman had whipped up his team and the coach proceeded slowly up the hill.

The Duke then turned to his own servants.

"He were drunk, Your Grace," the Coachman said defensively.

"He is sober enough now," the Duke replied.

He inspected his horses, which seemed in good shape, then bent to look at the wheel of his Carriage. It was buckled, there was no doubt about that. It was not badly damaged but it would have to be straightened by a wheelwright.

"How is it you have taken so long to get here?" the Duke enquired.

"It were young George, Your Grace," the Head-Coachman replied with the air of a martyr. "The lad felt sick and we had to stop twice on that account. I've now taken him up in the front beside me and put James at the back. But I told Mr. Graystone not to send him! There be motion with that new springing on the Carriage, Your Grace, and George has always been queasy about the stomach!"

"A nuisance!" the Duke observed, making a mental

note that in future footmen with queasy stomachs were not to leave Selchester House.

"A nuisance, indeed, Your Grace. No doubt the Baggage Chaise has been in Baldock an hour or more," the Head-Coachman remarked through gritted teeth.

The Duke, however, was not listening.

"Drive on slowly," he said. "We are meeting at the George and Dragon, is that not right?"

"The George and Dragon, Your Grace."

"Then we will all go there," the Duke said, "and find someone to repair the wheel immediately. Pay double what they ask if necessary. I do not wish to stay here any longer than I must."

"Very good, Your Grace."

The Duke found the George and Dragon passably comfortable and there was in its cellar a bottle of claret that he generously declared to be at least drinkable.

It was annoying, His Grace thought, that he must spend the rest of the day in Baldock, but he had no intention of arriving at Lord Upminster's house except in the manner which would be expected of him.

It would have been thought very shabby behaviour for any Gentleman in his position to call on another Nobleman who was in fact the merest acquaintance without a certain amount of pomp and ceremony.

To have driven up in his Phaeton would have seemed almost an insult, apart from the fact that the Duke had no intention of proclaiming the fact that his Coachman had been involved in an accident.

However much the fault lay with the other party concerned, one was always inclined to think that just as it takes two to make a quarrel, it also takes two coaches to cause a collision.

"No," His Grace decided, "the wheel must be mended, and while it is done I shall have to kick my heels in Baldock."

As it happened the Duke was well amused. He learnt from the Landlord of the Inn that there was a cock-fight in process, and asking for his Phaeton he drove outside the town to a small farm where he discovered quite a company of farmers, townsmen and cock-fighting fanciers.

Cock-fighting was not a sport to which the Duke was particularly partial at other times, but it certainly made the hours pass more pleasantly than they might otherwise have done.

When he returned to the Inn, the dinner which the Landlord provided was at least edible, even though His Grace's Chef at Selchester House would have declared it not fit even for the scullions.

When the Duke was embarking on his third glass of port, Mr. Carter, looking rather more white-faced and harassed than usual, entered the room and craved his attention.

A comparatively young man of some thirty-five summers, white-faced and of a nervous disposition, Mr. Carter was invariably reduced to a quaking jelly when anything went wrong.

"Well, Carter, what news?" the Duke enquired.

"The wheel should be finished late this evening, Your Grace," Mr. Carter replied with a composure he was far from feeling. "I had thought perhaps Your Grace would wish to continue your journey as far as Eaton Socon. But it is a dark night and we might encounter further mishap."

"I have no intention of moving at night as though we were highwaymen or sneak-theives," the Duke replied. "I can obtain a bed in this place, I suppose?"

"Yes, indeed, Your Grace, I have already commanded it," Mr. Carter replied.

"In which case see that the Coachmen and grooms are provided with reasonable accommodation," the

Duke said. "I have no wish for my staff to sleep in a hay-loft!"

"No, indeed, Your Grace, and may I add that Your Grace's consideration in this matter is greatly appreciated?"

"We will leave at nine-thirty tomorrow morning," the Duke said.

His Grace, however, was over-optimistic. The following morning when he descended for breakfast it was to find an irate farmer demanding to see him.

From his somewhat incomprehensible utterance the Duke discovered there had been a crate of live hens on the Stage-coach belonging to the farmer. In the flurry of repacking the vehicle, these had been forgotten and were not discovered on the roadside until late in the evening.

The farmer, who lived some distance from Baldock, had not been apprised of the mishap until he had come to market early that morning, and hearing that the Duke's chaise had been involved he had come to the George and Dragon filled with a sense of grievance.

He was extremely voluble about having lost a good sale for the hens as Smithfield Market, where his wife, who was a passenger in the coach, was taking them at dawn.

"Can they not leave today?" the Duke asked when the farmer paused for breath, having recited his grievances at the top of his voice with such violence that it seemed as if he might have a seizure at any moment.

Quite a hubbub broke out at this seemingly innocent question. The Landlord, the Landlord's wife, Mr. Carter, and several other people for no apparent reason were drawn into the controversy, all trying to explain to the Duke that there was no Stage-coach for another two days.

By this time the Duke was bored.

"Pay the man," he said to Mr. Carter. "Pay him what he thinks he is owed and let us be rid of his whining."

"But Your Grace!" Mr. Carter exclaimed in consternation, "it is not our responsibility. It is the Stage-coach owners who are liable. If they accept live-stock, then they are bound to deliver it to its destination within a certain space of time."

"My dear Carter," the Duke drawled in a manner which his servants recognised all too well as a danger signal, "I am not interested in the rights and wrongs of this case. Pay the man and put a stop to his shouting at me, which is something I most dislike!"

The farmer was paid and once again the Duke tried to get the Travelling Carriage and the Baggage Chaise on their way. This time there was a delay when one of the outriders came rushing from the stables to declare hysterically that the bridle of his horse had been stolen!"

But after a general hue and cry it was found that the Landlord's small son had taken it in a misguided effort to polish the silver of it even brighter than it was polished already.

He had been so obviously trying to be helpful that the anger directed at him by his father was, the Duke considered, undeserved and he ended the matter by handing the miscreant half a guinea.

This made the boy ecstatic and his parents so obsequiously grateful that finally the whole cavalcade left the George and Dragon in an atmosphere of beaming goodwill.

An over-soft feather bed and the Landlord's inferior claret and port had left the Duke with a slight headache, so he decided to ride.

"I need the exercise," he said to his Head-Groom. "I will take Salamanca and go across country. You can tool the Phaeton and we will meet at Eaton Socon. I believe the Inn is called 'The White Horse'."

"That is right, Your Grace," Mr. Carter interposed.

"You should be there early in the afternoon," the Duke said. "Perhaps about three o'clock. Wait for me! If I am late do not get in a pucker. I have no desire to arrive at Copple Hall before five!"

"No, Your Grace," Mr. Carter said, so doubtfully that it made the Duke glance at him sharply.

"Thinking of country times for dinner?" he asked. "I have thought of it too. I have no intention, Carter, of allowing any of my hosts to dine me before eight o'clock, and if they have other ideas, then they will just have to change them."

"Yes, Your Grace," Mr. Carter said humbly.

"So—" the Duke paused. "Perhaps to arrive at five o'clock will be too early! About six would be better! We will see. Anyway it is a fine day and Salamanca needs exercise."

"You are quite sure you would not like me to come with you, Your Grace?" the Head-Groom asked.

The Duke shook his head.

"And how would you keep up with me, pray? You know as well as I do that Salamanca can out-gallop and out-trot, if necessary, every one of my other cattle, however highly you think of them!"

"That is true, Your Grace," the Head-Groom admitted.

"Then we will meet at the White Horse."

The Duke mounted the stallion, who was fidgeting, tossing his head and rearing to show his impatience to be off.

The Duke obliged him by trotting briskly out of the town and then once they were clear of the last cottage, taking him into the fields. Shamelessly trespassing, he galloped over the flat land of Bedfordshire until both he and Salamanca felt a glow of well-being.

They rode on, Salamanca making short work of the hedges and walls they encountered. At lunchtime the Duke discovered an Inn tucked away in a small hamlet where he enjoyed a glass of ale and ate a large hunk of cheese with a crust of newly baked bread.

It was with a feeling of satisfaction that he proceeded, reflecting that few men had a finer mount than Salamanca and that few men could have passed a more enjoyable morning than he with the most delectable Zazeli.

He had indeed almost forgotten the reason for his journey, and it was with a sense of dismay that he realised suddenly that Salamanca had gone lame! He pulled in his reins and jumped down from the saddle to see what was amiss.

Raising Salamanca's off-side foreleg he saw at once a sharp stone embedded under the shoe. The Duke fortunately carried in his pocket a knife which contained exactly the right instrument for removing stones from a horse's hoof.

He applied this but the stone was so deeply embedded that in his efforts to dislodge it he also loosened the shoe itself. It came away in his hand.

Then he inspected the bare hoof in dismay! He realised that the stone in lodging deep had twisted Salamanca's fetlock. It was not a bad sprain but it was quite obvious the horse should not be ridden until he was rested and reshod.

Leading the stallion, the Duke left the farmtrack leading across a field which, with its rough stone surface, had caused the accident, and proceeded to a lane which bordered by high hedges, was not far away.

When he reached the lane he found a signpost. On it was written: "Eaton Socon 2 miles." The Duke gave a sigh. He did not relish a walk of two miles in his riding boots leading his horse. And then to his left he saw a small village.

There was the inevitable village green, a duck-pond in the centre of it, a few scattered cottages with thatched roofs, and an Inn, all black and white and agreeably picturesque.

There was also a Church and the Duke hoped that the village was large enough to boast a blacksmith. Leading Salamanca, who was limping dramatically, he walked towards the Inn.

As he neared it he saw sitting on a wooden seat outside a young woman. She was wearing a green riding-habit and there was a horse standing near her well-bred and well-groomed enough to tell the Duke that this was no village maiden.

He noticed that she glanced up as he appeared on the village green with an alert interest. Then to his surprise she turned her head away with a lack of curiosity which was not the reception the Duke had grown to expect from country wenches.

His Grace in fact had almost reached her side before she looked up again. Then she raised her head and he saw that she was surprisingly attractive.

Under a small green velvet tricorn the Unknown had russet-brown hair curling on each side of a heart-shaped face that was not strictly beautiful and yet at the same time was arrestingly attractive.

Her eyes were very large, also brown, but flecked with gold, and her nose was small, straight, had an aristocratic look about it which made the Duke sweep his hat from his head more impressively than he had intended to do at a first glance.

"Would you be obliging enough, Ma'am, to inform me if there is a blacksmith in this village?" he asked.

"Yes, there is," she replied in a soft, musical voice. "Has your horse lost a shoe?"

As she spoke she looked at Salamanca and her expression of indifference vanished.

"What a wonderful horse!" she exclaimed. Rising to her feet she stood staring at the stallion with an interest and an air of excitement which seemed to the Duke almost a subtle insult to himself.

"He is magnificent!" the Unknown cried. "Quite magnificent!"

"I am gratified that you should think so," the Duke said in one of his lofty voices which would have made Harry Sheraton smile. "But I would be grateful, ma'am, if you would direct me to the blacksmith."

"You go down the road," the Unknown began, then changed her mind. "I will take you. It is a trifle dfficult to explain."

"I would not wish . . ." the Duke began, but already she had turned away from him and going to the Inn door called:

"Billy! Billy! Where are you?"

"Oi be 'ere, Miss Verèna," a small boy answered, coming round the side of the Inn.

He was a sturdy urchin of about ten years old with a shock of untidy red hair, an impish grin and blue eyes that seemed to be seeking for mischief.

"Do ye want Oi, Miss Verena?"

"Of course I want you," she answered. "I should not be calling you otherwise. I am taking this Gentleman to the blacksmith's. Now stay here and watch the road. If you see a coach—a very grand coach with four horses and liveried coachmen, come and tell me at once. Do you understand?"

"A coach, Miss?"

"Yes, but a different coach from the ones which usually pass," Miss Verena replied. "And there will be two outriders—you know, men with white wigs and peaked caps."

"Lik'as be with 'is Lordship when 'e goes t'London?" Billy asked.

"That is right, and do not forget, come and tell me at once, and not waste a moment!"

"Oi've got me work t'do," Billy said doubtfully.

"If you watch until I come back I will give you . . ."

She felt in the pocket of her riding-jacket.

"Oh dear . . ."

"Pray allow me to be your banker," the Duke said with a faint smile on his lips, "especially as the money must be expended through my necessity."

He put his hand in his pocket as he spoke and drew out a handful of change. There were half-sovereigns and sovereigns, and several pieces of silver.

"Oh, thank you," Miss Verena said in an entirely natural manner and without embarrassment.

She took from his hand the smallest coin of them all.

"I am sorry to trouble you," she said, "but I have no purse and indeed nothing with which to bribe Billy except a handkerchief!"

She laughed as she spoke and the Duke noted that dimples appeared in both of her cheeks.

"Here you are, Billy, you mercenary rascal!" she said, handing him the coin. "And if you let that coach go by without telling me, I swear I will scrag you when I get back!"

"Oi'll keep me peepers skint, Miss," Billy promised.

His threatener turned to the Duke.

"Come along," she said. "We will have to make haste! I cannot trust Billy for long. A squirrel will distract his attention, or lost in his day-dreams, he will not even see the coach."

As she spoke she started to walk across the green and the Duke followed her leading Salamanca.

"Why is this particular coach of such import?" he asked.

"It belongs to a Duke," Miss Verena answered briefly.

She moved so that she was on the other side of Salamanca, her eyes solely for the horse.

"A Duke!" His Grace exclaimed, raising his eyebrows. "And you are so interested in this Nobleman that you are waiting here to see him pass?"

"Interested in him?" A peal of laughter rang out. "No indeed, except that I have a curiosity to see a selfish, inconsiderate, conceited, puffed-up creature who has set my friends in a turmoil!"

"I wonder of whom you are speaking?" the Duke asked with a rueful expression on his face.

"Oh, I will tell you if you are interested," Miss Verena replied, raising her hand as she spoke to pat Salamanca. "He is His Grace, the Odious Duke of Selchester!"

3

For the moment the Duke was too astonished to speak. Then before he could find words Verena said:

"But I should not be speaking like this to a stranger! Grandpapa always says that my tongue runs away with me, so please forget such an indiscretion."

As she spoke there came a whinny from behind them and the Duke turned his head to see that her horse was following close in the rear of Salmanca.

"Does your horse always follow you without being led?" he asked in surprise.

"Yes, always," Verena replied. "I have had him since he was a foal and he would follow me into the house if I allowed him to do so. He is so obedient that if I said: 'Go home!' he would leave us at once! And if Grandpapa wants me he only has to say: 'Assaye, find Verena!' and he discovers me however far I may be from the house!"

"Assaye?" the Duke questioned. "Is that his name?"

"It was Grandpapa's favourite battle," she replied, "and I have heard the tale of it so often that I almost feel as if I was there myself."

"Your Grandfather was in the Mahratta War, I gather?" the Duke remarked.

"He was at Seringapatam," Verena said, "and came home to England with Lord Wellington when he returned in 1805. And later he joined him on the Peninsula!"

"What was your Grandfather's name?" the Duke enquired.

"Winchcombe," Verena answered. "General Sir Alexander Winchcombe."

"Good Heavens!" the Duke ejaculated. "Old Bark and Bite!"

Then he added quickly:

"I beg your pardon, Miss Winchcombe, I should not have said that!"

"Do not apologise," Verena replied. "Grandpapa is proud of his nickname. He has so often told me how he acquired it. Do you know the story?"

"No, pray tell me," the Duke answered.

"It was when Grandpapa joined the Duke's army on the Peninsula. He walked into the Mess the first evening and heard a young Officer say: 'I hear a new General has arrived, one of these Indian Wallahs—all bark and no bite, I expect!' And Grandpapa turned round and said: "On the contrary, Sir, I both bark and bite!'"

The Duke laughed.

"I never met Your Grandfather, but I always heard him spoken of with great respect. He was a magnificent Commander."

"It is wonderful to hear you say that!" Verena exclaimed. "To me he is a very marvellous person and I know that if you were a soldier he would have liked to meet you, especially if you served in the Peninsula War. But Grandpapa . . ." She paused.

"He is not dead?" the Duke asked.

She shook her head.

"Not yet," she answered in a low voice. "But I am afraid he will not live long. He has had a heart attack and at the moment he is in a kind of coma. At times he is conscious, but he does not recognise anybody . . . not even me!"

There was a little sob in her voice which told the Duke how deeply she cared.

"I am sorry," he said.

"I try to be brave," she answered. "Grandpapa dislikes people who are over-emotional—especially females. The one thing he cannot abide is tears."

There was silence for a moment. Then she said with an obvious effort to change the subject:

"You have not told me the name of your horse."

"Salamanca," the Duke replied.

"Were you in that battle?" she asked, her eyes wide.

"Yes," he answered.

"And at Vittoria?" she enquired.

Again the Duke acquiesced and felt for the first time that Verena looked at him as if she really recognised that he was a man—not just the owner of a magnificent horse!

"Then you must have the Gold Cross," she said, "with your four battles inscribed on each arm."

"I admit to that honour," the Duke said. "But I would have been exceeding proud to sport the Mysore and Seringapatam Medals, which doubtless your Grandfather was awarded."

"Grandpapa has many decorations," Verena said. "But he lost the only person who mattered to him—my father was killed at Waterloo."

"I can see that you have military blood in your veins," the Duke said.

"I have indeed," she replied, lifting her chin with a little, unconscious gesture of pride. "All the Winchcombes have served their country, but now there is no one left in the . . . direct line."

There was a little pause before the last two words and the Duke sensed there was some reserve about this and wondered what it could be.

But he was most curious to know why she was waiting for his coach to arrive and he was turning over in his mind how to approach the subject when they reached the blacksmith's.

They had been walking down a narrow lane and now found themselves on the bank of a small stream with several cottages facing onto it.

Attached to one was the forge of a blacksmith. The cinders were glowing and the anvil was shining in the light from them. But the place was empty.

Verena took one look, went to the cottage door and knocked. A second or so later it was opened by a middle-aged woman wiping her hands on her apron.

"Good-day, Miss Verena," she said with a soft Bedfordshire accent. "Be ye wanting Fred?"

"Yes, indeed," Verena answered. "There is a Gentleman here whose horse has cast a shoe."

"Then ye'd best stable th'animal at th'back," the woman said. "Fred will not be home for n'hour at least."

"Where has he gone?" Verena enquired.

"Over to th'farm, Miss. There be trouble with one o' Farmer Wilk's cows and ye knows as well as Oi do that Fred's real handy when there be difficulty with th'calving."

"Yes, there is no one like him!" Verena replied. "But

I hope he will not be long. I expect the Gentleman wishes to get on his way."

"Fred'll be home for his supper, right enough," the woman answered. "Ye knows where to put th'horse, Miss Verena?"

"Yes, I know, do not trouble yourself, Mrs. Favel," Verena replied. "I expect you are busy with the children."

She turned away as she spoke and beckoning to the Duke went ahead to show him the way. At the back of the house there was a rough stall, open on one side, but bedded down with clean straw and a manger filled with hay.

The Duke tied Salamanca's bridle to the iron manger, then bent down to look at the sprained fetlock.

He felt it and found to his relief that it was not swollen. But Salamanca winced at the touch of his fingers and moved a little restlessly.

"You are hurting him," Verena said. "Let me see what I can do."

She crouched down, massaging the fetlock very gently with both her small hands, at the same time talking to Salamanca softly in a voice which seemed to the Duke to have something almost hypnotic about it.

There was no doubt that the great horse approved of what she was doing. At first he twitched back his ears, but after a moment or two, as if he understood she intended to help him, he started quietly to eat the hay in front of him, making no effort to move.

The Duke, after a moment's anxiety in case Salamanca should lash out at a stranger, moved away to stand leaning against the outside post of the stall, watching Verena.

He had heard of women who had healing in their fingers but he had always thought they were gypsies or ignorant country folk who were supposed to be nearer to nature than those who were educated.

Yet here was someone with the healing touch who looked like a Lady of Quality and undoubtedly was one!

At the same time, he thought, watching Verena's face as she talked to Salamanca, the girl had a kind of elfin loveliness about her. It was something he could not explain even to himself and was in fact a kind of beauty he had never encountered before.

Verena's eyelashes were long and dark against the clear transparency of her skin, and the curls of her brown hair seemed to have faint glints of gold in them to match her eyes. Her waist was tiny, her figure curved sweetly in budding maturity.

"She will make some country Squire or maybe a soldier exceedingly happy!" the Duke thought to himself.

Verena massaged Salamanca's fetlock for about ten minutes. Then she stood up and patting his neck, said:

"You will be all right, old boy, all you want is a shoe and you will be as good as new!"

And then for the first time since she had been attending to the stallion she looked at the Duke. He thought in fact that until this moment she had forgotten his very existence.

"There is nothing more we can do until Fred returns," she said. "I must go back. I only hope Billy has kept watch as I told him to do. We have been far longer than I intended."

"I will escort you," the Duke said.

"We shall see Fred when he comes home because Farmer Wilk's farm is on the other side of the village," Verena explained. "He will be riding a very old mare who only moves at about two miles an hour!"

The Duke drew his watch from his pocket. It was not yet five o'clock. If the blacksmith returned within the hour he could easily reach Eaton Socon by half past six, pick up his Carriage and arrive at Copple Hall soon after seven.

He would be late, but not inexcusably late. His Lordship might have to delay dinner a trifle, but that after all was of little consequence.

Verena turned up the narrow lane which was bordered with low hedges, green with the buds of spring, and beneath which nestled primroses and violets in vast profusion.

"Pray do not think me impertinent," the Duke said after a moment, "but I am consumed with curiosity as to why you should be so incensed with the Duke of Selchester."

"I told you that I should not have spoken with such devastating frankness," Verena replied, but her mouth was smiling and the Duke had a glimpse of her dimples.

"Please tell me," he begged, "otherwise you will condemn me to a sleepless night, while I lie wondering what His Grace can have done to incur your displeasure."

"He is utterly abominable!" Verena exclaimed. "Do you know that he was due at Copple Hall to stay with Lord Upminster two days ago! Pigs, calves and lambs have been slaughtered, a Boar's Head prepared, and they have already wrung the necks of no less than sixteen pigeons!

"Charmaine says that if she has to eat pigeon again when His Grace finally does appear, she will flap her arms like wings and fly!"

"His Grace is visiting Lord Upminster, I gather," the Duke observed.

"He is coming to pay his addresses to Charmaine," Verena replied, "and she is in floods of tears at the thought!"

"Do you know for certain that is the reason for his visit?" the Duke asked, choosing his words with care.

"It is obvious, is it not?" Verena replied. "His Grace writes from London to say he will be arriving to stay for two nights. He is barely acquainted with Lord and Lady Upminster, and it is well-known that his family have been pressing the Duke for years to produce an heir."

"And your friend Charmaine thinks that she may have taken the Duke's fancy?" the duke asked with what he hoped was a note of indifference in his voice.

"He has danced with her twice!" Verena answered, "and she is terrified of him! She says he looked down his nose at her as if she were a caterpillar crawling on his salad."

The Duke found it impossible not to laugh.

"Surely not a caterpillar!" he ejaculated.

"Well, any insect that he could flick away with a touch of his well-bred hand," Verena said scornfully. "Can you imagine the impertinence of it? He speaks to a girl on two occasions and decides she measures up to size as his future wife!"

"Perhaps it is not His Grace's intention to propose marriage," the Duke suggested mildly.

"Then why else would he wish to stay at Copple Hall?" Verena demanded. "It is a vastly uncomfortable house and Lord Upminster has no interest in anything save cattle! I cannot believe the high and mighty Duke of Selchester wants to talk calves for breakfast, cows for luncheon, and bulls for dinner!"

The Duke burst out laughing.

"It sounds a frightening prospect!"

"It is far worse for poor Charmaine!" Verena declared. "She had almost persuaded her father, as she had no other offers, to countenance her betrothal to the Honourable Clive Brothwicke.

"Of course he is only a second son with little sustenance, but he and Charmaine love each other, and if this had not happened I am convinced Lord Upminster would have allowed them to wed next year!"

"Well, surely it is quite easy," the Duke replied. "Miss Charmaine has only to refuse the Duke's addresses—if he makes them!"

"Refuse!" Verena exclaimed. "Can you be so cabbage-brained as to believe that Charmaine would be allowed to refuse a Duke? My Lord Upminster is hopping around like a gobble-cock at the prospect of having such a distinguished son-in-law, and Lady Upminster is already planning Charmaine's trousseau and contriving how to extract small sums from the housekeeping money when His Lordship is not looking!"

"Is that difficult?"

"You do not know Lord Upminster," Verena said. "He will not spend a penny-piece on his family. Everything must be saved for his cattle!"

"You make me feel quite sorry for his daughter," the Duke smiled.

"Everything would have been all right except for this odious Duke," Verena said. "Can you imagine, the monster actually announced that he was bringing ten servants with him! All of whom have to be accommodated, besides nine horses!"

Verena paused for a moment then continued in a different tone:

"The horses are what I hope to see. I am sure the Duke will have good horseflesh, however abominable he may be himself. I shall slip into the stables after he has arrived and have a look at his blood-stock! I doubt, however, if any of them will be as fine as Salamanca!"

"Will you not be meeting His Grace himself?" the Duke enquired.

"Certainly not! Lord Upminster does not approve of me. He says I am too outspoken, immodest and quite bereft of genteel graces! His Lordship prefers simpering creatures with down-cast eyes who sit tatting all day and only speak when spoken to!"

"I can see you do not fit into that category," the Duke said mockingly.

"Grandpapa always said that women are a damned nuisance anyway, and never more so than when they are being womanly."

The Duke laughed again. There was no doubt that this engaging girl was giving him furiously to think. At the same time he found her more amusing than any young female with whom he had ever conversed.

"But you still have not explained," he said as they reached the village green, "why you are waiting for the Duke."

"Do you not understand?" Verena said. "Copple Hall is a mile from here by road, the drive is nearly another half-mile. By riding across the fields I can be there in ten minutes.

"Charmaine is heartily bored with sitting about in her best gown waiting for the Duke when she might be meeting Clive in the shrubbery; and the cook has sworn she will not cook another pigeon until His Grace's horses are seen at the lodge gates."

She gave a little laugh.

"The moment I see the coach I will gallop across country to warn them that the conquering hero approaches! Charmaine will change her gown, cook will start roasting pigeons, and His Lordship will be waiting on the doorstep! And the Duke, because he is obviously a bumptious blockhead, will believe they are glad to see him!"

"His Grace also fought on the Peninsula," the Duke said quietly.

"I do not believe it!" Verena exclaimed in astonishment.

"I assure you it is the truth," the Duke replied. "I know he was there."

"Then if he was, he was like the Hanover Huzzars who later ran away at Waterloo!" Verena said scornfully. "I have often heard Grandpapa decry those young fops, those decorative young Gentlemen, who took to their heels and galloped all the way back to Brussels."

"They were not Englishmen, I assure you," the Duke replied frigidly, feeling he must defend himself.

There was a silence for a moment and then Verena said:

"I wish I could ask Grandpapa about the Duke; but anyway it is of no consequence. If those la-di-dah Society Bucks and Dandies did go to war, they found themselves swansdown jobs on the Staff and never got near enough to the enemy to see a shot fired."

Thinking of how cushy it had been to lie all night on the side of a mountain before the Battle of Bussaco and that the hunger and fever they suffered around Badajoz could hardly be described as swansdown, the Duke wanted to shake her. Nevertheless, he managed to say quite calmly:

"Many of the Bucks and Dandies you describe so scathingly did in fact fight with great gallantry, and a considerable number of them were killed in action!"

"Perhaps I am being unfair and prejudiced!" Verena said repentantly. "Grandpapa would rebuke me and I promise you that I have the greatest admiration for any soldier—whoever he may be—who suffered the discomforts of the Peninsula or who fought at Waterloo."

The Duke did not reply and after a moment she said almost shyly:

"Will you not tell me your name, Sir? For, if you have the medal of which we have just spoken, you must indeed be a brave man."

There was only an infinitesimal pause before the Duke replied:

"My name is Royd—Theron Royd."

"And your rank?"

"When I left the Army I was a Major."

"You must have hated to leave your Regiment," Verena said. "Grandpapa always told me it was the saddest day of his life when he said good-bye to the Grenadiers!"

"I think not only the Grenadiers, but the whole Army, must have missed your Grandfather."

"I am sure they did, and Oh, I do wish you could say that to him!"

They were by now nearing the Inn which the Duke noted was called the "Dog and Duck." There was no sign of Billy until Verena spied him half-way up an oak tree. She went to the foot of it.

"Have you seen the coach, Billy?"

"Nawta sight o'it, Miss Verena."

"Are you sure?"

Billy slithered down the tree.

"Slit me throat if Oi lie, Miss," he replied, making a gesture across his neck with a dirty finger. Then he ran off towards the back of the Inn.

"No Duke!" Verena exclaimed. "Do you think His Grace has been delayed by the turn of the cards in a Gaming Hell, or can he have succumbed to the charms of an over-toasted 'Incomparable'?"

The Duke smiled.

"What do you know of 'Incomparables', Miss Winchcombe?"

"Nothing, I am pleased to say!" Verena replied tartly. "But I am sure they and the odious Duke would deal well together!"

As she spoke Verena seated herself on the wooden

bench outside the Inn and the Duke followed her. Assaye, who had followed them, started to crop the grass.

"I like your horse," the Duke said. "Is it really true that he will obey everything you say to him?"

Verena smiled.

"Assaye!" she called. "Attention!"

The horse instantly straightened himself, his hooves together, his head held high staring straight ahead. He was completely motionless.

"At ease!" Verena commanded after nearly a minute had passed.

"I can make him die for the King," she said, "but when he gets up again he will roll and make such a mess of the saddle. What is the time? The Church clock has not worked for years."

The Duke drew his watch from his waistcoat pocket.

"A quarter after five."

"Then there is one thing certain," Verena said, "the Duke will not be coming now!"

"Why not?" the Duke enquired.

"Because the Upminsters dine at six," Verena replied, "and even if he arrived here this moment he could not reach the Hall in less than twenty minutes.

"And I do not suppose such a fastidious, conceited Coxcomb could change his clothes in under half an hour, do you?"

"I am sure His Grace would find it an impossibility," the Duke agreed, "although maybe he is not used to dining at country times."

"I thought of that," Verena confided, "and I told Charmaine to mention it to her father. But Lord Upminster replied that he was not going to have his belly rumbling with hunger for any ornament of the nobility, whoever he might be!"

Verena laughed and added:

67

"When His Lordship sees the Duke I suspect that he will be so delighted at His Grace's appearance that he will agree to dine at midnight if need be! Anyway, my vigil is at an end—for today at any rate."

She rose as she spoke.

"But you cannot leave!" the Duke said quickly. "Have you forgotten that I shall not recognise the blacksmith when he passes across the green? And I have no particular wish to sit with Salamanca in the stall until he returns."

"No, of course not. I had forgotten," Verena said. "But as a matter of fact I have something rather important to do."

"What is that?" the Duke asked.

She hesitated and the Duke knew she debated within herself whether she should confide in him. To his surprise he saw the brown eyes flecked with gold looking at him searchingly as if she seriously wondered whether he was trustworthy or not.

Verena was in fact thinking that the Duke seemed a very presentable man. She had thought at first that there was something rather conceited about him, as if he condescended to her, but now she thought that maybe he was shy of talking with strangers.

She had a strange feeling that he was not quite what he appeared to be. Why she had that impression she could not explain to herself. And then she suddenly thought that perhaps it was because men who had been habitually in uniform were never quite at their ease in civilian clothes, however elegant they might appear.

Major Royd was a soldier and that fact should commend him if nothing else did! How often since her Grandfather had been ill had she longed for someone to talk to who would be interested in the things with which she was concerned.

As if suddenly she made up her mind, Verena turned

round a little further on the seat and looking up at the Duke, said:

"If I tell you a secret, will you swear not to speak of it to anyone else unless I permit you to do so?"

"I swear," the Duke replied without hesitation.

"Then . . . something very strange is going on around here, and I am determined to discover what it is."

She hesitated for a moment and looked over her shoulder as if she was afraid someone was listening.

"I think," she said in a low voice, "it is something which involves Highwaymen. But if it is, there are quite a number of them and they are behaving in a most peculiar way!"

"What are they doing?" the Duke asked with a faint smile of amusement.

He had heard stories of this sort before and knew that the majority evolved from the superstitious fears of drunken yokels or the imagination of young women who had experienced nothing particularly exciting in their lives.

"Just down the road," Verena explained, "there is the Priory. It belongs to Grandpapa and was originally the family seat of the Winchcombes. But the top storeys were burnt out over fifty years ago and my Great-Grandfather moved to our present residence which was actually the Dower House. It was small and uncomfortable until Grandpapa made quite a large amount of prize money in the Mahratta War and spent it on enlarging the house and improving the Estate."

"I am glad the General received his prize money," the Duke interposed. "I always thought it extremely unfair that Wellington—or rather Colonel Wellesley as he was then—only received four thousand pounds after Seringapatam when the total treasure was estimated at well over a million!"

"Grandpapa thought it disgraceful too!" Verena agreed, "because he says it was really Colonel Wellesley who won the battle while General Harris received the credit and a hundred and fifty thousand pounds!"

"Prize money is always controversial," the Duke said, "but continue with your story."

"About a month ago the boys in the village began to talk about strange men being seen near the Priory," Verena went on. "I thought they were poachers or perhaps some travellers who had sought shelter there.

"And then a week ago Billy told me that he and another boy had seen four men going into the Priory carrying boxes or barrels on their horses.

"When I heard about it I rode over to the Priory on Assaye. There was no sign of anything unusual except that there were a lot of footmarks in the dust on the cellar steps and in the cellar itself."

Verena wrinkled her forehead.

"The boys are always truthful, especially Billy. He would not think of lying to me and I thought the men must have taken something to the Priory they wished to hide, then collected it again.

"I am sure they must have been Highwaymen. We are too far from the coast for smugglers to be bringing in brandy or other sorts of contraband."

The boys thought they were carrying barrels or boxes?" the Duke asked.

"That is what they told me," Verena answered. "And this afternoon, when I came here to wait for the Duke, Billy told me that the men had been seen again. He did not see them himself, but Tom, another village lad, swore that soon after dawn four men passed through the village and went up the old drive towards the Priory."

"Were they riding?" the Duke asked.

"Tom thought, although he could not be sure, that

each man carried a small barrel in front of him on his saddle."

"What are you going to do about it?" the Duke enquired.

"I had intended, if it became too late to expect the Duke, to visit the Priory on my way home," Verena answered. "It is not far from here. I suppose . . ."

She hesitated, then continued:

". . . I suppose you would not come with me?"

"I certainly do not think you should go there alone," the Duke answered.

"I am not afraid!" Verena retorted scornfully. "You must not think that! But it would be useful to have with me someone completely unprejudiced to see what is there and perhaps to decide if the footsteps in the dust are fresh."

"Let us hope that the contraband is still in evidence," the Duke smiled. "Footsteps are not very conclusive evidence."

"No indeed," Verena agreed. "And pray Heaven it is not any of our local men getting up to mischief."

"If it was, would that worry you?" the Duke asked.

"Grandpapa has always felt a responsibility towards all the families in Little Copple. A number of the men work on our Estate, and the Winchcombes had lived here for generations before Lord Upminster's father bought the Hall."

"So, if your local yokels have 'taken to the road', you will try to persuade them to embrace a more respectable calling," the Duke said mockingly.

"I am sure, Major Royd, that you felt you had a responsibility towards your troops in the War," Verena said severely. "We at home believe we have a similar responsibility towards those who serve us."

The Duke, who was a conscientious landlord, and showed both his tenants and his employees a generosity that was unrivalled in the vicinity of Selchester Castle, replied meekly:

"I stand rebuked!"

"That was rude of me," Verena said impulsively. "Forgive me? But since Grandpapa's illness I try to do what he would have wished and it is not always easy when there is no one to whom I can turn for advice."

"Do you live alone with your Grandfather?" the Duke enquired.

"Mama and I came to live with him after Papa was killed at Waterloo. Then Mama died, and since my Governess retired Grandpapa and I have been very happy alone. Grandpapa is somewhat crusty at times and a lot of people do not understand the manner in which he . . ."

Verena hesitated for a word.

"Barks at them!" the Duke interposed.

She dimpled at him.

"That is right! I have never felt his bite, but sometimes his wounds hurt him and he has had lumbago on and off ever since he served in India. Then indeed he can be very irritable!"

"Who could blame him?" the Duke enquired. "But I am certain of one thing, your Grandfather would not wish you to visit the old Priory alone. I will accompany you."

"That is very kind of you," Verena said. "And when we come back we can take a short cut to the blacksmith's shop. So if Fred is back by that time, we shall find him there. Anyway, when he does return home his wife will tell him that Salamanca is waiting for attention."

"Come along then," the Duke said with a smile.

He had a feeling he would like to put out his hand and hold Verena's—almost as if she were a child he was taking for a walk.

Instead, they moved side by side and the Duke thought he had never known anyone so unaffected, so completely lacking in self-consciousness as this attractive young woman in the green habit.

Assaye followed them without being told to do so. They progressed across the green and down the dusty roadway until about a hundred yards outside the village they came to a stone-flanked gateway covered with ivy and a drive on which the mass was growing thickly.

"This is the entrance!" Verena said.

The Duke, moving forward, saw there was an avenue of very ancient oak trees which had interlocked their branches overhead across the drive, so that it had become an eerie tunnel of darkness even in the clear light of the sun.

"I am sure the villagers think this place is full of ghosts," he suggested.

"Of course," Verena answered. "And indeed, we actually have several family phantoms. There is a white nun who wrings her hands for some crime for which she is doing eternal penance; and a Cavalier who clanks his chains and bumps overhead on floors that no longer exist."

"And you are not frightened of them?" the Duke enquired.

"You forget I am a soldier's daughter!" Verena said. "I would be ashamed to run away from some spooky creature that could not really hurt me."

"Let me, however, suggest you be wary of any human creatures who may frequent this place," the Duke said. "Highwaymen are desperate ruffians, and I must beg of you, Miss Winchcombe, never to come here alone."

"I have played in the Priory ever since I was a child," Verena retorted. "I am not going to allow a lot of ne'er-do-wells to scare me!"

"Do not be foolish," the Duke said sharply. "Surely you know that to walk deliberately into danger is as foolhardy as the charge of the heavy cavalry at Waterloo, of which your Grandfather must have spoken."

"He has described it to me a hundred times!" Verena answered. "No cavalry had ever before routed so great a body of infantry in formation. You may think them fool-hardy but it was extremely gallant!"

"Out of the whole charge only fifty remained alive," the Duke said harshly. "And the horses suffered abominably. I hope never to see again such a terrible slaughter!"

Verena looked at him searchingly. After a moment she said slowly:

"I have a feeling that far too often when there are wars those who remain at home, especially women, are regaled only with the glorious exploits! In actual fact war is cruel and evil, is it not?"

"That was what the Duke of Wellington said himself," the Duke replied, "or something like it. His actual words were: 'I hope to God I have fought my last battle. It is a bad thing to be always fighting.'"

"I had not heard he said that," Verena said. "But I have often thought that if I have a son I would wish him to serve his country and be a soldier. But I would also pray every night that he would never be called upon to fight in a war that involves so much sacrifice and suffering as the wars in which my Grandfather, my father, and you, have fought!"

"That is the right sentiment where women are concerned," the Duke approved.

"At the same time I would not wish my son to be a coward," Verena said quickly.

"I think that is extremely unlikely for one who were your son," the Duke replied.

She looked up at him and he saw her eyes shine.

"That is the nicest compliment anyone has ever paid me! Thank you, Major Royd! And now here we are at the Priory."

As she spoke she turned to Assaye who was still behind them and said commandingly:

"Hide, Assaye!"

The horse hesitated, then trotted off towards a clump of trees beyond the house.

"Will he really hide?" the Duke asked in amazement.

"Indeed he will," Verena answered. "We used to hide together when I wished to escape my Governess and then I taught him 'hide and seek'. I swear it would be almost impossible for you, as a stranger, to find him!"

"It is incredible!" the Duke exclaimed.

He saw that the Priory had once been a beautiful Elizabethan building. Of the two top floors there were only a few blackened walls standing and the roof had completely gone.

The garden was a wilderness, and a lake at the back of the house, where the monks had once caught their fish, was almost hidden by shrubs.

"I will take you down to the cellar," Verena informed him. "But walk carefully; some of the stairs have worn with age and it is easy to slip and land at the bottom on your back."

"I will certainly be careful," the Duke replied drily.

The ground floor of the house consisted of walls with empty windows, of burnt and blackened ceilings, the plaster now crumbling onto the floor.

A miscellaneous amount of rubbish had accumulated in what must have once been an elegant hallway, with a carved oak staircase curving upwards.

Verena preceded him across the Hall under the staircase and down a passage which led to what had once been the servants' quarters.

The place was festooned with cobwebs and dust lay thick on the floor. The Duke could see that tracks had been made fairly recently, which might have been caused by nothing more sinister than the feet of village children exploring the ruins, or by Verena herself when she came to search for contraband!

The Duke did not believe her story of the Highwaymen. At the same time, at the back of his mind he had the strange feeling that these were pointers to something important.

Verena stopped at the cellar steps. The door which once shut them off from the main passage had been torn from its hinges. As they descended, they got some light from long narrow windows at ground level, which were still secured by rusty iron bars.

The cellars, piled with all sorts of debris, appeared to run the whole length of the huge house. As the Duke and Verena went from room to room they were conscious of a feeling of damp and chill. Besides the main cellars, divided neatly with rough stone walls, each had an inner cavern secreted behind a huge oak door furnished with iron bolts and an impressive lock. These now stood open to reveal only an eerie darkness.

As the Duke followed Verena he noted an enormous number of rusting bottle-racks and ancient barrels of great size which had once contained ale.

"Your ancestors certainly enjoyed their liquor," the Duke remarked, and heard his voice echo round the empty caverns.

"My Great-Grandfather was a four-bottle man!" Verena smiled.

"So was mine!" the Duke replied.

They went into yet another cellar, where there were

dozens more empty barrels, but the door of the inner cave was closed and barred.

Verena stopped suddenly.

"When I was last here," she said in a low voice, "that door was open."

"Are you sure?" the Duke asked her.

"I am quite certain," she replied.

"Well, let us open the door now and see if there is anything inside," the Duke said.

He walked towards it as he spoke and saw that the lock had been turned but there was no key.

"It is locked!" he exclaimed.

"I know where the keys are," Verena told him.

"Where is that?"

'It will take me a minute or two because it is at the far end."

She sped away from him leaving the Duke staring at the door. He inspected the lock carefully. It was quite obvious that someone had oiled it recently. It was very large—the type of lock the monks used in the old days on Church doors and apparently in the cellars of their Priories.

There were also two bolts, and these moved surprisingly easily as the Duke pulled them back. Then he inspected the keyhole again. He was wondering now whether Verena would find the key where she had expected.

If anyone was using this particular cellar for illicit purposes he was not likely to restore the key to its normal place; and it was extremely unlikely, in view of the craftsmanship of the monks, that the locks in any of these cellars would be identical!

He was just wondering if it would be possible to force an entrance but doubting that even with the right tools it would be possible, when he heard a step behind him.

"Have you found the key?" he intended to ask, thinking it was Verena.

But as he opened his lips to speak he felt a blinding crash on his head followed immediately by another. He found himself falling . . .

Then he knew no more.

4

Verena went to the far end of the cellar where in an alcove there was a concealed cache which the monks had made centuries ago to hold their keys.

Even if the Duke wished to accompany her she would not have let him into the secret which her Grandfather had shown her years ago, telling her it was known only to the Winchcombe family and had been handed down from father to son.

"No I have no son," he said sadly, "I must show it to you because, Child, you are the last direct descendant of a line that has existed for five centuries."

This had all seemed very impressive to a little girl of ten, and when the General had pulled a lever hidden behind a pillar and slowly a huge stone had moved to disclose a small opening, she had been thrilled.

The hole was just large enough for a man to insert his hand. In a hollow space inside the pillar was a huge hook and on it was hung, attached to a circular piece of wire, the huge keys of the cellar.

Verena used to wonder why the monks had taken such precautions about their wine; for there was no doubt that it would have been impossible for anyone not knowing the secret of the keys to find them. What was more, she had always believed it would be impossible for anyone to force open the cellar doors.

Now, when she reached the alcove in which the secret cache lay, she looked back to make quite certain that the Duke had not followed her.

Then, still with a little thrill of excitement which had never left her all down the years, she pulled the iron lever and slowly the stone moved.

She slipped her small hand inside only to find there was nothing attached to the iron hook. She thought the keys must have fallen off but the cache was not deep and there was nothing at the bottom of it except dust and a few pieces of stone.

Verena stood looking at the age-old hiding-place with a frown between her eyes.

"Who could have learnt that the keys were hidden here?" she wondered.

It could not have been someone who had discovered the secret by mistake; for, if so, it was unlikely that he would have closed the stone again and thrust back the lever.

Slowly, puzzled and worried, she walked back towards the Duke. She did not intend to let him know even now of the secret place. Instead, she thought, she would just say that the keys had been stolen.

But someone knew of the keys and their whereabouts! Someone had taken them and locked the cellar door! And that person, whoever it might be, had come to the Priory since her visit last week!

Verena was so deep in her thoughts that she did not

even realise that she had now reached the cellar where she had left the Duke. Then, as she walked into it, she saw as if in a flash of a second, a man hit the Duke with a large knotted cudgel. The first blow spun his high hat from his head and made him stagger—then at a second blow he fell.

For a moment Verena was too paralysed with horror to cry out. Then as the Duke hit the floor with a dull thud she heard footsteps coming down the stone stairs.

Swiftly, without even consciously thinking about it, she slipped behind the great empty barrels which lay between her and the man with the cudgel.

It was the instinct of self-preservation which made her crouch down low on the dusty floor. Her heart was thumping so loudly with fear that she thought it must betray her. She could hear the footsteps coming nearer and nearer until they entered the cellar where she was hiding.

It was then she heard the Man with the Cudgel speak—

"I found a stranger here, Sir. He be down for the count but do you think he was seeking for evidence against us?"

The man did not speak with an educated voice, yet at the same time he was not illiterate and had no particular accent. It was rather the tone, Verena thought, of a superior servant.

There was no doubt that the man who replied to him spoke with the cultured drawl of a Gentleman:

"A man! The Devil take it! He is not a Bow Street Runner?"

"Not in those boots, Sir!"

Verena thought that the Gentleman inspected the fallen Duke.

"No, you are right! He is certainly not a Runner!"

"Shall I turn him over so that you can see his visage, Sir?"

"To what purpose? Maybe he is just a traveller seeking refuge from the inclemency of the weather. It is raining hard."

"Shall I blow a piece of lead in him, Sir?" the Man with the Cudgel asked.

"You damned fool!" the Gentleman ejaculated. "Dead men cause questions to be asked and tales carried to the Magistrates! Let us get on with our task. It is a cursed nuisance that he has come here because it means we dare not use this place again, not at any rate for a month or two! Have you got the key?"

"Here it is, Sir," the Man with the Cudgel replied.

"Then get the door opened, and be quick about it," the Gentleman commanded.

Peeping through the barrels Verena could see the Man with the Cudgel inserting a key in the lock. He had his back to her but she could see the profile of the Gentleman quite clearly.

Sharp-featured, with a pointed nose over a thin, tight-lipped mouth, he was dressed with exceeding elegance. His expensively-cut coat fitted tightly to his body, his cravat was tied in the most intricate folds and the points of his collar were high above his chin.

He wore his high hat at an angle and he had, she thought, the look of a Dandy, or at least a Gentleman of Fashion.

The Man with the Cudgel had opened the cellar door and now he plunged into the darkness to return carrying what appeared to be a heavy wooden box, heavily corded and sealed.

"How many?" the Gentleman enquired.

"Four, Sir. The coach was bound for York and I think we can definitely have an exceptional haul this time!"

There was a crash as the Man with the Cudgel set the box on the floor, and as he straightened himself, seeking in his pocket for a knife with which to cut the cords, Verena could see his face quite clearly.

She had expected someone evil-looking, a desperado or a ruffian with perhaps sword-cuts on his face, and definitely coarse-featured. But instead the man had almost a sanctimonious air.

His hair was grey, turning white at the temples, he had unremarkable features, but sharp, shrewd eyes beneath thick eyebrows. He might have been a tradesman or a Butler, she thought, and was not in the least like her idea of a Highwayman!

He bent down and a moment later she heard the Gentleman exclaim with a note of triumph in his voice:

"God! What a prize! Gold! Thousands of sovereigns!"

"That was what I suspicioned, Sir! If you'll start putting the coins into the sack I'll bring out the rest."

Under cover of a loud clinking of coins, very, very cautiously Verena edged her way a little further behind the barrels until she could see round them and perceive the face of the Gentleman.

He was taking handfuls of gold coins from the box and placing them into a long, narrow sack such as grocers sometimes used to hold rice and other such commodities.

He had, as she suspected, a well-bred countenance, but there was something far more unpleasant about him than about the man and the Cudgel. His face was thin and dissipated while the expression in his eyes as he transferred the gold from the sack was one of such outrageous greed as to be repulsive.

The Man with the Cudgel came from the cavern carrying four more boxes. He opened them and Verena heard him exclaim:

"Bank of England Notes in this one, Sir."

"Used or unused?" the Gentleman enquired.

"The majority, Sir, appear to be used!"

"Good, then they will be safe. Have you another sack for them?"

"Yes, Sir. I brought four with me."

"That should be enough," the Gentleman drawled. "Open the other boxes."

There was a noise of the lids of the boxes being pressed back on the floor.

"More sovereigns!" she heard the Gentleman drawl.

Then the Man with the Cudgel remarked:

"Bonds in this one! Do we dare keep them, Sir?"

"No, too dangerous!" the Gentleman replied. "Chuck them into the water with the other boxes, but cord it first—they might float!"

"I had thought of that, Sir," the Man with the Cudgel said with just a hint of rebuke in his voice.

There was no answer and he continued:

"I'll be taking this sack up to the curricle, Sir. I'm only hoping there will be room for the lot in the hidey-hole!"

"You will just have to pack it tight," the Gentleman replied. "I said when the hiding-place was being made that it was not big enough!"

"'Tis the first time there's been a squeeze," the Man with the Cudgel replied. "If we'd had it any bigger, Sir, it might have appeared suspicious. As it is, it'd take a sharp eye to notice the difference from any other Gentleman's vehicle!"

"Hurry up, you fool, and stop nattering!" the Gentleman suddenly said testily. "Get it all aboard and let us clear out! It gives me the creeps to be here with that man lying on the floor!"

"He'll not be hearing anything we're saying, Sir," the Man with the Cudgel said with a snigger. "But if you are worried, let me make sure he won't blab. There's no point in taking risks!"

"There will be far more risk if we leave any more dead bodies about," the Gentleman snarled.

"Very good, Sir," the Man with the Cudgel replied.

Putting the sack of gold under one arm and one of the boxes under the other, he went from the cellar and up the steps.

Verena kept absolutely motionless. She knew that it was dangerous to stare too fixedly at the Gentleman now that he was alone. She was well aware how easy it was for someone to feel instinctively that he was being watched.

Because she was afraid of being discovered, she shut her eyes, listening to the clink of coins as the Gentleman filled the sack.

The Man with the Cudgel returned. Again, he carried a sack and a box up the cellar stairs. And now there was only the soft rustle of notes as the Gentleman transferred them from the third wooden box.

"Fifteen thousand pounds at least!" he muttered once to himself.

The fourth box, which contained the bonds, was recorded when the Man with the Cudgel returned. Now the whole operation was finished.

The Gentleman straightened himself and Verena saw him look towards the fallen Duke.

"I wonder if he was really suspicious?" he asked. "No, just a traveller, Hickson! I am certain of it. Perhaps thirsty and in search of a drink! Well, let us make sure those who find him will be convinced that he wandered in here by a drunken mistake!"

"How are you going to do that, Sir?" Hickson asked.

"Quite simple," the Gentleman replied with an unpleasant smile on his lips.

As he spoke he unscrewed the gold top of the elegant

malacca cane which he had been carrying when he came into the cellar. He drew from the stick a long, thin glass phial which Verena knew contained brandy. She had seen such a stick before; in fact her father had owned one.

As the Gentleman opened the phial and poured the contents over the Duke's neck she heard him say:

"Waste of good brandy, but it is doubtful if anyone will believe him if he blabbers of locked doors when they find him smelling strongly of the grape!"

"You are clever, Sir, that's what you are!" Hickson said. "I've never known a Gentleman with such a mind for detail!"

"That is why we are successful, Hickson," the Gentleman replied with satisfaction. "Always remember that in operations like ours it is the details that count, every one of them! That reminds me—you had no trouble this morning?"

"None at all, Sir, it happened just as you planned. That bit of marshland near the river was that misty you couldn't see a hand in front of your face. The guards were dead before they knew what had hit them, and the coachmen, unconscious, were tied up and inside the coach before they could utter an oath!"

"They did not see any of you?"

"No, Sir, and anyway we all had our faces covered."

"Good man, I congratulate you, Hickson!"

"I was only carrying out your orders, Sir," Hickson said with a note of servility.

"And mind you always do so!" the Gentleman admonished. "That is a hundred guineas in your pockets, Hickson, and fifty for each of your men! Not bad for a morning's work!"

"Not bad at all, Sir," Hickson replied. "But I did hope that you would see your way, Sir, to increasing the remuneration. I've my expenses, Sir, as you well know, and I've to make certain that the men I employ on your behalf are trustworthy. 'Tis not always easy."

There was silence. Verena could see that the two men were facing each other and she knew by the tenseness of the Gentleman's figure that he was angry and at the same time alarmed.

"What are you asking?" he enquired at last and the resentful note in his voice was very obvious.

"Five hundred sovereigns, Sir," Hickson replied in an almost silky tone. "I can't manage with less. 'Tis quite impossible. And seeing the size of this haul, Sir, the men are expecting a trifle more. Say now a hundred sovereigns each."

"Curse you! This is blackmail!" the Gentleman exclaimed.

"No indeed, Sir," Hickson said in shocked tones. "Just a generous gesture on your part and an expression of your satisfaction, Sir, at the way in which your plans were carried out."

"Blast you, but you know I cannot refuse!" the Gentleman exclaimed. "Very well, you can take the blasted money when we get to London. But do not drive me too far, Hickson, or I might find other agents to carry out my commands."

"I think it might be a mistake, Sir, at this juncture, were we to fall out over a few paltry coins."

Hickson's voice was still that of a well-trained servant but at the same time there was no mistaking the threat underlying his words.

There was a moment's pause and Verena saw the men were eyeing each other. Then the Gentleman turned towards the cellar steps, carrying the sack in one hand.

"Let us get out of here," he said harshly, "before it becomes too curst dangerous!"

He walked away. Hickson put the sack containing

the notes under one arm and picked up the two remaining boxes. His cudgel dangled from the fingers of one hand.

Looking round the cellar, he seemed to stare for a moment at the Duke, and then chuckling beneath his breath he followed in the wake of his master.

Verena did not move. She waited, half afraid one of them might return, until listening intently, far away in the distance she thought she heard the sound of horses' hooves.

The Duke was suddenly aware of voices—voices speaking in low tones. Yet at first he could not understand what they were saying.

He had thought, on the few occasions when he had been capable of coherent thought, that he was on a battle-field and that he had been wounded. He could remember wondering why the ground felt so soft.

The pain in his head had been very real, and he imagined that a French bullet might be lodged in it or maybe he had been close-shaved by a cannon-ball.

He could recall crying out because he was so thirsty, and wondered who could have brought him a drink in a cup rather than in an Army water-bottle. What he had drunk had not had the brackish taste of water that had travelled for several days on the saddle of a horse!

Then he thought how infuriating it was to be wounded after having survived for so long unscathed.

"Damn the Frenchies!" he murmured to himself and thought that a woman answered him—which was of course ridiculous!

But now he knew that he was lying in a bed—a soft bed. His head still hurt and it was too much effort to open his eyes. He heard a man's voice say:

"You're sure it's not too much for you, Miss Verena,

staying up yet another night with the gentleman? You had best let Dr. Graves send us Mrs. Doughty!"

"I would not have that drunken old midwife in the house," a young voice replied scornfully, "let alone allow her to look after a sick man! Do not worry about me, Travers, you have Grandpapa on your hands and that is enough for anyone!"

"I don't like it, Miss Verena, and that's a fact!"

"Well, you will just have to put up with it!" Verena answered with a hint of laughter in her voice. "You know as well as I do, Travers, that I am well able to care for anyone who is sick. Now go to bed, and if I need you I will ring the bell. That I promise."

"If the Gentleman comes conscious you let me know at once, Miss Verena! And also if he begins throwing himself about again in delirium!"

"If he does I will take care of him as I have done before," Verena interrupted. "You must admit, Travers, that I was the only person who could handle him."

"That's true enough, Miss Verena. Well, if there's anything you want you've but to ring the bell or give me a call. I'm only just down the passage, as well you know."

"Go to bed, Travers, and stop clucking over me like a broody hen!" Verena said. "The Doctor expects that Major Royd is unlikely to regain consciousness until tomorrow. Good-night, Travers."

"Good-night, Miss."

There was the sound of a closing door and now the waves of darkness started to recede from the Duke's brain and he began to remember the girl in the green habit waiting for the Duke of Selchester! The ruined Priory where she had taken him! The locked door in the cellar—yes, that was where it had happened!

He could recall the sudden crash on his head, the sensation of falling, then darkness—a darkness in which he had felt himself struggling for hours—or was it days?

With what seemed an almost superhuman effort the Duke opened his eyes. He was lying in a large canopied bed, a curtain was pulled on one side to shield him from a lighted candle, and sitting beside the bed in a high-backed chair, was Verena.

He remembered her now. The small heart-shaped face with its elfin loveliness, the gold speckled eyes, the dark brown hair which fell over her shoulders—he did not recall it was so long.

Then he realised she was wearing a wrap of white wool, corded round her slim waist, with wide sleeves almost like a monk's robe.

There was a book in her hand and she was holding it sideways so as to catch the light from the candle.

The Duke did not speak, but all at once she looked up at him as if she sensed he was no longer unconscious.

She set down her book, rose and came to his side.

"Are you awake at last?" she enquired in a soft musical voice.

He did not reply and she put a small, cool hand on his forehead. It made him recall how often in the torturous darkness of his dreams he had felt the coolness of that hand and had thought it was the cold wind blowing over the mountains in Portugal.

"Where am I?"

His lips could hardly form the words but she understood.

"You are in my Grandfather's house," she answered. "You are quite safe and I am nursing you."

"How long?"

"This is the second day you have been here," she replied, "and it will be the third night since you received the blows on your head."

"Who was it?"

"I will tell you later," she replied. "Go to sleep."

He felt her fingers moving on his forehead and the gentle pressure seemed almost mesmeric. There was so much more he wanted to ask her but somehow it was not of consequence. He was tired, he wanted to sleep, and the insistence of those fingers was quite irresistible . . .

When he awoke again it was morning. There was no sign of Verena but a manservant was tidying his bed. He was not a young man but there was something in his carriage, in the manner in which he held his head and shoulders that told the Duke that he had been a soldier.

Then he remembered he was in the house of General Sir Alexander Winchcombe—"Old Bark and Bite"— and it was his Grand-daughter who had brought him here! The same girl, curse her, who was responsible for the pain in his head.

"I see you are awake, Sir," a respectful voice said before him. "Would you care for something to eat or drink?"

"I would like a shave," the Duke replied.

"Very good, Sir, and may I suggest that you partake of the light gruel that Miss Verena has prepared for you?"

"I will take nothing of the sort," the Duke wanted to retort, but somehow it was too much of an effort.

When the gruel came he drank it.

He was not asleep when the servant shaved him although most of the time he kept his eyes closed. However, he must have dozed off because it seemed only a few minutes later that it was the afternoon and Verena came into the room with the Doctor behind her.

The Duke had thought himself annoyed with her, and yet when she came to his side and stood smiling at him engagingly, he found it impossible not to smile back.

She looked so young, so fresh, and so infuriatingly well in the sunlight coming through the windows.

"Here is Doctor Graves to see you, Major Royd."

The Doctor was a jovial, middle-aged man, who, despite a practice extending over many miles of country, found time to hunt three days in the winter and to enjoy many boating expeditions in the summer on the River Ouse.

He examined the Duke's head.

"It's a good thing you are so tall, Major," he said. "If the blow had been on the top of your head we might have been in trouble! As it is, the cudgel, or whatever those villainous footpads used, stunned you but has done no particular damage. We need not be afraid you will end up in Bedlam!"

The Doctor chuckled at his joke, which the Duke thought singularly unfunny.

"Rest is what you require," the Doctor continued. "Rest and sleep. Eat anything you fancy, but do not try to get up until you are quite certain the floor will not rise and hit you in the face!"

Again the Doctor chuckled.

"You've got a good physique, young man, which is half the battle! Incidentally, as you are a soldier, that is the right expression, if I may say so!"

"How long shall I have to stay here?" the Duke asked.

"If you take my advice you will stay here as long as possible," the Doctor said. "You are comfortable, you have not got to exert yourself; and you have an excellent nurse!"

He smiled at Verena as he spoke.

"Thank you kindly, Sir," she replied. "Unfortunately your patient does not appreciate me. Indeed, when he was delirious he kept thinking I was one of Bonaparte's soldiers and trying to shoot me!"

"Make him apologise!" the Doctor said, "or dock his rations."

Enjoying his own sense of humour the Doctor patted the Duke on the shoulder.

"Now be sensible, Major. If you get up too soon you'll feel as if your head is being split open with a chopper. And what is more, you may well find yourself back in bed for a week or so! I will call in two days' time, and no heroics until I see you again!"

He walked across the room with Verena following him. The Duke listened to them talking about the General until he could hear them no more.

His head was still hurting more than he cared to admit to himself. Because he disliked the feeling of being helpless he scowled at Verena when she came back into the room.

"One thing should cheer you up," she remarked. "You are not going to be a turnip-brain as a result of all this!"

"That is, of course, a great comfort to me," the Duke remarked drily. "And I would like to point out, young woman, that this would not have occurred at all had you not persuaded me to go seeking for Highwaymen in that peculiarly unpleasant cellar of yours!"

"It was not Highwaymen who attacked you, nor a footpad as I told the Doctor," Verena answered. "It was the Bullion thieves!"

The Duke forgot his own grievances.

"Bullion thieves!" he ejaculated. "How do you know?"

"I saw them," Verena replied. "Oh, I am so glad you are better! I have been aching to tell you what happened. Are you well enough to listen?"

"Of course I am well enough!" the Duke replied sharply. "Tell me exactly what occurred."

She hesitated.

"The Doctor said you were to be kept quiet!"

"If there is one thing that is likely to put me in a fidget," the Duke replied, "it is that after having whetted my curiosity you should refuse to tell me what occurred after I was ignominiously disposed of by an unseen hand!"

"The hand which held the cudgel belonged to a man called Hickson," Verena replied. "He did not look in the least like a Highwayman or indeed the desperado which in fact he is. I heard him admit to having killed the two guards on the Bullion Coach and to have bound and gagged the coachmen."

The Duke was so interested that he made a movement as if he would sit up. But instantly there was a sharp, excruciating pain in his head which made him sink back against the pillows.

"No, do not move!" Verena said sharply, adjusting the pillows carefully behind him.

"I cannot see you properly," he complained weakly. "I do not want to miss a word of what you are telling me."

"Then I will sit on the bed so that you can see me," she replied.

Without any sign of shyness or embarrassment she perched on the side of the high bed which was wide enough to be intended for two people. The Duke could lie at his ease looking up at her, and he thought once again that she was unlike any young woman he had ever met before.

Her hair was neatly arranged with fashionable curls falling on each side of her cheeks, and the rest was coiled neatly on the top of her head.

He remembered how, when he had first come back

to consciousness, it had fallen over her shoulders, reaching, he thought, almost to her waist. And now in the sunlight coming through the window he could see there were shimmers of gold in the russet brown.

He could also see the sparkling gold in her eyes as she started to tell him what had occurred in the cellar.

The story took a long time in the telling, and when Verena had finished speaking the Duke knew that there were a thousand questions he wanted to ask her.

But he was too tired. Slowly, his eyelids covered his eyes and he was conscious that Verena had bent forward to put her hand once again on his forehead.

There was something very comforting in the soft coolness of her hand which he remembered had massaged Salamanca's fetlock. The thought of his horse roused him from the sleep that was seeping over him like a warm wave.

"Salamanca?" he murmured.

"He is quite safe in Grandpapa's stables," Verena answered. "Do not worry about him."

The Duke was asleep before she had said the last word.

When he awoke again it was to see to his astonishment a shock of untidy red hair and a pair of impudent blue eyes staring at him curiously.

"Billy!" the Duke ejaculated, saying the word to himself more to be sure he remembered it than in addressing his new visitor.

"Be ye better, Major?" Billy asked. "Miss Verena has gone t'th'big house t'see Miss Charmaine. She says Oi'm to tell ye she'd be back shortly an' t'sit here in case ye wanted summat!"

The Duke considered for a moment before he asked:

"Do you think you could run an errand for me without telling Miss Verena or anyone else?"

"Cos Oi could!" Billy answered. "Oi dinna talk, not if Oi gives me promise!"

"Then I want you to take a note for me to Eaton Socon," the Duke said. "Can you manage that, Billy?"

"'Course Oi can," Billy replied scornfully. "Oi'll walk there in under th'hour if Oi goes across th'fields. 'Tis like as not Oi'll get a lift back in Farmer Wilks' gig!"

"Then find me a pen and some paper," the Duke said. "I have to write a note."

It all took time. The Duke found it difficult lying on his back to hold a piece of paper firm against a book while he wrote with the white quill pen which Billy informed him he had purloined from the General's desk downstairs.

Once or twice the words he was writing seemed to swim before his eyes but finally he managed to inscribe quite legibly:

"I have been Detained. Stay where You are Until I Send for You. On no Account let this Boy learn my Name, but Reward him with Two Crowns.
Selchester."

The Duke addressed the note to Mr. Carter, The White Horse Inn, Eaton Socon. He wondered what his anxious clerk would make of it. But he knew that, whatever his private feelings, Mr. Carter would obediently carry out his employer's instructions.

Giving the letter to Billy, the Duke asked:

"Can you read?"

"Nay."

"Then take this note to The White Horse at Eaton Socon. You know the Inn, I suppose?"

"Everyun knows th'White Horse," Billy replied.

"Ask for a Mr. Carter. When you see him, hand him the note and he will give you two crowns."

"Two crowns!" Billy exclaimed. "Be ye sure o' that?"

"If he does not I will give them to you on your return," the Duke promised. "But I think you will find that Mr. Carter will not fail his obligation."

"How soon can Oi be off?" Billy enquired, obviously eager to receive such untold wealth.

"As soon as Miss Verena returns and has no further use for you," the Duke replied. "And Billy, give me your word you will not divulge our secret to her."

> "Break me promise or tell a lie,
> High on th'gibbet may Oi die!"

Billy recited breathlessly.

The Duke felt such an oath should be fairly foolproof, and then feeling quite exhausted with the effort he had made he closed his eyes.

It was not long before Verena returned and Billy was relieved of his charge.

"I hope he has been no trouble to you?" Verena asked.

"On the contrary. He has been most helpful," the Duke replied and saw Billy wink at him behind Verena's back with a faint sense of amusement.

It was a long time, he thought to himself, since anyone had treated him with such scant courtesy, but there was a comradeship about it that somehow was vaguely heartwarming.

As soon as Billy had gone from the room Verena pulled off the tricorn hat which she wore with her velvet riding-habit and perched herself on the side of the bed.

"I have such excitements to tell you!" she exclaimed. "The Duke has not appeared!"

"Not appeared!" the Duke echoed. "What can have happened to him?"

"Lord Upminster is almost convinced that the letter he received announcing his Grace's visit was a hoax, written by one of his envious competitors whose cattle did not win so many prizes at the local Show as His Lordship's.

"Anyway, he is so incensed at the Duke's apparent ill-manners that Charmaine says she is quite convinced that he will allow her engagement to Clive Brothwicke to be announced before Christmas!"

"My Nurse used to say it is an ill wind turns none to good!" the Duke remarked with a smile.

"Thomas Tusser! 1524 to 1580," Verena exclaimed. "I was made to learn all his poetic versions of old proverbs, and there is one which would have been a useful warning to the Odious Duke!"

"Which is that?" the Duke enquired.

"It is about buying or selling of pig in a poke!" Verena replied. "And that is exactly what His Grace was doing in deciding to marry Charmaine without knowing anything about her!"

The Duke tried to find words in which to excuse himself, but Verena continued:

"But that is not what I wanted to tell you. Lord Upminster was declaiming quite inordinately about a terrible hold-up along the road just outside Eaton Socon which took place three days ago!

"His Lordship is a Magistrate and it was reported in Court this morning that the dead bodies of two guards were discovered in the ditch and that the two coachmen who had been driving the Bullion Coach were found gagged and bound inside it.

"The horses had been cut from the traces and had been allowed to wander about the fields; so nobody found and examined the coach for some time.

"And the wretched men inside were half dead with fear, hunger and thirst! What was more, His Lordship is convinced that the bullion contained in the coach, which was on its way to York, was of immense value."

"Did you say anything to His Lordship about what happened in the cellar?" the Duke asked.

"I am not such a cork-brain as that!" Verena said scornfully. "The men have the money. We have no idea of who they are or where they may be! What use is it to talk? What we have to do is to plan somehow to catch the thieves red-handed. You would have been able to do so if they had not knocked you out!"

"I see your point," the Duke said drily. "But have you not forgotten they said they would not be using the Priory again?"

"The Gentleman said not for a month or two. All we have to do is to wait!" Verena said.

"Are you seriously suggesting," the Duke enquired, "that we should say nothing and allow those murderers to ramp about the country, attacking other Bullion Coaches in the same manner, in the hope that eventually they will return to the Priory?"

"What else can we do?" Verena retorted. "If I tell His Lordship now what has happened, he will overwhelm you with questions but you can tell him nothing! While I can merely describe what the Gentleman and Hickson look like! There must be thousands of other people almost exactly the same in appearance."

The Duke considered for a moment. Then he said:

"Have you mentioned my presence to Lord Upminster?"

For the first time since he had known her a faint flush came into Verena's cheeks.

"I did not!" she answered. "Perhaps it was wrong of me, but I felt it might be slightly difficult to relate how I met you and why I should be concerning myself with a stranger whose horse had dropped a shoe to the point of inviting him to stay with Grandpapa! Besides, how was I to explain the wounds on your head?"

"I think you have proved that discretion was very much the better part of valour," the Duke said with a smile. "Incidentally, how did you get me back here? I am interested to hear the end of the story!"

"I rode home on Assaye and told Travers what had happened. He collected three of the gardners and they carried you here on a gate! It is not more than half a mile but they found you extremely heavy! You are a very big man, Major Royd!"

"Are Travers and the other men to be trusted?" the Duke enquired.

"Travers was with Grandpapa at Waterloo," Verena replied, "and the others will do as they are told. I have told them it is of the utmost import that they do not talk, and I do not think they will. They are all used to taking orders from Grandpapa and I believe in this instance they will obey me!"

"Then, what we have to decide," the Duke said, "is how we can find the Gentleman with the astute mind who organises the Bullion robberies, and his servant Hickson, who carries them out!"

"It sounds exciting," Verena said. "Oh, I wish Grandpapa could help us! I know it is something he would enjoy more than anything else!"

"I am sure the General would not approve of us just sitting back and waiting for it to happen again," the Duke said. "I heard about these Bullion robberies before I left London and they are causing a great deal of concern amongst the Military."

"The Military?" Verena asked in surprise.

"It is the Army which guards the Bank of England, from where the bullion comes," the Duke explained.

"There does not seem much point in guarding the

Bank of England when the robbers ambush it on the roadways," Verena said. "It would be so much better if they sent a military escort with the coaches."

The Duke remembered that Harry Sheraton had said very much the same thing. He wondered what Harry would think of Verena. Of one thing he was quite sure, that his friend would be exceedingly amused at the position in which he now found himself!

By now he should have been leaving Copple Hall for Lord Wilmington's Estate in Derbyshire. Instead he was the secret guest of a brown-eyed country wench who had got him mixed up in the sort of unsavoury trouble he had always made sure of avoiding.

There were some among his friends who enjoyed hunting down Highwaymen or trying to trick card-sharpers and other cheats into positions where they could be exposed and denounced.

It was the type of thing he personally had always abhorred, and yet here he was in a situation where it would be impossible for him to pretend ignorance of what had occurred.

And yet at the same time he had no desire to reveal the somewhat ignominious part he had played, as he must if he were to report how the Bullion robbers had used the Priory as a place of hiding.

For a moment the Duke wondered if Verena had dreamt the whole thing. Could what she had seen and heard really be true? And then he realised what a cleverly thought out and yet simple plan the whole thing was.

Hickson, whoever he might be, employs three men on behalf of the unknown Gentleman. The latter informs Hickson where the Bullion Coach can be intercepted, choosing, as in this instance, early in the morning when the road is misty. The guards are shot before they can even see who is attacking them; the coachmen are tied up by men who wear masks.

The bullion is loaded on their horses, and after travelling a short distance across country the treasure is hidden in a ruined house, which must have been decided on previously by the Gentleman and Hickson.

Then three of the robbers immediately ride away and disappear, doubtless into the underworld of London.

Only Hickson is left to contact the unknown Gentleman; to come with him to the place of hiding, to deposit the evidence of the crime, in the shape of the empty bullion boxes, in the lake, and then return to London with the booty carefully hidden in a secret place in the Gentleman's curricle, where no one would ever suspect it to be.

It was almost a foolproof operation from beginning to end! The only unanswered question being, how the Gentleman knew when the Bullion Coaches were leaving the Bank and what was their destination.

The Duke must have looked as if he was concentrating hard on the problem; for after a moment he realised Verena was watching him, a smile on her lips, her dimples very much in evidence.

"Well," she asked, "have you found a solution?"

"Not yet," he replied.

"One thing is quite certain," she told him. "I am going to practise shooting again!"

"Shooting?" he asked.

"Yes, I am a good shot with a musket," she replied. "Grandpapa taught me, until I can hit the centre of a target at fifty yards. But I have grown somewhat rusty with a pistol. I have a feeling, Major Royd, we will need to be good shots before we have finished this chase!"

"There is no question of 'we'," the Duke replied.

"You are not going to be mixed up in anything so unpleasant and dangerous."

"Do you really believe that I would accept that?" Verena asked scornfully. "You cannot treat me as if I were some swooning female who would faint at the sight of a pistol, or scream at the sound of a shot!

"I am to be a soldier's wife and ride with the Army like Lady Waldegrave. Grandpapa told me how before the Battle of Salamanca he had seen her for four days together amongst the skirmishers. And Mrs. Dalbiec rode at the head of the Fourth Dragoons on the march and was constantly exposed to fire! Did you not see those Ladies?"

"I did!" the Duke replied grimly, "and it only confirmed my unshakable conviction that a battlefield is no place for any female!"

"Is that your opinion?" Verena asked. "Then you can leave your wife at home! The man I marry will be proud to have me by his side! Of that I am certain!"

"You are to be married?" the Duke asked.

Verena nodded her head.

"It is a secret," she answered.

"Another one?"

She smiled, her eyes shining.

"The most important of them all," she answered. "Unfortunately Grandpapa does not approve of Giles, so I can never talk about him. But he is a soldier, brave, intrepid and adventurous, and I intend as soon as we are wed to go with him wherever he may be serving the King. I have no intention of being a dismal sit-at-home wife!"

"I think you are being quite nonsensical!" the Duke said sharply, and wondered why the thought of Verena on a battlefield annoyed him so intensely.

5

"Check-mate!" Verena declared.

The Duke stared at the chess-board with a rueful expression on his face.

"You cannot have won again?" he said almost incredulously.

"I have!" Verena replied. "You left your King exposed. That is something you should never do!"

"I have until now believed myself a good player!" the Duke remarked.

"Would you like another game?" Verena asked.

The Duke put his head back against the high, velvet armchair which had been drawn up to the window so that he could get some air from the open casement and the sunshine on his face.

It was the first day he had been dressed, and the Doctor had said that he could be up for three or four hours unless he felt especially fatigued.

It was amazing to the Duke when he thought about it

that he had now been the uninvited guest of General Winchcombe for six days, and yet strangely enough he was neither bored nor in any hurry to leave.

It was true that for the first few days his head had felt as if it might split open and a continual headache had been hard to bear. But as his head improved he found himself amused by Verena and content to be with her in a manner that he could not explain to himself.

Previously in his life he had always wanted to be entertained. In the evening by witty, scintillating and elegantly gowned women; in the daytime by hunting, shooting, a mill, or racing.

If he had been told that it was possible for him to be content for six days to rest quietly and to enjoy the company of a young girl who, apart from the Doctor and a servant, was the only person he saw, he would not have believed such a suggestion credible.

But Verena amused him simply because she appeared to make so little effort to entertain him. It was true that she played chess with him, at which she always won, and piquet, at which he was undoubtedly her master, but her main attraction was that she was simply herself!

The Duke was used to women who deliberately set out to be alluring, who flirted with their eyes, their lips and the movement of their bodies! They meant to attract him as a man; they used every trick and artifice to arouse his desire for them.

Verena looked at him with a wide-eyed frankness which told him that not for one moment did she think of him as a potential beau, or indeed—a sobering thought—even as an attractive male!

But when she entered the room, sunshine seemed to come in with her and there always seemed to be something exciting that she had to relate to him.

It might be nothing more sensational than that a fox had nipped the heads off six old hens the night before;

that Farmer Wilks' prize cow had given birth to a calf with two heads; or that Lord Upminster's prize bull had escaped and been found servicing a herd of very ordinary cows belonging to a small-holder who had never been able to afford the fees of a stud bull!

It was just country talk and country lore, and yet the Duke found himself laughing uproariously at some ridiculous situation simply because of the manner in which Verena described it to him.

While she brought him laughter she also brought him solace when his headache was unbearable.

He could not have believed that a woman's hands against his forehead could bring so quickly a relief from intolerable pain, or make his eyelids droop so that he fell asleep almost before he knew what was happening.

He had questioned the credibility of Verena's powers the first day when she had massaged Salamanca's fetlock, but, having now found how quickly and easily she could dispel his pain, he knew that never again would he be a disbeliever.

Now Verena sensed that he was tired and putting aside the chess-board, said:

"You must not do too much today or Doctor Graves will be incensed with me. Would you care for me to read to you?"

"What literature do you suggest?" the Duke asked. "*Love at First Sight* or *The Lost Heir?*"

She laughed.

"How do you know the names of such nonsensical novels? But because of the insult you imply by suggesting them, I think I will read you *Vindication of the Rights of Woman* by Mary Wollstonecraft!"

"God forbid!" the Duke exclaimed. "And do not tell me you desire to be one of those strident women who talk about their rights!"

"I certainly think that as a sex we are downtrodden and imposed on by men," Verena flashed at him.

"Never have I heard such fustian!" the Duke replied.

"Do you really consider it right," Verena asked, seating herself beside him on the window-seat, "that a man should have complete control over a woman's fortune and her Estate from the moment he makes her his wife?"

"Why not?" the Duke enquired. "She would be incapable of managing either by herself!"

"That is an outrageous statement!" Verena cried. "Do you realise that I have helped Grandpapa administer this Estate for the last three years, and now that he is ill everything is carried on by me exactly as before."

"Maybe," the Duke admitted. "But the General planned it all in the first instance. Think what a mess the average woman would make of any Estate if she had to start from scratch without the help and guidance of an intelligent man!"

"You infuriate me!" Verena declared, her eyes flashing at him. "Not all women are nit-witted, without a thought in their heads save of pretty gowns and babies!"

"What else would a man wish them to have in their heads?" the Duke asked with a twinkle in his eye.

"You are deliberately provoking me," Verena said accusingly. "And it is dangerous for you to be excited, seeing to what a weak state a great big man like yourself has been reduced! So I shall not talk to you any longer but shall read to you from a nice soothing book!"

"The weak and humiliating state to which I am reduced is, may I point out, Miss Winchcombe, due entirely to the hazardous enterprise into which you enticed me! Had I minded my own business and not gone into a haunted house in an effort to protect a frail female, my head would not be in the state it is now!"

"If you call me a frail female," Verena exclaimed, "I shall fetch my musket and blow a hole in you!"

"Wound an unarmed and injured man!" the Duke protested in mock horror. "Where could you have learnt such iniquities such as practised only by the French?"

Verena dimpled at him.

"It is no use," she said. "You always manage to have the last word. Well, which is it to be—*Caesaris Commentarii* in Latin, or *Plutarch's Lives*? I have read both to Grandpapa and he told me that the Duke of Wellington took these books with him on his voyage to India."

The Duke raised his eyebrows—no young woman of his acquaintance could read Latin and few were interested in Plutarch!

"I wish, at the moment, to hear neither," he replied. "I want to talk to you, Verena. Do you not understand that you are the only person who has the slightest chance of catching the 'Evil Genius'? If you refuse to use your knowledge of what he looks like, more guards on Bullion Coaches are likely to be killed! Can you really bear to be responsible for their deaths, Verena?"

Verena rose from the window-seat and walked across the room.

"That is an unfair argument, as well you know!"

"It is a factual one," the Duke answered. "There is no one else who can help solve not only the robberies but the murders—for they are nothing else—of the wretched men who guard the Bullion!"

"Do you really think that if I went to London," Verena asked, "there is the slightest chance of my encountering the 'Evil Genius'? I cannot believe he spends his time at Assemblies or attending Balls!"

"Why not?" the Duke asked. "Let us argue this out

logically, Verena. You tell me that he has the appearance of a Gentleman, youngish, well-dressed, somewhat of a Dandy. Having obtained all this money, what is he likely to spend it on?"

"Horses, I suppose," Verena said almost reluctantly.

"But of course," the Duke answered. "Every fashionable Buck wishes to own good bloodstock. So we imagine he will go to Tattersall's and purchase the finest horseflesh available.

"Next, he will wish to show them off to the *Beau Ton,* of which from your description, I would imagine he is a member! He will be invited to Balls!"

"Then that precludes me!" Verena interposed. "You know quite well I am not of the *Beau Ton,* and if I go to London I shall certainly not be asked to the Balls frequented by such a Buck, such a Dandy as the 'Evil Genius'. And what is more, I am not all all likely to receive a ticket for Almack's!"

Just for a moment there was a suspicion of wistfullness in Verena's voice. It was the ambition of every *débutante* and every young woman of fashion to be admitted to the most aristocratic, the most exclusive Club in the whole of Society.

Almack's, which was run by the great London hostesses like Lady Jersey, Lady Cowper and the Princess de Lieven, made its own rules and had even refused the great Duke of Wellington himself when he tried to gain admittance one evening after eleven o'clock and was not wearing knee-breeches!

"I could arrange that for you," the Duke said without thinking.

"You could arrange it?" Verena cried incredulously. "That I cannot believe!"

It was obvious, the Duke thought wryly, that as a person of consequence he did not stand very high in this country chit's estimation.

"I have some—distinguished friends," he said somewhat hesitatingly. "And my sister, though you may not credit it, moves with the *Beau Ton*."

"I was not being rude," Verena said hastily, "at least not intentionally. But I had thought of you simply as a soldier."

"I have a feeling that is not a compliment," the Duke replied.

"It really is! I cannot imagine that you would wish to associate with those dressed-up, empty-headed chatter-boxes! And before you ask me what I know about them, I will tell you!

"I have twice been to London—once when I was only fifteen and Grandpapa took me to see all the sights. He even showed me the wild beasts at the Royal Exchange. It was thrilling and I enjoyed every moment of it.

"The second time was two years ago after I had passed my seventeenth birthday, and Grandpapa thought that I should see a little of the social world. I went to a number of dinner parties and two Balls.

"It was not gay all the time because my Godmother—Lady Bingley—with whom we stayed, is not young and she was leading a quiet existence since her husband, who was a Judge, did not enjoy good health.

"But she did invite her friends to meet me at her 'At Homes'. They were mostly rather old and of course most of Grandpapa's acquaintances were soldiers and his contemporaries."

Verena paused for a moment and then she continued:

"Lady Yarde, who had once been one of Grandpapa's flirts, chaperoned me to a Ball given by the Duchess of Bedford and to another by Lady Cowper. I saw the *Beau Monde*, and although I thought some of the women were beautiful, the men were decidedly overdressed, affected and puffed up with their own conceit!"

"Now I wonder who your partners could have been?" the Duke enquired, his eyes twinkling.

"I suppose I did seem to them a trifle rustic!" Verena said frankly. "But they need not have been quite so stiff-necked. I felt they expected me to go down on my knees in gratitude because they had condescended to a country wench!"

"I promise that anyone to whom I introduce you will treat you with the utmost respect," the Duke said.

Verena laughed, the dimples showing in her cheek.

"And how will you contrive that?" she asked. "Command them to do their duty as you command your troops? No thank you, Major Royd, I will stay in the country where people like me for myself, and the cut of my gown is of no consequence!"

"And let the 'Evil Genius' off scot-free?" the Duke asked. "Even at this moment the wife of some wretched guard may be sobbing her eyes out because she has just been made a widow. I do not suppose there is even a pension for such women. Their children may starve, and who will be to blame but you?"

"Stop it!" Verena exclaimed angrily. "You are being monstrously unfair and you know it! That is the most sneaky underhand method of trying to coerce me!"

"Nevertheless it is the truth!" the Duke said quietly.

"You know that I cannot leave here whilst Grand-papa is so ill," Verena argued. "If the . . . dies then I might consider your suggestion."

"And when your Grandfather dies," the Duke asked, "what do you intend to do? You will not be able to live here alone!"

"I know that! I am not completely green!" Verena retorted. "My old Governess, Miss Richardson, will come to me until I can make proper arrangements. Then I will get in touch with Giles and we shall be married."

"Where is he at the moment?" the Duke enquired.

"I think he may be in India," Verena answered. "I have not heard from him for a long time. Of course, if he is abroad, the letters will take months by sea! Anyway, when we meet I will tell him what you suggest and ask his approval. I should not be surprised if he thought the whole idea as ridiculous as I consider it to be!"

She tossed her head as she spoke and went from the room, closing the door sharply behind her.

The Duke sat with a smile on his lips, thinking how easy it was to tease her and how automatically at the mere mention of Society she became incensed and full of condemnation of the people, especially the men, who were described as the *Beau Ton*.

He imagined that she must have felt out of place and rather lost in London when she had gone there with her Grandfather.

And he could understand that with her upbringing she had found the restrictions and conventions of the Social world very different from the freedom she enjoyed at home.

He guessed that at seventeen Verena had been perhaps a little ungainly, like a foal not yet fully grown. And this, combined with her sense of insecurity, and her unfashionable forthrightness, perhaps had laid her open to a number of snubs and set downs.

But now that she was nearly twenty, if she were dressed in the height of fashion and introduced by the right people, the Duke was prepared to wager that she would be a sensation.

She would certainly, he thought, with her dark hair and huge gold-speckled eyes, make girls who were fair and blue-eyed seem positively insipid, and he was not surprised that a parent like Lord Upminster did not invite Verena to his house when so important a suitor for his daughter's hand as the Duke of Selchester was expected.

The Duke had learnt that Mr. Carter had sent off his letters of apology; for Verena returning from Copple Hall had been full of Lord Upminster's fury on learning that the Duke after all did not intend to honour his residence.

"The preparations to receive His Grace were an entire waste of money," he had raged. "It is your fault, Charmaine, for having encouraged the man in the first place. He would not have suggested such a visit had you not led him to hope that his addresses might be favourably received."

"I certainly did not encourage the Duke, Papa," Charmaine had faltered. "In fact, His Grace hardly spoke to me."

"Your fault! Entirely your fault!" Lord Upminster snapped. "I shall deduct what has been expended out of your dress allowance!"

Verena described the scene graphically to the Duke and then added:

"Lady Upminster, however, consoled Charmaine with the information that she had extracted no less than ten pounds from the housekeeping money! So nobody will suffer because the odious Duke has cancelled his visit, and Charmaine and Clive are now convinced they can plan their wedding for the Spring!"

"I told you it was an ill wind," the Duke said, his eyes twinkling.

"I wonder why the odious Duke changed his mind?"

"Perhaps he was unavoidably detained."

"I am sure it was 'An Incomparable'," Verena said. "Well, I wish her joy of him! I only hope she makes him really miserable—it would teach him a lesson!"

"You are a vindictive little monkey," the Duke exclaimed. "Do you always feel so vehemently about those for whom you have no liking?"

"I can see you want me to be a bread-and-butter Miss," Verena said accusingly, "without a thought in my head, without a conviction of my own! Well, Major, you will be disappointed! I have very positive opinions on most subjects—especially men!"

"What is your opinion of me?" the Duke asked.

He saw her brown eyes searching his face as if she looked for something beneath the surface.

"Shall I tell your fortune?" she parried.

"A witch as well as a healer?" the Duke enquired. "Is there no end to your talents?"

"I am clairvoyant," Verena explained, "because my mother's mother was a seventh child of a seventh child. That gives one special powers, you know."

"I have heard of that belief," the Duke remarked. "Who was your mother before she married your father?"

"My mother was the daughter of Lord Merwin," Verena replied. "Her family did not consider Papa a suitable suitor; so Mama climbed out of her bedroom window and ran away with Papa!"

"Very romantic for them!" the Duke said drily. "I imagine you do not know your Merwin relatives."

"I have no wish to meet them!" Verena exclaimed positively. "How dare they look down on Papa! He was so handsome, so brave, and a brilliant soldier!"

"Old quarrels have a habit of punishing those who had no part in them," the Duke said reflectively.

He was thinking that the Merwin family could have introduced Verena into the Social world very much more successfully than an aged General, however distinguished on the field of battle!

"Do not let us talk of Mama's high-nosed relatives,"

Verena pleaded. "It always makes me cross. Let me hold in my hands something you have always worn."

She reached out as she spoke and picked up his gold watch which Travers had put beside his bed. It was fat and heavy and the Duke had a moment's fear that she might recognise the crest engraved on the back of it.

But Verena was not looking at the watch, she was merely holding it in both hands. She shut her eyes.

"You have been very near to death," she said slowly. "But of course I know that! I can see blood and darkness all round you and yet you are not afraid. I think, had I never seen you before this moment, I would have known you were a soldier and a good one!"

She was quiet for a few moments before she continued:

"You received a decoration, but I can see other tributes, something that looks like a . . . Crown. I cannot quite understand it, but you have either held an important position in the past or will do in the future. Had you not left the Army I should imagine you would have been made a Field Marshal!"

"Perhaps there will be another war," the Duke suggested, "and I shall rejoin my Regiment."

"I do not think you will do that," Verena said in a far-away voice. "But you will be in a position of . . . great authority and you will help many . . . people. I am not quite certain how, but they look to you to guide them—perhaps to command them! But there is danger for you . . . danger from a man—a man who hates you! There is something he wants from you and he is determined to obtain it! But you will be saved . . . it is a woman who saves you!"

"What is she like?" the Duke asked.

"I cannot see her," Verena answered. "I can only see danger . . . danger in the darkness . . . and danger in a building . . . and there is blood!"

She opened her eyes and said seriously:

"You must be careful, Major, very careful!"

"I think you are seeing the past, not the future," the Duke suggested. "I have been in danger, thanks to you, and I was rescued, again thanks to you. I could have told you all that without the aid of clairvoyance."

Verena put the watch back on the table.

"You can scoff at me, but I promise you it will come true. And be careful, I would not wish anything to happen to you!"

"I am grateful for your solicitude," the Duke said.

Then looking into Verena's eyes he realised she was really troubled.

"You do not honestly believe all that moonshine, do you?" he asked.

For a moment she did not answer. Her gold-flecked eyes were held by his grey ones and he had the strange feeling that something passed between them. Something neither of them had sought or expected. Verena drew in her breath and turned away.

"I wish I did not believe it, but my predictions have an unfortunate habit of becoming true!" she answered in a low voice as she went out of the room.

Now the Duke remembered what she had said and wondered if in fact by trying to persuade Verena to come to London he was taking them both into danger.

He knew only too well that the Bullion robbers were killers and that if they had the slightest suspicion that Verena knew their secret, her life would be forfeit!

But why should they know, he asked himself. Why should they suspect anyone from Little Copple? Not even the stranger they had pole-axed in the old Priory was likely to guess how their robberies were contrived.

"It is clever, brilliantly clever!" the Duke thought. "And so simple!"

The door opened and Travers came into the room.

"Miss Verena thinks it's time you went back to bed, Sir," he said respectfully. "You've been up for nearly four hours and the Doctor said you were to take it easy today."

The Duke was about to protest when he realised that he was in fact aching with fatigue. His head was swimming although he tried to tell himself it was just his imagination!

Because he really was longing to lie down he capitulated.

"Very well, Travers," he said, "I do not feel strong enough to argue with Miss Verena, so I will go to bed. But tomorrow I intend to stay up all day!"

"I expect Miss Verena will have something to say about that too, Sir," Travers said with a chuckle.

"Does she always get her own way?" the Duke enquired.

"Miss Verena is one of the pleasantest young Ladies I have ever known," Travers said, "but she is a trifle like her Grandfather—it was always said in the Regiment it was easier to bend the barrel of a cannon than to change the General's mind! Miss Verena is a chip off the old block! But where the Master does it by command, Miss Verena has a coaxing manner which one finds it hard to gainsay!"

"I think she commands me!" the Duke said ruefully.

"That is because you're sick, Sir," Travers replied. "There is nothing a female, whatever her age, enjoys more, than having a man dependent on her. Real tyrants they become if one is indisposed, and Miss Verena is no exception!"

"I have noticed that," the Duke agreed. "Tell me, Travers, who is this Gentleman to whom Miss Verena considers herself engaged?"

"Captain Giles Winchcombe-Smythe, Sir."

"So that is his name," the Duke remarked. "I had not thought to ask."

"The Captain is a sort of relation, Sir," Travers explained. "Calls himself a cousin but in my opinion it is nothing but a connection!

"The Captain's mother was the Master's second cousin. Her name was Winchcombe, right enough, but she weds a man called Smythe and later adds her name to his! The marriage was not smiled upon by the family, from what I hears, Sir."

"And does the General approve of his Grand-daughter's engagement?" the Duke enquired.

"He does not!" Travers said sharply, "and if without offence I can make a correction, Sir, it is no engagement! Just an understanding, as one might say, between Captain Giles and Miss Verena—and something that is kept secret from the Master."

"Why is that?" the Duke asked, climbing thankfully into bed and thinking nothing had ever seemed more comfortable than the softness of the feather pillows which Travers arranged behind his head.

Travers glanced towards the door.

"I do not know that I should be saying this to you, Sir, but seeing as you're a soldier and seeing there's no one else in whom I can confide, I'll tell you the truth! 'Tis worried to death I am!"

"Tell me why," the Duke encouraged him.

"Well, Sir, Captain Giles has been coming to see the Master on and off ever since I can remember, and the only reason he has ever called has been to extract money! It started years ago when we first came home from India."

"How old is the Captain?" the Duke interposed. "I have thought of him as a very young man!"

"No indeed, Sir, Captain Giles will not see thirty-eight again as sure as I am standing here!"

"Thirty-eight!" the Duke exclaimed. "A trifle old for Miss Verena surely?"

"Much too old in many ways," Travers replied darkly.

"Go on with your story," the Duke suggested.

" 'Twas always the same, Sir—Money! Money! The Captain was in debt, the duns were after him; there would be a scandal; he would have to leave the Regiment—and not much of a Regiment at that!"

"What was it?" the Duke asked.

"The Eleventh Foot, Sir," Travers replied with all the contempt of a Grenadier Guardsman for lesser breeds.

The Duke prevented himself from smiling.

"Continue!"

"Well, Sir, after the Master and Miss Verena comes back from London two years ago, Captain Giles arrives unexpectedly and I sees the moment I sets eyes on him, Sir, he be below hatches. As I expects, at the first opportunity he seeks out the Master for a private chat.

" 'Twas not a good moment—as I could have told him—seeing as how the Master was in real pain from an attack of gout, due, as I said at the time, Sir, to the smart boots he insisted on wearing in London and which were too tight for him!"

"They can indeed be troublesome," the Duke remarked.

"Be that as it may, the Master were feeling crusty-like and Captain Giles did himself no good! I could hear their voices raised as I was passing the door of the Study and, quite by accident, as you'll understand, Sir, and because they were a-speaking so loud, I couldn't help but hear what they said."

"I am sure there was no difficulty about it," the Duke remarked.

" 'I will give you two thousand pounds and not a

penny-piece more!' the Master thunders. You could have heard him right across the Barrack Square, Sir, I swears to it.

" 'And if you come here again," he went on, "I will kick you out! You have bled me long enough and I do not intend to deplete Verena's inheritance for a bumble-splasher like you!' "

Travers paused. Then he continued:

"The Captain says something which I couldn't catch and then the Master shouts: 'Leave you anything in my will? You must be addle-pated! Everything I possess— the Estate, my house and my fortune—is Verena's and that is my last word! Take the two thousand and go to the devil with it as far as I am concerned. I have finished with you. Do you hear me?' "

Travers drew his breath.

"That was certainly conclusive," the Duke remarked.

"You'd have thought so, Sir," Travers agreed. "But owing to the horses having to rest seeing they had just returned from London, the Captain had to stay for two more days and he made the most of the opportunity!"

"What do you mean," the Duke enquired.

"The Master had as good as told the Captain that Miss Verena was an heiress, hadn't he?" Travers asked. "He'd always ignored her before as if being little more than a child she was of no interest to him! But now he sets out to captivate her!

"I promise you, Sir, 'twas like watching them damned natives slither up the side of a fort! Like monkeys I used to think they were when we were in Mysore!

"All charm and graces, Captain Giles was to Miss Verena! She was hypnotised by him as if he were one of them phoney snake-charmers that used to hang about the Barracks and make us pay to watch their tricks!"

There was a frown between the Duke's eyes as Travers continued:

"It fair made me sick, Sir, I don't mind telling you, to see a cheap charlatan hoodwinking a lovely young Lady like Miss Verena with tales of his bravery! From the way he talked you'd have thought he'd fought Boney single-handed!"

"Miss Verena was fascinated by him, I suppose," the Duke said in a low voice as if he spoke to himself.

"Of course she were!" Travers replied. "She'd come back from London, Sir, having not enjoyed herself half as much as she had expected—the Master did his best, but is old and the Lady with whom we stayed were getting on in years.

"Miss Verena met no one young with whom she could enjoy herself and although I knows nothing of such matters, Sir, it seemed to me that the gowns her Governess bought her in Biggleswade made her appear a bit of a dowd!"

Travers shook his head.

"Now Miss Verena has developed tastes of her own, and very pretty she looks, but in those days she was naught but a child and I think she were a trifle cast down—as if at the parties she had attended she had not been a success!"

"I am sure you are right, Travers," the Duke said.

"Then, Sir, almost as soon as we returns, Captain Giles arrives and manoeuvres himself into a position of advantage, so to speak! I could see it happening before my very eyes!

"The compliments he paid her! The manner in which he kisses her hand good-night; pulls her chair out; opens the door; helps her on with her coat—all the things he'd not troubled to do on previous occasions but which Miss Verena had never known from any other Gentleman!"

Travers dropped his voice.

" 'You're entrancing, Verena,' I hears him say to her. 'When I am bivouacking on some windy plain or in the hot darkness of an Indian night, I shall think of your eyes and all my discomforts will be of no consequence, for I shall only remember you!' "

Travers gave a disdainful snort.

"That be just the sort of stuff young females fall for, Sir, 'specially when they've not heard it all before!"

"I will take your word for it, Travers," the Duke said with a faint smile.

"Before the Captain left I learns, Sir, exactly how he had tied things up! When I calls him on the morning of the day he was leaving, he says:

" 'Travers, when the General dies, I wish you to get in touch with me immediately. My Club will always find me. You must send a message to me there so that I can post here with all speed to look after Miss Verena.'

" 'I dare say the Master had already made proper arrangements, Sir,'' I replied. 'Perhaps he will be appointing a Guardian or such like should Miss Verena not be of age.'

" 'There's no need for you to trouble your head with such matters, my man,' the Captain says, all lofty-like. 'I shall be Miss Verena's Guardian because as soon as the General is dead we will be married! Though don't you go tittle-tattling to him, Travers, because it is none of your business. And if you were to do such a thing, I would see that you were turned away without a pension!' "

Travers snorted again.

"There were a lot of things I could have said to him, Sir, but I've learnt after being with the Master so long that nothing is ever gained through speaking back to a superior officer, whatever Regiment he might be in! So

122

I says—polite-like: 'At which Club would you wish me to address you, Sir?'

" 'The United Services,' he replied, 'and send the message post-haste, do you understand?'

"I thought of course that the Captain would slip me a coin for my pains, which I half-intended to refuse to accept, but not a bit of it! Off he goes with his cheque for two thousand pounds from the Master and a lot of smarmy, affectionate farewells for Miss Verena!

" 'I shall be thinking of you day and night,' I hears him say, 'until we meet again.' "

"I am surprised at Miss Verena agreeing to deceive her Grandfather," the Duke said.

"In a way she did nothing of the sort, Sir," Travers answered. "Because she's always been so open, that very night I hears her say to the Master:

" 'Grandfather, Giles said he will look after me if anything happens to you.'

" 'I am quite certain he would be willing to do so!' the Master replied with a sarcastic note in his voice. 'But you will oblige me, Verena, by having nothing to do with that young man! He is a bad lot, just as his father was a bad lot before him. And his mother had no right to add my name to his! Winchcombe-Smythe indeed! Smythe is what he is called—and snide is what he is by nature!'

" 'I like him, Grandpapa,' Miss Verena says bravely.

" 'Then you can just unlike him,' the General shouted. 'He will not enter this house again, do you understand?'

" 'Yes, Grandpapa,' she answers."

"Was that all?" the Duke asked as Travers stopped speaking.

"The General was never clever with women," Travers remarked sadly. "An exceptional Commander, as you know, Sir, a Martinet expecting to be obeyed whatever he asked of his troops and a man one was proud to serve! But where very young females were concerned he were as lunk-headed as a plough-boy!"

Travers sighed.

"If the Master had more experience, Sir, he'd have asked Miss Verena to give him her word of honour to have nothing to do with Captain Giles. And because she loves him I believes she would have kept it!

"But no, the Master just abuses the Captain and orders her to forget him, and you knows as well as I do, Sir, if there's one thing that makes a female partial to a man it's to think that he be hard done by!"

"That is true enough!" the Duke agreed.

"So there we are," Travers exclaimed, "with Captain Giles waiting to hear of the Master's death, and Miss Verena spending her time training herself to be a soldier's wife!"

The Duke was to be well aware that this was the truth, because later in the afternoon when Verena poured out his tea, she asked his help.

"I am determined not to be an ignoramus if it comes to another war," she told him. "Travers has shown me how to peg down a tent, how to cook on an open fire with the type of utensils that are used in the field-kitchens. But there must be other things I can learn. What do you suggest?"

"I suggest you stay at home," the Duke replied.

"That is the sort of remark you would make!" she said scornfully. "Giles has much more fire and enthusiasm than you. Did I tell you what the Duke of Wellington said to him after the Battle of Waterloo?"

"Several times," the Duke said tartly.

"Well, you shall hear it again," Verena said defiantly. "He said: 'Captain, if I had more young men like you under my command this Battle would have been over yesterday!'"

The Duke, who did not believe a word of it, asked sourly:

"And who, may I ask, related this to you?"

"Giles, of course," Verena replied.

Then she paused.

"I know what you are thinking!" she said accusingly, "you think that he was boasting because he told me about it. But I do not believe any man could receive such a glowing compliment and not wish to tell it to someone for whom he has an affection. As Giles himself said to me: 'I would rather have heard that than received fifty decorations!' "

"You have seen his medals, of course," the Duke said.

Verena shook her head.

"Giles was not wearing uniform when he came here," she said. "But, oh, how I would love to see him in his red tunic. He must look magnificent!"

"I am sure he does!" the Duke remarked coldly.

"He is not as tall as you," Verena went on, "but, do you know, I have never asked you what Regiment you were in?"

"The Life-Guards," the Duke replied.

"The Regiment the Duke of Wellington led himself at Waterloo!" Verena exclaimed. "I might have known, having seen Salamanca, you could not bear to go to war without your horses, could you?"

"I should certainly feel very lost without them," the Duke answered.

"If I were rich," Verena said with a wistful look in her eyes, "I should buy horses! Horses and more horses. I would have an enormous stable and then I would not want friends or a husband or children, or anything else. Just horses! They do not mind what you wear or what you say, or how you look. They love you for what you are and they know instinctively that you love them!"

"I see that any man who captures your fancy will have to look like a horse," the Duke remarked.

She gave a gurgle of amusement.

"Perhaps he will be a centaur!"

The Duke laughed, and then Verena said:

"But people do resemble animals. I wish you could see Lord Upminster. He looks exactly like a large porker who is ready for market!"

"Of what animal do I remind you?" the Duke asked curiously.

She considered for a moment and then she said:

"But of course, it is not difficult where you are concerned. Napoleon called the Duke of Wellington 'The Leopard'. Grandpapa said he meant it as an insult! But 'The Leopard' and those close to him who were called Leopards, destroyed the 'victorious eagles'!"

"Indeed we did!" the Duke said, remembering the jokes there had been about Napoleon's sneering disparagement of the hideous Leopard!

"I thought when the gardeners carried you here on the gate," Verena went on, "that you looked like a Roman gladiator who had lost his fight in the Colesseum. But now I know you are a Leopard, like the Iron Duke—tenacious, unconquerable, and triumphant!"

"Thank you," the Duke answered. "I would rather be a Leopard than any other animal, I can assure you!"

"And what am I?" Verena enquired.

"A small, irritating and extremely noisy mosquito," he replied instantly.

"How can you be so horrid?" she exclaimed. "For that you shall only have gruel for supper. I will go now and countermand the very succulent dishes Cook is preparing for you."

"I apologise, I do really!" the Duke answered. "But it is impossible not to tease you!"

"Then what am I like?" she asked.

"I really do not know," he answered. "At times you spit at me like a tiger-cat, but at other times you are almost endearing, like the little red squirrel I used to have as a child. It would sit on my shoulders and snatch at the nuts I offered him."

"I think I would rather be a song-bird," Verena suggested.

"No resemblance!" the Duke replied. "Shall I tell you instead that when I first made your acquaintance I thought you were like an elf! Those supernatural little creatures who hide in trunks of old trees, peep at one through the thick branches and leave rings on the green lawns where they have danced the night away!"

He realised as he stopped speaking that Verena was looking at him with an incredulous expression in her eyes.

"So you know about elves," she said softly.

"I was a lonely child," the Duke explained. "My sister was older than I, and I imagined many things until they beat them out of me at school!"

"What sort of things?" Verena asked intently.

He knew that he had intrigued her and for the first time they had found a closeness, quite different to the frank friendly relationship they had enjoyed since they met.

"Elves in the woods," he replied, "goblins burrowing inside the hills and mountains, nymphs and sprites in the streams and waterfalls, and dangerous frightening dragons hidden among the pine trees!"

As the Duke spoke he thought of Harry Sheraton and mocked at himself. Then Verena's voice, breathless with wonder, made him forget everything but the two gold-specked eyes.

"Dragons!" she said, her voice thrilling with excitement. "So you believed in them too! I thought there was no one else who would understand!"

"Of course, I was the Knight in shining armour," the Duke said, "who killed the dragons!"

"And the goblins helped you?"

"They showed me the way. I hid in their tunnels inside the hills, and they left messages for me under the ancient trees and by the side of the enchanted stream."

"And the birds warned you when the dragons were abroad!" Verena cried. "I never dreamt . . . I never knew there was a man in the whole wide world who knew of such secret things!"

"It must have been because you were also aware of these mysteries," the Duke said, "that I thought you were like an Elf."

"Oh, I wish with all my heart that I were really an Elf," Verena replied passionately, "and that I could bring you some very special magic you have never known before!"

There was silence and then, almost beneath his breath, the Duke murmured:

"Perhaps you have!"

6

The Duke was awake for a considerable part of the night worrying over Verena, trying to decide how he could induce her to go to London, at the same time wondering whether it was really wise for her to do so.

It was—although he did not realise it—the first time he had ever been seriously concerned about someone else's actions that did not directly affect his own comfort or contentment.

And he awoke in the morning to find himself irritated by the knowledge that he still had no solution to the problem.

Fate, however, was to make the decision for him!

Having told Travers the night before that he would rise early the next morning and come downstairs, the servant arrived with a jug of hot shaving water as soon as the Duke had finished breakfast.

Having shaved the Duke in a most competent manner, he then assisted His Grace to dress.

The Duke was ready and glad at finding himself clear-headed and with a deal more energy than on the previous day when Verena knocked on the door.

"How are you?" she asked when the Duke had commanded her to enter. She stood just inside the room, inspecting him with a critical eye, before she exclaimed:

"You look better! You do really, and there is so much I want to show you in the house and grounds. I am well aware also that you are longing to see Salamanca!"

Travers had gone from the room as she spoke and the Duke, standing in the sunshine by the open window, watched her move towards him, noting that her simple sprigged muslin gown revealed the slim perfection of her young body and how the sunshine was somehow reflected in her eyes.

"What does it feel like," she asked as she reached his side, "to be going back to the world again?"

"It is a strange feeling," the Duke answered quite seriously. "For seven days I have been isolated in this room. It has been a little world in itself. It was almost like being in a small ship on the wide ocean with yesterday behind me and tomorrow somewhere over the horizon!"

"Have you been very bored?" Verena asked.

"You know I have not!" he answered in his deep voice.

There was something in his eyes which made her turn her face towards the window.

"Salamanca is waiting," she said quickly. "Would you like Travers to help you down the stairs or will you lean on me?"

"I assure you I can manage quite competently by myself," the Duke replied.

"You must be careful," she said. "Remember the

Doctor has said you must not do too much too quickly!"

The Duke had no time to answer her because at that moment Travers appeared in the doorway.

"Miss Verena, come quickly!" he cried with a note of urgency in his voice.

Without question Verena turned, ran from the room and the Duke heard her speeding down the passage towards her Grandfather's bedchamber. He waited and knew instinctively what had occurred.

In less than five minutes Verena came back. There was no need for the Duke, seeing the stricken expression in her eyes and the pallor of her cheeks, to be told what had happened.

Then, almost as if she moved without conscious thought, compelled by some instinct stronger than her own will, she walked towards him and like a child seeking consolation hid her face against his shoulder.

The Duke's arms went round her. He held her close without speaking and knew she was not aware of him as a man, but merely as a source of comfort. As he smelt the sweet fresh fragrance of her hair, he was conscious that above all else he wanted to protect her.

She had turned to him in her distress, and he knew if it was in his power he asked only that he could stand between her and anything that might disturb and frighten her.

Verena was trembling, but she was fighting valiantly to stop the tears that her Grandfather dispised. After some time she said in a low voice:

"I was expecting it but . . . somehow it is so . . . final."

"It always is," the Duke said gently.

"He would not have wished to linger as he was," Verena said almost beneath her breath. "He wanted to die like a soldier!"

The Duke's arms still enfolded her, but she now moved a little and he set her free. She walked to the window to stand staring out into the garden.

"I must be brave," she whispered almost to herself.

"You are being brave," the Duke told her.

She turned her head at his words, her eyes searching his face as if she saw him for the first time.

"I did so want . . . you to . . . meet him," she murmured tremulously.

"I am proud to remember the General as I last saw him," the Duke replied, "riding across the battlefield at Waterloo after our victory, his Grenadiers behind him."

He saw the tears well into her eyes at his words.

"I must go back and help Travers," she said hastily.

"I am sure there is nothing you can do," the Duke answered quietly. "Stay here, I will see if I can be of assistance."

Verena would have argued but he put his hand on her shoulder and forced her down on the window-seat.

"Do as I tell you, Verena," he said. "I promise you it is best."

There was something authoritative in his voice which she obeyed without further question, and the Duke went from the room and down the passage to where he knew he would find the General's bedchamber.

Travers was just coming from the room as he reached it. He had covered his Master's body with a sheet and lowered the blinds.

"Can I help in any way?" the Duke enquired.

"No, thank you, Sir," Travers answered. "I am about to send a groom for the Doctor and for the lodge-keeper's wife, who does the laying out in Little Copple. He will also carry a message to the Master's attorney as lives in Biggleswade."

Travers closed the bedroom door before he continued:

"The firm has, I knows, full instructions as to what the Master wished to be done immediately on his death. The Gentleman should be here in about two hours' time. Until then if you could care for Miss Verena, Sir—she'll take it hard!"

"I will look after her," the Duke promised.

He went back to his bedroom. Verena was still sitting on the window-seat. The Duke held out his hand.

"Come," he said. "Travers has seen to everything. You promised to show me Salamanca!"

It was nearly two hours later that the Duke and Verena, having visited the stables and sat under a shady tree in the garden, arrived back at the house to see a gig outside.

"That will be Mr. Laybarrow," Verena announced. "I knew Travers would send for him. I believe that Grandpapa has left some special instructions as to how he wishes to be buried."

"I will wait until you have heard what he has to say," the Duke told her. "Then I must be on my way."

"You are not intending to leave?" she asked in surprise. "But you cannot travel so soon!"

"I am well enough," the Duke replied. "And you must be aware, Verena, that now your Grandfather is dead, I cannot stay in the house."

"Travers will send for Miss Richardson," Verena replied. "She will chaperone me if you think it so necessary. Please do not leave until I know what I am to do!"

The Duke looked surprised.

"Grandpapa always told me," Verena continued, "that when he died he had made special arrangements not only for his burial but also for me. I have no idea what they may be but I promised on my honour that I will carry out his wishes!"

She gave a little sigh that was almost a sob.

"The thought of what Grandpapa may ask frightens me. Perhaps it is foolish of me but please, Major Royd, please do not leave me until I know what it may be!"

As she pleaded with the Duke Verena stretched out her hand and placed it on his arm. It was a small hand with long, sensitive fingers. There were several brown freckles on the whiteness of the skin. The Duke felt a sudden urge of compassion towards this lovely child—for she was little more—who, living in the country, knew so little of the outside world.

"What will become of her?" he wondered and realised with a perception that was unusual for him that with the death of her Grandfather Verena's whole world had fallen apart!

"I will stay while you have need of me," he said quietly.

"Thank you! Thank you!" Verena answered.

And impulsively, like a child, she laid a cheek for a moment against his arm.

"I am ashamed of feeling afraid," she said in a low voice, "yet I cannot help being apprehensive."

"Let us go into the house and find out exactly what your Grandfather has asked of you," the Duke said. "It is just as foolish to over-estimate one's enemy as to under-estimate him!"

Verena managed a wan smile.

"You must not call Grandpapa an enemy!"

"I was referring to these mysterious instructions," the Duke answered. "I am sure you will find they are not so formidable as you anticipate!"

"Perhaps you are right," Verena agreed.

Lifting her chin a little higher she walked into the house.

Mr. Laybarrow, an elderly, wizened little man with a bald head, was waiting for them in the Salon talking to a Lady with grey hair who at Verena's appearance held out both her hands.

"Oh, Richie! I am so thrilled to see you!" Verena cried. "How kind of you to come."

"You knew, dear, that I would be with you as swiftly as possible immediately I received the sad news of the General's death," Miss Richardson replied.

She kissed Verena then looked at the Duke with undisguised curiosity.

"This is Major Royd," Verena explained. "He has been staying here after suffering a slight accident in the village. I will tell you all about it later. Major, this is my former Governess, of whom I have spoken—Miss Richardson."

The Duke bowed and Miss Richardson curtsied. The Duke liked her calm, sensible face and the way in which she asked no unnecessary questions.

"If you will pardon me for saying so, Miss Winchcombe," Mr. Laybarrow said in the dusty, dry voice of his profession, "I have a most important interview this afternoon and wish to return to Biggleswade with all possible speed. It would be exceedingly considerate on your part if you would permit me to inform you immediately of the late General Sir Alexander Winchcombe's instructions to be carried out in the event of his death."

"Yes, indeed, Mr. Laybarrow," Verena replied. "There is no reason for any delay and I am very willing to listen to anything you have to impart. Is it correct for Miss Richardson to be present? And I would wish, if possible, for Major Royd, who is our guest, also to hear you."

"It shall be as you desire, Miss Winchcombe," Mr. Laybarrow replied.

"Then shall we sit down?" Verena suggested.

Mr. Laybarrow seated himself in a high-backed chair and started fumbling with a well-worn black leather bag. The Duke, realising his need, brought a small table to his side and Mr. Laybarrow thanked him as he placed his bag upon it, prising it open to reveal a number of papers.

It all appeared very impressive, but actually what Mr. Laybarrow finally extracted from the bag was only one sheet of parchment. Then, adjusting his spectacles, he looked up to see that Verena, Miss Richardson and the Duke had seated themselves in chairs facing him.

He cleared his throat.

"You are aware, Miss Winchcombe," he began, "that Mayhew, Bodkin and Critchwick are your Grandfather's lawyers and I am in fact only acting on their behalf until they can be informed of Sir Alexander's most regrettable decease."

"Yes, I know that," Verena replied in a low voice.

"All deeds and documents concerning the house and Estate are with these Gentlemen in Lincoln's Inn Fields," Mr. Laybarrow continued. "What I am about to read now is a summary of your Grandfather's will and his instructions regarding his burial."

"Please continue, Mr. Laybarrow."

The Duke, watching Verena, realised that this formality was a great strain, but she held herself proudly and, although she was very pale she was in fact completely composed.

"These instructions," Mr. Laybarrow went on, "were written and signed eighteen months ago, on July the fifth, eighteen hundred and twenty-two:

'I, Alexander Frederick Conrad Winchcombe bearing the Rank of General and being a Knight Commander of the Order of the Bath, leave Everything I possess—my Estate, House and Monies—to my Grand-daughter Verena Winchcombe to inherit at the Age of twenty-one or sooner should she Marry.

'However, in the event of my Dying before she attains her Majority I ask my good Friend and Lawyer, Arthur Critchwick, to Appoint a Guardian to Administer her Possessions and to Ensure that She does not make an Unsuitable Marriage.

'I had hoped, being a Soldier, to Die as a Soldier—on the Battlefield. As this Wish cannot now be Fulfilled I Desire to be Buried on the Consecrated Ground of the Old Priory, the only Person present besides the Parson to be my Servant William Travers.

'My death is to be kept completely Secret for Three Months. After this Period has passed a brief Notice may be inserted in the *Gazette*.

'Locally there is no reason for Anyone to be informed that I am Dead and I have no Wish for expressions of sympathy in the Shape of Flowers, Letters or Mournings to be offered either by anyone in my Household or by Strangers and Acquaintances in Whom I have no Interest.

'Bearing this Secrecy in Mind and Being Aware that it is my Deepest Wish that No One should know of My Demise, I Desire that as soon as my Eyes are Closed my Grandchild shall Leave the House and travel with her former Governess, Miss Richardson, to London.

'Here she can Stay with her Godmother, Lady Bingwall, or failing Her, Miss Richardson can contact Lady Yarde and solicit Her Ladyship's help and advice.

'I wish my Grand-daughter, who has Nursed Me so Devotedly these past Years and for whom I have the Deepest Affection, to Enjoy some of the Social

Life of which She has been Deprived owing to my Infirmities.

'I Desire Her to become Acquainted with People of Her own Class and of Her own Age. She is Well-Provided with Money, which should be Expended on Everything that Appertains to Her Comfort. It is my Wish that she should not Wear Mourning or Indeed that Anyone outside our immediate Household should know that She is Bereaved.

'If My Granddaughter has an Affection for Me I Believe that my Wishes in these Matters will be carried out by Her and Everyone else Whom it Concerns.

'My Servant, William Travers, will, I Believe, Serve my Grand-daughter as He has Served Me faithfully and well until He reaches the Age of Retirement. He is to Receive Five Hundred Pounds Immediately, a Pension of Three Pounds a Week for Life and when he requires it one of the Cottages at the Drive Gates.' "

Mr. Laybarrow stopped speaking to find Verena staring at him in utter astonishment. Hastily she rose to her feet.

"It is impossible!" she cried. "How could Grandfather have asked it of me?"

Miss Richardson went to her side.

"I think, dearest," she said quitely, "that your Grandfather was always distressed that owing to his age and his infirmities he could provide you with so little gaiety.

"I remember when he returned with you from London he told me that he was not at all satisfied by the people with whom you had become acquainted. He had thought them too old and too dull for someone as young as yourself."

"I have no wish to meet London people!" Verena retorted.

As if she felt she was speaking too intimately in front of Mr. Laybarrow, she walked away from Miss Richardson towards the elderly lawyer who was closing his black bag.

"Thank you for your attention, Mr. Laybarrow," she said. "If I visit London I will be in touch with Mr. Critchwick."

"I will write to him tonight," Mr. Laybarrow replied. "But there is one more thing, Miss Winchcombe, I must impart to you: you are now an extemely wealthy woman, and any monies you may require for travelling, for your expenses in London, and of course for the upkeep of this house, can be obtained either from my firm in Biggleswade or from Mr. Critchwick in London."

"You say I am wealthy," Verena answered. "I had no idea that Grandpapa was a rich man."

"Indeed, Miss Winchcombe, the General was extremely well situated," Mr. Laybarrow replied. "Mr. Critchwick will of course be able to give you more detailed accounting, but I think it is within my province to say that you will inherit a fortune of nearly ninety thousand pounds, besides of course the house and the Estate."

He realised that Verena was too surprised to speak and bowing to her politely he added:

"May I convey to you my deepest condolences, Miss Winchcombe. It must be a consolation to remember that your Grandfather had a very distinguished career and that he was admired by everyone who knew him, especially those who served under him."

"Thank you, Mr. Laybarrow," Verena said in a low voice.

Then briskly, obviously eager to be gone, Mr. Laybarrow shook hands with Miss Richardson and the

Duke and went from the Salon into the Hall where Travers was waiting to hand him his hat and to assist him into his gig.

No sooner had the door closed behind him than Verena put her hands up to her cheeks and exclaimed:

"I cannot believe it! I cannot credit what I have heard! I will not go to London! How indeed could Grandpapa ask it of me?"

"I think that is the most sensible will I have ever heard," the Duke remarked.

"But why?" Verena demanded.

The Duke glanced at Miss Richardson and saw by her expression that she approved of his words.

"What good can you do here, feeling lonely and miserable, bereft of someone who has been your constant companion for nearly ten years? What the General asks of you, Verena, stems from his desire to save you both pain and loneliness."

"And of course, dear," Miss Richardson interposed briskly, "you must do as your Grandfather wished, whatever your personal feelings in the matter. I will go upstairs now and ask the housemaids to start packing. If we start early tomorrow morning we will reach London comfortably before it is dark."

Without waiting for a reply Miss Richardson went from the room. Verena turned towards the Duke.

"Must I go?" she pleaded. "I know now that is what was frightening me! I had a presentiment of some such devastating plan! I hate Society . . . you know how much I hate it!"

"I promise you it will not be so bad as you anticipate," the Duke answered. "And at least if you go to London it gives us an opportunity to search for the 'Evil Genius'!"

If he had wished to distract Verena's mind from her own distress he could not have found a better way.

"So you have won!" she cried resentfully, her eyes flashing at him. "If I did not know that you had never met Grandpapa, I would have believed that you contrived this between you!"

She made an exasperated sound before she continued:

"This is what you wanted was it not, that I should go to London? That I should search the streets, the Park, the Balls, the Assemblies, for a man I have only seen once and whom I may not recognise again?"

"That is not true," the Duke argued. "You know as well as I do you will recognise 'The Evil Genius' the moment you set eyes on him!"

"He may appear very different in London," Verena said crossly.

"Anyway, it will be interesting to search for him together," the Duke suggested.

Verena glanced up at him and saw the smile on his lips.

"You are delighted!" she said accusingly. "Delighted because you have got your own way! Well, let me tell you, Major Royd, I do not intend to do exactly as you command me, whether in London or here.

"Besides, despite your assurances, it is very unlikely if I stay with my Godmother that I shall go to any places smart or exclusive enough to be the haunt of the 'Evil Genius'!"

"We shall see!" the Duke said enigmatically.

Verena walked across the room to stare out into the garden.

"I want to stay here!" she said forlornly. "I want to ride Assaye over the fields, to talk to Billy at the 'Dog and Duck', to plan Charmaine's wedding-gown, to . . ."

". . . come home to an empty house and feel miserable without your Grandfather," the Duke finished.

"Perhaps you are right," she admitted with a sigh. "Anyway, I must do what Grandpapa wished, and if we find the 'Evil Genius' perhaps it will be worth while. You promise that you will call on me in London?"

The Duke realised it was the cry of a child who was suddenly afraid of being alone in a vast and unknown city.

"I will see you as often as you permit me," the Duke assured her.

Verena gave a little cry.

"But I was forgetting—you are not well enough to travel! I am sure the Doctor will not allow you to go to London for at least two or three days."

"I shall leave here tomorrow, as soon as I have seen you and Miss Richardson on your way," the Duke replied. "Do not worry about me, Verena; I have people to visit in Eaton Socon and Salamanca can easily carry me there."

"You are sure you are strong enough?" Verena asked anxiously.

"Quite sure," the Duke replied. "Would you like me to arrange for a carriage to convey you to London or a groom to ride Assaye?"

"We can travel in Grandpapa's landau," Verena answered. "And one of the grooms can ride Assaye. There is, however, one thing which troubles me. I would like to rent some stables when I am in London. The horses can at first be accommodated at my Godmother's stables which are near her house in Manchester Square. But I would not wish to incommode her by inflicting my horses on her for long."

"I will find you a stable," the Duke said.

"Thank you," Verena answered.

"Now I can buy horses of my own!"

She said the words in a voice of awe as if suddenly

she realised she could fulfil her greatest wish but was half afraid it was still a fantasy.

"I can help you," the Duke remarked.

"Could you find me horses even half as wonderful as Salamanca?" Verena asked.

"I promise that I will put you in the way of purchasing the finest horseflesh available," the Duke promised. "Although of course I shall never admit that they could possibly be as fine as Salamanca."

"Or as clever as Assaye," Verena added with a little smile.

"That of course goes without saying," the Duke agreed.

Their eyes met.

"Do not be afraid," the Duke said softly. "You are young and very lovely, Verena. The world can be a wonderfully attractive place when you have both those attributes!"

"I shall make mistakes . . ." she whispered, almost as if she spoke to herself.

"Not if you trust me," the Duke replied.

She put out her hand towards him as if in need of comfort. The Duke took it and felt her cold fingers tighten on his.

"I will destroy the dragons, Elf," he said softly.

Verena drew in her breath.

"I hope you can . . . Leopard!" she whispered in a very small voice.

It was, however, a woe-begone little face under a pretty straw bonnet to which the Duke said good-bye the following morning when Verena and Miss Richardson left for London.

Their landau was solid and old-fashioned, and the Coachman had been thirty years in the General's service. But the horses were good bloodstock and the Duke had confidence in the footman escorting the Ladies. A swarthy young country man, His Grace was convinced he would deal competently with any dangers that might be encountered on the journey.

A groom followed behind, riding Assaye.

"Good-bye, Travers," Verena said, holding out her hand.

Travers took it in his.

"I'll carry out the Master's orders, Miss, and keep the house ready for your return."

Miss Richardson, who had already said good-bye to the Duke, stepped into the carriage. Verena held out both her hands to him, her large eyes filled with unshed tears.

"You will come and see me . . . soon," she asked.

"The day after tomorrow," the Duke promised.

"You have my Godmother's address?"

"You wrote it down for me," he answered. "Take care of yourself, Verena, and I promise you I will do my best to see that you enjoy London. It will be very different, I swear to you, from your last visit!"

"I doubt it!" Verena replied. "Good-bye, Major. You must travel slowly. I think you should take at least two or three days on the journey."

"You will be pushing me in a bath-chair before you are finished!" the Duke answered, and saw a ghost of a dimple before she turned away and stepped into the landau.

The Coachman started up the horses. Verena's hand waved from the window until the carriage was out of sight.

"Poor child!" Travers muttered beneath his breath.

"She will be all right," the Duke answered. "I will see to that."

"Indeed, Sir, I sure hopes so!" Travers replied. "And you can be certain of one thing—I'll be sending no messages to the United Services Club!"

"How much did you influence the General to write that will?" the Duke asked with a twinkle in his eye.

There was an answering smile on Travers' lips.

"I may perhaps have put it into the Master's head, Sir, that Miss Verena might get tied up with some undesirable person seeing as how she'd had so little experience of eligible suitors."

"That was sensible of you!"

"And of course, Sir," Travers continued, "I did point out to the General that being in black gloves made it hard for a young Lady to make any new acquaintances. After I says that, the Master was not beyond guessing who'd be acalling as soon as he was under ground!"

"I congratulate you," the Duke said.

He left a little while later on Salamanca for Eaton Socon. He had thought himself strong enough to endure such a short journey on horseback, but by the time he reached the White Horse he was glad enough to give Salamanca into the hands of his own groom and to repair with a throbbing head to the private parlour Mr. Carter had engaged for him.

After partaking of a light luncheon the Duke left for London and only the excellent springing of his new travelling-landau and the fact that he was able to sleep part of the way made the journey bearable.

It was indeed a very tired, exhausted man who reached Selchester House after midnight and sank thankfully into his own bed to sleep heavily and dreamlessly until late the following morning.

When the Duke awoke, he wondered for a moment where he was. Then as the events of the past week crowded back into his mind, he found himself planning certain operations with a zest and an interest which made him exceedingly impatient of any physical weakness.

The Duke had thought at Eaton Socon that he would send for his own Physician on his arrival at Selchester House. But he decided on rising that apart from a certain soreness his head was in fact well on the way to recovery and he had other more important things to do.

Mr. Graystone, however, delayed him and it was not until after luncheon that the Duke travelling in his Town Landau repaired to a Mansion in Charles Street, Mayfair. Here, on asking for Lord Adolphus Royd, he was informed by the Butler that His Lordship was in the Study and was led to a quiet room at the back of the house.

Lord Adolphus, who had put on weight considerably in the last ten years of his life, looked up in surprise at his nephew's entrance. Heaving himself from the comfortable armchair in which he had been enjoying a quiet snooze, he exclaimed:

"Good Heavens! Theron! Why was I not informed that you would be calling on me?"

He held out a fat hand remarking as he did so:

"Is there an urgent reason for such unusual attention? Surely you have returned exceeding swiftly from your intended trip to the country."

"I arrived back last night," the Duke said.

"Your addresses have already been accepted?" Lord Adolphus enquired curiously.

"I have made no addresses," the Duke replied sharply. "What I have come to ask you, Uncle Adolphus, is whether we have a relationship with Lord Merwin?"

"Merwin?" Lord Adolphus repeated. "Why should you expect that we have a connection with that prosy and loquacious windbag for whom I have had a deep aversion from the time I was at Oxford?"

"Most Noble families are linked by marriage somewhere in their family tree," the Duke replied. "You yourself have made that statement to me on many occasions in the past!"

"It is true," Lord Adolphus replied, "but I would have no wish to be connected with Merwin! Tiresome chap—very tiresome!"

"Uncle Adolphus, the one subject on which you are an authority, the one subject on which no one can fault you, is lineage," the Duke said. "Surely to oblige me you can find some small connection, however trifling, between our family and that of Lord Merwin's?"

"There is none!" Lord Adolphus replied adamantly. "And I cannot conceive, Theron, why you should desire a cognation so distasteful or—to put it stronger— abhorrent to me!"

"What can Lord Merwin have done to you?" the Duke asked with a hint of laughter in his voice.

"I have no wish to dig up any skeletons," Lord Adolphus replied. "It is enough for me to say, Theron, that I do not include any of the Merwin family on my visiting list! Anyway, the Lord Merwin I knew has been dead these past ten years!"

"Then why could you not say so?" the Duke enquired. "Although I imagine he had an heir!"

"I believe a cousin inherited the title," Lord Adolphus replied coldly. "But I have equally no desire for his acquaintance. What bat is flapping in our belfry, Theron? There is enough blue blood in the *Beau Ton* without your needing to rub shoulders with those who are quite beneath your touch!"

"You disappoint me," the Duke said, walking restlessly across the room. "And Winchcombe? We have no connection with that family, I presume?"

"Winchcombe!" Lord Adolphus repeated. "Now that is a very different kettle of fish!"

The Duke, who had asked the question in an offhand

way as one who already knew the answer, was suddenly alert.

"Yes, indeed, very different," Lord Adolphus continued. "As a matter of fact, my dear boy, your Great-Grandfather married a Winchcombe."

"He did?" the Duke ejaculated. "Then why have I never been told of it?"

"As it happens I have not included the union in my history of the family."

"Why the devil not?" the Duke asked.

"Because it was a *mésalliance*—something of which none of us could be proud!"

"What happened?" the Duke enquired.

There was now no mistaking his curiosity and Lord Adolphus, who seldom found his relatives interested in the family archives which were his particular hobby, was gratified to notice the manner in which the Duke seated himself in a comfortable chair and was apparently prepared to listen raptly to anything his relative had to impart.

"Do you mean to say," he asked as Lord Adolphus seemed to pause for reflection, "that my Great-Grandmother was a Winchcombe?"

'Nothing of the sort!" Lord Adolphus snapped. "Your Great-Grandmother was a Newcastle—an excellent family, good blood. The quarterings embellish our own with great distinction!"

"Then explain yourself," the Duke begged.

"The Winchcombe *mésalliance* was a family misfortune, which is why I have not incorporated it in the family tree."

"Cheating, are you?" the Duke asked. "Well, I have always been suspicious that you bend the branches a trifle, Uncle Adolphus."

"I have done nothing of the sort!" his Uncle retorted.

"But it seemed rather pointless to record for posterity the senseless action of a young profligate."

"Suppose you tell me what happened?" the Duke suggested. "And let me judge for myself."

"When your Great-Grandfather was up at Oxford," Lord Adolphus began, "he became infatuated with a young female of the name of Winchcombe—daughter of some Army chap.

"The boy was nineteen at the time—a wild blade who had been in innumerable scrapes—when he asked his father's permission to marry the wench. You can imagine the reply!

"Her father as it happened also refused his consent. Your Great-Grandfather in those days had no title, there being several lives between him and the Dukedom, and he was also in a state of impecunity habitual to most Undergraduates."

"What happened?" the Duke asked with a smile.

"Young Royd and Arabella Winchcombe ran away to Gretna Green!"

"That must have caused a scandal!" the Duke ejaculated.

"It did, indeed," his Uncle replied. "Both fathers set off in pursuit only to reach Gretna Green without having a sight or sign of the eloping couple. They thought they must have been hoaxed and after abusing each other in respect of their erring offspring for over a week, they returned south striving on their journey to discern the whereabouts of the lovers."

"What had occurred?" the Duke asked with deep curiosity.

"The runaways had been involved in a carriage accident," Lord Adolphus replied. "It happened after they had lost their way on some Yorkshire Moor. Anyway, they were both injured, your Great-Grandfather broke his leg and several ribs.

"They accepted the hospitality of the Country Squire who had been driving the other vehicle, and he certainly paid handsomely for his part in the collision; for they stayed with him for months!

"Arabella Winchcombe making a swift recovery apparently nursed her lover back to health. I imagine she was a competent chit—being a soldier's daughter."

"I am sure she was," the Duke remarked reflectively.

"Four months elapsed before they finally reached Gretna Green and were married!" Lord Adolphus continued.

"My God, that must have given the gossips something to chatter about!" the Duke remarked.

"It was all hushed up," his Uncle replied. "When they returned south Miss Winchcombe, or rather, Mrs. Royd, went back to live with her parents and died in childbirth five months later and the child was still-born. Your Great-Grandfather returned to his studies, or rather to his gay life at Oxford!

"The prodigal was welcomed home by the family and no one was sure of what had happened until he announced to his parents he was a widower!"

"They must have been curious!" the Duke murmured.

"I have a suspicion after reading the existing correspondence that young Royd, having a vast dislike of the penury in which he had been existing in the north, was a quite convincing liar," Lord Adolphus answered, "while my own opinion is that by the time they reached home he was bored with Arabella!"

"Obviously a shyster of the first water!" the Duke remarked. "And yet from all the accounts he was a conformable Duke and in his declining years deeply religious!"

"Another example of the poacher turned gamekeeper!" Lord Adolphus smiled. "No man is more pontifical than a reformed rake!"

The Duke laughed, then remarked seriously:

"Nevertheless, my heart bleeds for Arabella!"

"Never knew you had one," his Uncle retorted.

"It has for some years been a matter of conjecture," the Duke agreed, "but, Uncle Adolphus, you have told me exactly what I wished to know: my Great-Grandfather was in fact married to a Winchcombe!"

"Secretly, and as I have already said, I shall not acknowledge the connection in the family history which I am at this moment compiling," Lord Adolphus retorted.

"On the contrary, you will oblige me by telling the truth," the Duke replied. "I find the story most intriguing and in the interest of accuracy it should be recorded."

"Well, I'll be damned," Lord Adolphus remarked. "Never known you interested in your ancestors before now, and certainly not in any seamy incidents which do not reflect well on the family character."

The Duke did not reply and Lord Adolphus stared at his nephew reflectively with narrowed eyes.

"Is it a Merwin or a Winchcombe who has a particular interest for you?" he enquired.

"Both," the Duke replied, and went from the room without gratifying his relative's curiosity any further.

From Curzon Street he drove to Lincoln's Inn Fields and after some difficulty in finding the premises of Messrs. Mayhew, Bodkin and Critchwick he finally climbed a small, dark, twisting staircase to their offices on the first floor.

A somewhat disdainful clerk was inclined to query the possibility of the Duke seeing Mr. Critchwick seeing as he had no appointment. But when he learnt the distinguished visitor's name, with low bows of obsequious servility he escorted His Grace into an inner office.

There the Duke discovered an earnest-visaged and bespectacled but comparatively young man seated behind an imposingly large desk, who made him a long verbose speech on the honour His Grace was conferring on the firm by entering their offices.

"Are you Mr. Critchwick?" the Duke enquired, as soon as he was given an opportunity of speaking.

"That is my name, Your Grace, but I surmise you were in fact expecting to meet my father, Mr. Arthur Critchwick."

"I was," the Duke replied.

"Then I must inform Your Grace that my father is indisposed. In actual fact, I must be frank and tell you he has suffered a stroke which has impaired his faculties, and there is no likelihood of his resuming work here in this office."

The Duke seated himself on a chair which was not only uncomfortable but was, he suspected, unpleasantly dusty.

"That is unfortunate," he said. "I was anxious to meet your father, Mr. Critchwick, as I understand he is by General Sir Alexander Winchcombe's will empowered to appoint a Guardian for Miss Verena Winchcombe until she should attain her majority."

"That is correct, Your Grace," Mr. Crtichwick replied. "We received a letter this very morning informing us of the General's demise. My father if he were capable of understanding what has occurred, would I know be deeply distressed at losing an old friend and a valued client."

"But as you have apparently taken your father's position," the Duke said, "I presume you have the authority, Mr. Critchwick, to appoint a Guardian for Miss Winchcombe."

"I have, Your Grace," Mr. Critchwick replied.

"Excellent!" the Duke replied. "Then I will be obliged, Mr. Critchwick, as a relative and a person of responsibility, if you will appoint me!"

7

Verena was so downcast for the first ten miles of the journey towards London that she could hardly bring herself to reply to Miss Richardson's conversation and when her former Governess spoke of the General she began to weep.

Almost immediately she made an effort to regain her self-control but the atmosphere in the landau was lugubrious in the extreme until Miss Richardson in her calm, matter-of-fact voice remarked:

"I never thought, Verena, to find you so poor-spirited!"

"I have no wish to go to London."

"Then indeed I wash my hands of you," Miss Richardson declared. "You used to have a sense of adventure, to be prepared to meet difficulties with a smile and make an effort to overcome obstacles. You are certainly not the same girl who had three falls in trying to leap a five-barred gate but succeeded in the end!"

Verena managed a smile.

"I would not like to believe that you are ashamed of me."

"Well, I am!" Miss Richardson replied frankly. "And I can only be thankful that the General cannot see you now. If there was one thing for which he had a distaste it was a wet pea-goose in a fit of the dismals!"

This made Verena laugh and after they had partaken an early luncheon at Baldock her spirits noticeably revived.

They reached the outskirts of London about five o'clock and the landau, wending its way through narrow roads congested with drays, coaches, carriages and smart phaetons, eventually reached Lady Bingley's residence in Manchester Square.

It was a tall, narrow, unpretentious house with, however, large windows looking onto the garden in the centre of the square and a private garden of its own at the back.

As the Coachman drew the horses to a standstill Verena wondered a little anxiously whether her Godmother would be pleased to welcome her, arriving unexpectedly and without an invitation.

But she need have had no fears on that score. Lady Bingley, after a first exclamation of sheer astonishment at the sight of her God-daughter, held out her arms and there was no mistaking the sincerity of her welcome.

Her Ladyship had been widowed the previous year, and after a lifetime of attending to the needs and whims of a somewhat demanding husband, she was finding time heavy on her hands. She could have asked for nothing more enlivening than the company of her God-daughter.

On the way to London Verena and Miss Richardson had decided they would tell Lady Bingley that the General had sent them to London because he was convinced that Verena needed a rest after having nursed him so devotedly and for so long.

"A rest?" Lady Bingley exclaimed. "What you need, my dear, is some gaiety! I have often thought of you mouldering away in that flat, damp, insalubrious part of the country without, I am convinced a sign of a beau or even the chance of a flirtation!"

"I have been very happy with Grandpapa," Verena said with just the faintest tremor in her voice.

"I am sure you have," Lady Bingley replied, "but there is no gainsaying the fact that your Grandfather will never see seventy-five again, and although he was a handsome, dashing buck in his time, he is hardly the type of partner one would choose for the delightfully improper new-fashioned waltz!"

Verena laughed at that and Lady Bingley continued:

"The Season is just starting and I am sure we can contrive that you will enjoy yourself, even if I must be honest, my dearest, and say that I cannot see my way to getting you invited to Balls of absolutely the first flight."

Lady Bingley, who had been attractive in her day and still had a certain corpulent charm, came from a well-known County family and was well aware of the difference that lay between the invitations received by a *débutante* of the finest blood and by one who must hang somewhat precariously on the fringe of the *Beau Ton*.

Then she gave an exclamation:

"I have just thought of something which is indeed fortunate. I am having an 'At Home' the day after tomorrow and quite by chance I encountered an old friend of mine last week—Lady Studholde. We were at school together but since her husband is exceedingly wealthy and has some minor position at Court, she now moves in a very different world from mine!

"However, I invited Her Ladyship to honour my little party on Thursday and she has accepted! If she comes and should take a fancy to you, Verena, then things could be very different!"

"Why would they be?" Verena asked in an uncompromising voice.

"Because, dear child, Lady Studholde not only has two sons of marriageable age but she is also chaperoning a daughter in her second season. What could be more delightful than that you and Sybil Studholde should attend parties together?"

Lady Bingley drew in her breath rapturously at the thought, then added with a little sigh:

"Unfortunately, Sybil has not much countenance, poor girl! I doubt after all if Lady Studholde would risk the comparison between you and Sybil, which would be all too obvious!"

"You mean I am too pretty?" Verena asked.

"You have grown into a beauty," her Godmother told her. "In fact for a moment I could hardly believe my eyes when you walked in through the door! Remember, child, I have not seen you for two years, and the change is remarkable!"

Her Ladyship sighed again before she continued:

"If only I had taken pains to keep up my acquaintance with Lady Jersey and Lady Cowper, both of whom I knew in my youth, then your success, my dearest God-daughter, would be assured."

At the mention of the names of the two patronesses at Almacks, Verena remembered that Major Royd had told her that he could ensure her entry to that "Holy of Holies!"

She thought to mention to her Godmother what he had said and then decided against it. She was certain he must have been mistaken. It was unlikely that he knew such glittering stars in the Social firmament and if he did they would be unlikely to accept her on the introduction of a young man!

Verena put her arms round her Godmother's shoulder and kissed her soft cheek.

"It is far too kind of you to worry about me," she said. "I shall be happy just by being with you. I have no wish for Balls and Assemblies. It is only Grandpapa who is anxious for me to enjoy them, which I am sure I will not."

"That is sheer fustian, my love!" Lady Bingley exclaimed. "But you may leave everything to me. I promise you I will do what is best for you. After all, we already hold in our hands the most important introduction of all."

"And what is that?" Verena asked curiously.

"That you are exceedingly pretty, my dearest," Lady Bingley replied.

Her Ladyship in fact expressed more confidence in her powers to introduce Verena to the Polite World than she actually felt was possible. No one knew better than she did the obstacles and difficulties that the great Social Hostesses were all too swift to raise if they sensed there was the slightest presumption on the part of some country wench to enter their magic circle!

An exemplary wife, Lady Bingley had been content with the company of Lord Bingley's friends who had been mostly connected with the legal profession or of aged peers whom he encountered in the House of Lords.

Now she regretted bitterly her indolence in not making a push to include in her hospitality the friends she had known when she herself had been a girl, or to have kept up a correspondence with country neighbors of her family whose aristocratic lineage entitled them when they did visit London to move in the most lofty circles.

However, she did not despair. Her Ladyship had

often regretted not being able to give Verena a more amusing time on her last visit. But the child had certainly then not been the beauty she was now!

"The first thing Verena must have," Lady Bingley said to Miss Richardson when they were alone, "is some really fashionable gowns. Has the General made any provision for her expenditure on this visit?"

Miss Richardson was ready with her answer.

"Yes, indeed, My Lady," she answered. "The General has said that Verena can spend any money she wishes, in fact he has commanded her to buy everything of the best!"

The former Governess paused for a moment before she added:

"I do not think, My Lady, I shall be betraying a confidence if I tell you that on the General's death Verena will inherit a fortune of over ninety thousand pounds besides her Grandfather's Estate!"

"Ninety thousand pounds!" Lady Bingley exclaimed faintly. "Then the child is an heiress! With her looks and that wealth we can indeed find her a husband of the very first stare!"

Miss Richardson, who knew the story of Captain Giles Winchcombe-Smythe and the General's opinion of him, hoped Lady Bingley would not be disappointed. At the same time, she realised the General had been wiser than anyone had expected in planning that Verena should at least have her chance to see the world before she threw herself away on someone completely unsuitable.

The following day Verena spent a most enjoyable time in Bond Street. Armed by Lady Bingley with the addresses of the most expensive dressmakers and spending over an hour in Miss Tuting's millinery shop in St. James's, she returned to Manchester Square with the landau so filled with boxes, parcels and bags that there had been hardly room when they collected all their purchases for the vehicle to include herself and Miss Richardson.

Like Verena's looks, her taste had improved too, and Lady Bingley was delighted with the gowns she had chosen.

"I am somewhat appalled at such fantastic extravagance!" Verena said.

"It is never an extravagance to buy something in which you not only look your best but feel your best!" Lady Bingley replied.

Verena, remembering the gowns she had worn on her last visit to London, had been determined that this time she would not look rustic whatever her feelings might be.

And the gauzes, satins, lamés, laces, ribbons, feathers and flowers were all, she felt, the ammunition with which her Grandfather would have wished her to be provided in making an onslaught on the Social World.

She recognized with some bitterness that this was an enemy she had to fight with all her strength were she to achieve even a minor victory.

When it was time for bed Verena lay awake for some time thinking of her home and of Major Royd. She had in fact several times during the day wondered how he was faring and regretting that he could not have convalesced a few days longer before setting out to ride Salamanca to Eaton Socon. It was but two miles, but she feared that the motion of the horse beneath him would aggravate his head and perhaps start it aching again.

The Duke had attempted to hide the pain which had at first been almost intolerable but Verena knew how much he had suffered.

Now, remembering his bravery, she was ashamed that she should have bewailed both to him and to Miss

Richardson her Grandfather's instructions instead of making the very best of them!

Her thoughts lingered so long on the Major that she chid herself for not being more elated by the realisation that she could now marry her cousin Giles.

She told herself it was only through reluctance to break her promise to her Grandfather that she had not determined immediately on her arrival in London to discover Giles' whereabouts.

"The War Office could inform me where his Regiment is stationed," she thought.

It was, however, a difficult decision. Should she find Giles and tell him that the General was dead? Or should she respect her Grandfather's wishes and wait three months until the notice appeared in the *Gazette*?

On Thursday morning Verena remembered that Major Royd had promised that he would call that day, but there was no sign of him before luncheon although when she went once again to the shops with Miss Richardson she left a message with the Butler to say what time they would return.

Miss Richardson left after luncheon to return to the country. She had done her duty in bringing Verena to London, but now that her former pupil was safely in the hands of Lady Bingley, she wished to return to her cottage, her dogs and her cats.

"I have invited my guests for four o'clock," Lady Bingley told Verena, when Miss Richardson had departed. "I have sent out quite a number of extra invitations yesterday and this morning informing my friends of your arrival in London and hoping that they will honour us this afternoon and make your acquaintance."

"How kind you are!" Verena exclaimed.

"I went through my address book yesterday," Lady Bingley continued, "and found several friends who have daughters about your age and a number who have sons!

But you know as well as I do, dear, it is the older women who can take you up or give you a set-down. So I do beg of you, my dearest child, to make yourself charming to the Dowagers!"

"I will try," Verena promised.

When finally she was dressed she looked at herself critically in the long mirror in her bedroom before repairing downstairs to the Salon.

Her gown, from Madame Bertine, the most exclusive, most sought-after Court dress-maker in the whole of Bond Street, had cost what seemed to Verena an inordinate sum. But there was no doubt that it set off successfully the darkness of her hair with its golden lights and made her skin seem almost dazzlingly white.

Of pale yellow silk over a heavy satin of the same hue, it was ornamented at the hem and round the neck with tiny frills of lace and embellished with bows of velvet ribbon which could only have come from France. The same ribbons encircled her tiny waist.

Satisfied with her reflection Verena turned to go downstairs only to be called to her Godmother's bedchamber.

"Come here, child," Lady Bingley said, looking resplendent in rustling black taffeta trimmed with Chantilly lace. "I have a present for you!"

"A present?" Verena echoed.

"I hope you will like it. I wore it myself when I was your age."

Verena opened a velvet box and found inside a string of beautifully matched pearls. Their soft lustre, when she clasped them round her long white neck, gave her appearance a touch of glamour which she had never known before.

After an affectionate embrace Verena and Lady Bingley descended to the Salon on the first floor where more extensive preparations had been made than was usual at one of Lady Bingley's "At Homes."

Arrangements of carnations, lilies and roses decorated the side tables in the spacious L-shaped Salon which with its long windows, high ceiling and Adam fireplace was a very convenient room in which to hold a reception.

The furniture was heavy, having been inherited by Lord Bingley from his father, but it was nevertheless of solid worth, and the satin-damask curtains and covers on the sofas and chairs were pleasing to the eye—if not particularly sensational.

"As I have asked so many more people than usual," Lady Bingley said to Verena, "I have engaged two extra footmen and as old Johnson is growing deaf I nearly always on these occasions hire an experienced man to announce my guests."

Verena had already caught sight of an awe-inspiring individual, looking uncommonly like an Archbishop, standing at the top of the stairway. She was not surprised when his voice matched his appearance—seeming to intone the names of the arrivals almost melodiously as he announced them.

Lady Bingley's friends had rallied to her clarion-call —or perhaps her description of her God-daughter had been flattering enough to make them curious.

Anyway, they came up the stairs one after another, the majority of them on the wrong side of fifty. Nevertheless there were a few elegant young bloods who took one swift appraising glance at Verena and decided they were not wasting their time in such an unfashionable area as Manchester Square.

Then just after half after four of the clock Verena caught sight of an exceedingly handsome face and a pair of broad shoulders behind an aged Gentleman who was propelling himself slowly upwards with one hand on the banisters, the other on an ivory stick.

"Mr. Justice and Lady Pollard," the Butler announced.

As the elderly couple moved forward to shake Lady Bingley's hand and to be introduced to Verena, she managed to catch the Duke's eye and to smile dazzlingly at him.

There was no mistaking, he thought, the gladness in her face and he waited to be announced, wondering as he did so what name he should give.

But the pontifical announcer had been engaged over the years by most of London's leading Hostesses. He was surprised to see the Duke in Manchester Square. Nevertheless he had announced His Grace on so many previous occasions that there was no need for the formality of enquiring his name.

As Lady Pollard took her hand from her hostess's and offered it somewhat perfunctorily to Verena, the Duke was announced in stentorian tones:

"His Grace, the Duke of Selchester."

For a moment Lady Bingley felt paralysed. Then she thought humbly there must be some incredible mistake. Never in her most ambitious dreams had she anticipated that the most sought after, the most eligible bachelor in the whole of the *Ton* would ever grace a party of hers.

She had indeed imagined a little foolishly that with Verena's looks she might contrive to inveigle Lord Cumberford or even the young Earl of Paddington to one of her receptions.

But never would she have aspired to the Duke of Selchester, who was known to be so exclusive and so fastidious in his choice of entertainment that it was said that the Regent before he came to the Throne had on many occasions to plead with him to accept an invitation to Carlton House.

"You must forgive my intrusion, My Lady, when you are entertaining," the Duke was saying in his deep voice, and Lady Bingley had almost to force herself to listen to him.

"I am—honoured, Your Grace," she managed to falter before the Duke continued:

"My excuse is that naturally I wish to welcome to London my relative, Miss Verena Winchcombe."

"Your relative?" Lady Bingley queried, feeling that in her astonishment she must be stammering.

"Yes indeed," the Duke replied. "Did the General never tell you that my Great-Grandfather married a Winchcombe?"

"No, I do not think he did," Lady Bingley answered.

Even as she spoke she realised with a swelling sense of satisfaction that after the announcement of the Duke's name there had been a sudden silence in the crowded reception room.

The chatter had started again, but Lady Bingley saw with a full heart that Lady Studholde was not far from the door and could not have failed to notice the new arrival.

The Duke moved one step from Lady Bingley to Verena and encountered two eyes flashing at him with an anger so vehement that he could hardly believe that only a few seconds before they had been lit with a smile.

"Allow me to wish you well, Verena," he said.

"How dare you?" she asked almost beneath her breath. "How dare you deceive me?"

"Lord and Lady Carthwraite and the Honourable Florence Carthwraite."

The Duke, looking down into the white and furious face raised to his said quietly:

"We will discuss it later. I must not prevent you from greeting your guests."

He walked further into the room to be immediately buttonholed by Lady Studholde. She was a woman who had always bored him and he soon extracted himself with dexterity, having seen an aged Peer by the window whom he often encountered in the House of Lords.

He talked to him for a short time, greeted one or two other familiar faces, and then walked back to where Lady Bingley and Verena were still receiving guests.

There was, however, by now only a trickle of late-comers ascending the stairs and the Duke, when there was a pause, said to Lady Bingley:

"I wonder if you'll permit me to have a few words alone with my relative. My family is eager to meet her and I thought that if I could talk over with Miss Winchcombe certain invitations I have received on her behalf, especially one from my sister, she could convey them to Your Ladyship when you are less preoccupied."

"Yes, of course, Your Grace," Lady Bingley replied. "And I hope we may have the pleasure of your company when the house is not so crowded."

"That is exactly what I wish to discuss," the Duke answered.

"I do not . . ." Verena began, only to be silenced by Lady Bingley saying:

"Take the Duke to the Morning-Room, Verena. There is no hurry. No one will leave until they have partaken of the refreshments."

"Your Ladyship is most gracious," the Duke said, raising Lady Bingley's gloved hand perfunctorily to his lips.

Verena wanted to protest, to refuse to go with him. But he merely stood aside at the top of the stairs and waited for her to precede him. There was something in the expression of his eyes or maybe in his air of calm authority which made her obey.

She ran down the stairs as if in a hurry and led the way to the Morning-Room situated at the back of the house, its french-windows opening onto the small garden.

The sunshine picked up the lights in Verena's hair but her eyes were dark and stony as the Duke shut the door behind him.

"How could you?" she cried. "How could you behave in such an abominable, deceitful, underhand manner?"

"It was you who assumed that I could not by any possibility be the Nobleman for whom you were waiting," the Duke replied with a twinkle in his eye. "It was extremely mortifying, I may assure you, to find that I have so little presence without the trappings of a smart coach, outriders and liveried servants!"

"You could have told me the truth when I asked your name!" Verena retorted. "Why were you so dishonest?"

"I have a strong distaste for roast pigeon," the Duke replied promptly.

Just for a moment Verena's irresistible dimples betrayed her. Then moving across the room she stormed:

"You have behaved in the most outrageous, contemptible, and despicable manner!"

"I think 'odious' is the word you need," the Duke replied. "And there are two other descriptions of me you have forgotten."

"What are they?" Verena asked crossly.

"A bumptious Blockhead and a conceited Cockscomb! How could you expect me after those scathing definitions to reveal who I was? Besides, I did not lie to you—my name is Theron Royd."

"You are contemptible! I will never forgive you," Verena declared.

"Never?" the Duke asked. "Then what indeed are we to do about the 'Evil Genius'?"

"Nothing," Verena snapped. "This exonerates me from all responsibility where he is concerned. Your behaviour has only confirmed my feelings where you are concerned."

She drew in her breath and continued thunderously:

"When I think of the preparations that were being made for your arrival at Copple Hall; when I recall how you deliberately enticed me to reveal my opinion of you; when I remember how you beguiled me into asking your help and support—well, all I can say, Your Grace, is that I despise you now more than I despised you before we met!"

"That is unfortunate," the Duke said quietly, "because, Verena, I have made you my special responsibility."

"What do you mean by that?" Verena asked. "And what is all this nonsense about our being related? You know that is a lie like all the other lies you have told me!"

"It is in fact the truth," the Duke answered. "My Great-Grandfather married a girl called Arabella Winchcombe!"

"I have never heard tell of it," Verena said suspiciously.

"Apparently it was quite a scandal. They ran away together to Gretna Green just as your father and mother did. It was very romantic! You must get my Uncle, Lord Adolphus Royd, to tell you the whole story."

"I am not intending to meet your Uncle, your sister or any other members of your family," Verena replied in a hard little voice. "My Godmother has made very extensive plans to introduce me to the Social World that Grandpapa desired for me. I have no need of your assistance and certainly not of your patronage. You will oblige me, my Most Noble Duke, if you will just leave me alone!"

"That, Verena, is something which unfortunately I am unable to do," the Duke said. "I have been to see Mr. Critchwick and he has appointed, as your Grandfather's will suggested, a Guardian who will administer your fortune and protect you from undesirable suitors until you reach the age of twenty-one."

"You have been to see Mr. Critchwick!" Verena exclaimed. "I intended to see him tomorrow! What right have you to interfere?"

"Mr. Critchwick was delighted to see me," the Duke answered. "In fact, so delighted, Verena, that he has appointed me your legal Guardian!"

For a moment Verena was speechless. Her eyes, sparkling with anger, searched the Duke's face as if she half-believed he was deliberately teasing her.

Then when she knew that he had told the truth, she gave a cry of sheer rage and stamped her foot.

"How dare you? How dare you?"

"You may be incensed with me," the Duke replied, "but I assure you, Verena, I could make things far easier for your Social début than anyone else can contrive.

"All you have to do is to trust me, and I promise you that, when you cease wishing to eat me, you will find I have in fact acted for the best."

"I will never forgive you!" Verena said fiercely.

She turned her back on him to stare blindly out of the window.

"As your Guardian," the Duke said quietly, "I cannot allow you to cause speculation and gossip by talking with me here alone for too long.

"I have arranged to take your Godmother and yourself to a small party my sister—the Countess of Ereth—is giving this evening. We will dine first at Selchester House and I will call for you in my carriage at seven-forty-five."

"I will not come!" Verena stormed. "Nothing will induce me to dine with you!"

The Duke gave a sigh as if he were dealing with an exasperating child.

"If that is your last word," he said, "I will go upstairs and explain my plans to your Godmother. She, I feel sure, will not wish you to miss the opportunity of meeting not only my sister, but enjoying the informal dance which her daughter, who is about your age, is holding for her friends."

He paused and added more gently:

"It is quite a small occasion, Verena, so there is no need for you to be afraid."

"I am not afraid," Verena retorted. "I am just disgusted by your behaviour."

"That is something we can discuss on another occasion," the Duke replied loftily. "As it is, unless you wish me to trouble your Godmother when she is so occupied, I will leave now and return, as I have already said, at a quarter before eight."

The Duke stopped speaking and looked at the tense, incensed little figure facing him with clenched hands.

"Wear your prettiest gown, Verena," he said. "First impressions are important and I want my family to be proud of their new relative. Incidentally, I congratulate you on the choice of the dress you are wearing now."

"I hate you!"

Verena thought even as she spoke that she sounded like a petulant child rather than an affronted adult.

The Duke moved towards her, took her by the shoulders and turned her round to face him. Before she realised what he was about he had lifted her hand to his lips.

"Forgive me, Elf," he said beguilingly, with laughter in his eyes.

Then before she could rage at him again he was gone from the room, leaving the door open. She heard him cross the Hall and knew that he took his hat and gloves from an attendant footman. The front door closed behind him and Verena, still seething with indignation, slowly went upstairs to rejoin her Godmother.

She half hoped, although knowing that such an idea was unlikely in the extreme, that Lady Bingley would feel too tired or have some valid excuse why they should not dine at Selchester House.

But as soon as Verena imparted the Duke's invitation to her Godmother she was in such a flutter of excitement and delight that Verena could not even begin to explain why she herself was not looking forward to the evening.

"Why did you not tell me, dearest, that you knew the Duke of Selchester?" Lady Bingley asked curiously.

"I have not known him for long," Verena answered diffidently.

"But how could you have met anyone of such import living in the country?"

"He . . . he was on his way to stay with the Upminsters," Verena replied, feeling it was wisest to tell the truth.

"Oh, now I understand!" Lady Bingley exclaimed. "The Upminsters have a pretty daughter, have they not? I suppose they are angling for His Grace like every other ambitious parent. But from all I hear the Duke is extremely elusive!"

Verena did not answer and then Lady Bingley continued:

"But how is it I have never before heard there was a connection between the Winchcombes and the Royds?"

"It all happened a long time ago," Verena replied.

She longed to deny there was any truth in the Duke's assertion. At the same time she knew that he would not have announced in public that she was his relation unless he was sure of his facts.

"It is gratifying, most gratifying!" Lady Bingley said. "And Lady Studholde has overwhelmed us with invitations: to her Ball, to dinner, to luncheon next week. My dear, I could have laughed in her face. I am quite certain that had the Duke not called when he did, we should, if we were lucky, have been palmed off with a card to her Ball and not a suggestion of a meal."

"Are you sure you are not too fatigued, Godmama, to dine out tonight?" Verena began tentatively.

"I am certainly not too fatigued to visit Selchester House!" Lady Bingley replied. "Oh, Verena, if you only knew how I have longed all my life to see the inside of that magnificent mansion! But never, never once have I had the chance of entering Selchester House or indeed Ereth House, which you tell me we shall be visiting later. You are indeed the luckiest girl in the world!"

"Only because I have you for my Godmother," Verena said.

Feeling she could not listen any longer to Lady Bingley's effusiveness she ran upstairs to her bedroom.

Despite her first decision to teach the Duke a lesson by making herself look a dowdy country Miss, she could not on reflection resist wearing a new gown of pale green gauze over a foundation of shimmering green lamé.

It was only when she was dressed and the maid was giving a finishing touch to her hair, that she realised that the Duke might think she had deliberately tried to remind him of the woods, the waterfalls and the pine forests.

Then she told herself defiantly that such talk had only been a part of his deceit—that he really had no interest in such childish nonsense.

"I hate him!" she told herself.

"Did you speak, Miss?" her maid enquired.

"No! No!" Verena answered quickly.

But all the way in the carriage, as Lady Bingley chatted happily to their Ducal host, Verena repeated over and over again beneath her breath:

"I hate him! I hate him!"

She had, however, been unable to forestall a sudden irrepressible start of admiration when he had first come into the Drawing-Room where she and Lady Bingley were awaiting him.

Verena had never before seen the Duke in evening dress, and it would have been impossible for any man to appear more handsome, more elegant.

His blue satin evening-coat, with its long tails and rolled revers, was worn over a plain waistcoat but with a frilled cravat so intricately tied that Verena, with a curl of her lips, felt it must have taken hours of painstaking endeavour to achieve.

As it was an informal party the Duke wore trousers instead of knee-breeches, but they fitted so closely and gave him such a slim yet athletic grace that Verena was irresistibly reminded of the nickname she had given him. He might be a Leopard, she thought, but Napoleon had been right in disparaging the "Hideous Leopards" if they were all like the Duke!

"I hate him!" she said beneath her breath, and refused to meet his eyes, dropping her eyelids and sitting in the Carriage with her face turned towards the windows.

Her little straight nose and firm chin, though she did not realise it, were exquisitely silhouetted against the darkness of the well-padded town-landau in which the Duke was conveying them.

"I have long desired to see the magnificence of Selchester House," Lady Bingley gushed as they entered the great Marble Hall with its Greek statues, Roman mosaics, huge silver sconces and enormous crystal chandeliers.

"My ancestors were great collectors of antiquity," the Duke answered. "My collection, if it is worthy of the name, is housed in the stables!"

He glanced at Verena as he spoke and knew she could not prevent the little flicker of interest which leapt into her eyes.

"As a matter of fact," the Duke continued, "I have today heard of an exceptional pair of bays to be sold by Lord Manson, a friend of mine, which I think would interest you, Verena."

Just for a moment there was silence. Verena longed to tell the Duke she was not interested, to inform him that should she buy horses for her stables she would choose them herself without his help.

But then there came before her eyes a mental picture of Salamanca tossing his head, the muscles rippling beneath his shining coat, his long black tail switching away the flies.

"I am prepared to look at them," she capitulated.

Her voice was cold and distant but she knew as she spoke that the Duke thought he had won at any rate part of the battle!

"He is intolerable!" she thought. "I hate him!"

It was, however, hard to remain frigidly silent when the Duke, after a delectable dinner at which he talked most interestingly, showed her and Lady Bingley some of the treasures of Selchester House. He then conveyed them in his carriage to a mansion in Berkeley Square which belonged to his brother-in-law.

The Countess of Ereth was six years older than the Duke but was still at the height of her beauty, which had astounded the Social World when she had first emerged from the schoolroom.

Princes, Dukes, Ambassadors, had all solicited her hand, but the Earl of Ereth had fallen in love with her at first sight and with but a few stormy episodes they had been extremely happy in the nineteen years they had been married.

Their eldest daughter was now eighteen and nearly as lovely as her mother had been. Lady Ereth, a doting parent, naturally desired that her child should have the pick of all the most eligible bachelors that the *Beau Ton* could provide and had therefore arranged to entertain extensively all through the London Season.

Although she did not yet know it, the Duke was determined that Verena should take part in many of the festivities already planned.

He had sent a footman to warn his sister that he would be attending her party that evening and that he was bringing two friends with him. As he had not given her their names, the Countess, knowing her brother, had expected to see Captain Harry Sheraton and perhaps another of the Duke's special cronies.

When the Duke reached the top of the wide staircase at Ereth House, leading the way so that he could introduce Lady Bingley and Verena, his sister held out her hand and kissed his cheek affectionately.

"I did not expect you back so soon, Theron," she exclaimed. "You cannot have had time to visit all three of the blonde beauties I chose for you! Was the Upminster chit so attractive that you had no reason to go further?"

"My plans were changed," the Duke answered quickly, realising ruefully that Verena must have heard his sister's words, which she had made no effort to muffle. "Instead, Evelyn, I have brought you a surprise guest. May I introduce Lady Bingley, who is so obliging as to offer her hospitality to a relative of ours who has just arrived in London——Miss Verena Winchcombe."

The Countess of Ereth looked at her brother with a slightly puzzled expression.

"A relative?" she queried.

"Yes, indeed," the Duke replied. "Have you forgotten that our Great-Grandfather married a Miss Arabella Winchcombe?"

The Countess of Ereth had of course never heard of Arabella Winchcombe, but she was too well-bred to show her ignorance.

"Oh, Great-Grandpapa!" she exclaimed knowingly, and greeted Lady Bingley.

She held out her hand to Verena, noting how pretty the girl was but recalling at the same time that she was not the Duke's type—fair hair and blue eyes was what he had insisted was the right colouring for his Duchess.

Then why, the Countess of Ereth asked herself, had he troubled to admit a relationship which she guessed only existed in some dusty archive pored over by Lord Adolphus!

She had, however, over the years of dealing with her brother learnt that if he wished to impart information of any sort he would do so in his own good time.

She therefore introduced Lady Bingley to an elderly Admiral and took Verena to another Salon where her daughter, Emmaline, was entertaining her young friends with a small orchestra of but a dozen instrumentalists to play for them.

Left alone in a strange room with a number of people she had never set eyes on before, Verena felt a moment of shyness. But it was an emotion that was quite impossible to feel for long when Emmaline was present.

In a short time she had introduced Verena to all her friends, admired her gown, asked a whole host of impertinent questions to which she apparently did not require answers, and set the whole party dancing to some absurd country romp which Verena had never expected to see in Polite Society.

They "Stripped the Willow," took their partners for "Sir Roger de Coverley" and ended up ridiculously playing "Oranges and Lemons" and "Musical Chairs!"

It was all rather childish and a great deal of fun, and it was only when the band was not playing and Verena heard the marble clock on the chimney-piece strike midnight, that she realised she had already been a guest at Ereth House for over two hours.

Resolutely she walked into the other Salon where the older members of the party were talking and drinking champagne.

The Duke was standing by the fireplace. Verena took one look at him and walking to his side, said:

"Your Grace must be well aware that you should not be up so late. If I had known the time I should have insisted that we went home an hour ago!"

"Are you making a suggestion or commanding me?" the Duke enquired.

"I would not wish all the trouble Doctor Graves and I have taken to be wasted," Verena answered.

Then, as the Duke hesitated, she said crossly:

"Do not be so nonsensical! You know as well as I do you are not yet well enough to stay up as late as this! Indeed, you should not have travelled to London yesterday. I expected you to take longer on the journey."

The Duke looked at her speculatively for a moment before he said:

"If it is your wish, Verena, I will take you home and then retire. I had thought you were too angry with me to remember my injuries!"

"My anger, Your Grace, has nothing to do with your health! And as I am responsible—as you have often pointed out—for the wound on your head, then if you intend to escort Godmama and me back to Manchester Square, we should leave at once."

"If that is what you desire," the Duke replied.

He collected Lady Bingley, and more swiftly than Verena could have imagined possible they made their farewells and the three of them were in the Duke's coach driving home.

On arrival Lady Bingley thanked the Duke profusely; Verena only said as she dropped a curtsey:

"For goodness' sake be sensible and go straight to bed!"

"I will obey your instructions," the Duke said, "but I hope you will permit me to call for you tomorrow morning in my Phaeton. I wish to take you driving in The Park."

He glanced round to see if Lady Bingley was out of hearing and added in a low voice:

"We must search, as you know, for the 'Evil Genius'."

"And if I refuse to come with you?" Verena asked.

"Then I might have to compel you," the Duke replied in an amused voice.

"Compel me?" she questioned, glancing up at him.

"As a Guardian I have certain rights. I should not hesitate to exercise them, Verena."

She uttered a sound of exasperation and tossing her head, stalked away from him. But the Duke was smiling as he stepped back into his landau and was driven towards Selchester House.

8

The Duke was finishing his breakfast when Captain Sheraton was announced.

He entered the room in the magnificent glory of the uniform of the Life Guards, his breastplate shining in the sunshine from the window, the spurs clinking on his thigh-high boots; and he carried under his arm the classical helmet with horsehair crest and plumes designed by the Prince Regent.

"God, Harry!" the Duke ejaculated, looking up from a dish of lamb cutlets embellished with truffles and cream. "You clank like the bell in a damned belfry! Sit down before you deafen me!"

"On way to Barracks," Harry Sheraton replied. "Heard you back, Theron. Could not resist looking in to hear had you found a blushing bride!"

"I have not," the Duke answered, "but I have found your Bullion thieves!"

"Found what—" Harry Sheraton ejaculated.

"It is a long story," the Duke replied with a smile. "You had best be seated, Harry, or you will fall down from exhaustion! I well know the weight of that fancy attire is intolerable!"

"Trouble is," Harry Sheraton replied, seating himself carefully on one of the high-backed dining chairs, "only time even passably comfortable is on a horse! Never mind that, tell your tale! Not much time!"

The Duke obliged, relating in detail his encounter with Verena, the curiosity which led him to the old Priory, and the manner in which he had suffered—as he put it—"in the interests of law and justice!"

"Good God, Theron!" Harry Sheraton ejaculated when he had finished. "Know you to be truthful cove or would swear you bamming with all the Cheltenham theatricals rolled into one!"

"It is the truth," the Duke said soberly.

"Cleverest scheme I have ever heard!" Harry Sheraton exclaimed.

"Exactly what I thought," the Duke agreed. "It is almost foolproof as far as the 'Evil Genius' is concerned."

"That what you call him?" Harry Sheraton asked. "Apt name! Genius right enough!"

"I think it was Verena's name for him," the Duke remarked, "but as you say he certainly has a brain-box to think out a plan which would be very difficult to pin on him unless we catch him in the very act."

"What we shall have to do," Harry Sheraton said positively.

"Exactly!" the Duke agreed. "That is why I was so anxious that Verena should come to London. After all, she is the only person who can identify him!"

"About this girl," Harry Sheraton said with a change of tone. "Sounds an Amazon! Intend to marry her?"

The Duke put down his knife and fork with a clatter.

"Marry her!" he exclaimed. "I can assure you,

Harry, by the way Verena raged at me yesterday she would sooner marry a gorilla at the Royal Exchange! She considers me abominable, deceitful, contemptible and in her favourite epithet—odious!"

"Sounds rum sort of wench!" Harry Sheraton said, his eyes on the Duke's face.

"She is certainly different from most young females of her age," the Duke remarked. "She hates Society and would rather associate with village children; has a vast disdain for anyone she considers top-lofty; and a passion for horses. She has trained her own horse to do the most incredible tricks! She has healing hands, can read Latin, handle a musket with considerable skill; and she has not the slightest conception of how to flirt or ingratiate herself as a female!"

Harry Sheraton's eyes twinkled.

"Makes me cursed curious, Theron! Think you already half-way to altar!"

The Duke rose from his seat at the table.

"You can save such idle speculation for the romances from the Lending Libraries. Verena considers herself promised to some fortune-hunting footslogger. In fact, I am almost convinced it is my duty to make a push to find him or at least have some idea of his whereabouts! Heaven knows where the 11th Foot are stationed at the moment!"

"Must be off," Harry Sheraton said, rising with difficulty from his chair. "See you later. Talk further on this matter."

The Duke was not listening.

"I suppose," he said reflectively, "I could visit the War Office."

"Not accompany you there," Harry Sheraton remarked. "Gives me the creeps to see those old Generals hanging round hoping war will break out some obscure part of world."

He paused half-way to the door to ask:

"By the way, what the footslogger's name? Have Uncle who commanded the 11th one time!"

"The name is Captain Winchcombe-Smythe," the Duke replied.

"Giles Winchcombe-Smythe?" Harry Sheraton asked.

"Yes!" the Duke answered in surprise. "How the devil did you know?"

"Unless a twin," Harry Sheraton answered. "In my Regiment!"

"In the Life Guards!" the Duke ejaculated.

"Right," Harry Sheraton replied. "Bought a transfer to us two months ago."

"What is he like?" the Duke enquired.

"Not spoken with him over much," Harry Sheraton answered. "Not done to be effusive to newcomers. But see him of course. Thought at first he would pass, then . . ."

Harry Sheraton paused.

"Then what happened?" the Duke prompted.

"Begun to sport his blunt, deal too ostentatiously," Harry Sheraton continued. "Boasts of conquests in petticoat line; gives parties for Covent Garden frails which send the younger officers on parade with such hangovers they cannot see the point of their swords at two paces."

"Interesting," the Duke said quietly.

"Personally think him an outsider and will tell you more later," Harry Sheraton said with a quick glance at the clock. "Roasted if late, the Colonel in none too good a humour these days. One thing would cheer him to hand over 'Evil Genius' in irons!"

"You will have to persuade Miss Winchcombe to come looking for him," the Duke said with a sudden smile.

"Certainly do that," Harry Sheraton promised. "Gad, Theron, you are most unaccountable chap! Never expected you be one for adventure, heroics, all that type swashbuckling!"

"I am not," the Duke answered ruefully. "I was forced into it, you might say, by circumstances over which I had no control."

He found, however, he was talking to himself in an empty Dining-Room. Harry Sheraton was already proceeding across the Hall, his accoutrements clanking as he moved.

The conversation had, however, given the Duke much food for thought and when he collected Verena just before noon to take her driving in the Park, he had not made up his mind whether he should tell her Captain Winchcombe-Smythe was in London or whether he should wait until she asked for his help.

He had an idea that she might visit the War Office on her own, and this—which would give rise to gossip and speculation—was something the Duke was determined to prevent.

He wondered whether he should speak to Lady Bingley about it, and then decided that perhaps the wisest course would be to determine how anxious Verena herself was to meet her cousin.

He had, however, an idea that because she was incensed with him at the moment, her thought inevitably would turn with affection and perhaps longing towards Captain Winchcombe-Smythe.

When the Duke arrived at Lady Bingley's house in Manchester Square, his groom, who had accompanied him in his High Perch Phaeton, jumped down to ring the bell.

"You can walk home from here, Fowler," the Duke said.

"Very good, Your Grace."

The man, however, waited when Verena appeared, to help her up into the Phaeton beside the Duke.

Verena had intended to treat her Guardian with a cool indifference, to answer him in monosyllables and try by an air of dignity and frigidity to make him realise that while she is obeying his command she was still extremely incensed by his unforgivable behaviour.

Unfortunately, as she descended the steps, her chin held high, her expression telling him all too clearly that she was prepared to do battle, she stole a quick glance at the horses pulling the High Perch Phaeton, and was lost!

Two perfectly matched geldings, both black as jet, they were as dashing a pair as she had ever seen!

She stopped dead on the pavement to stare at them. They were tossing their heads, moving a little restlessly, and as they sidled and fidgeted, proclaimed all too clearly that they were anxious to be off!

With difficulty Verena bit back the words of admiration which hovered on her lips, and climbing into the Phaeton with the assistance of Fowler, took only a brief glance at the Duke.

He was looking more handsome and more impressive than usual, wearing a high beaver at an angle on his head, a grey whipcord coat into which he seemed to have been poured, and pale yellow pantaloons above hessians whose shine rivalled the silver accoutrements on the black and yellow Phaeton.

If the Duke was magnificent, Verena herself, though she did not realise it, was the perfect accompaniment for him in a new driving-coat of pink batiste, trimmed with pink braid of slightly darker hue and fastened with pearl buttons.

The high-crowned straw bonnet which framed her brown hair was ornamented with tiny ostrich feathers of the same pink, and matched by the ribbons that were tied under her small pointed chin.

The Duke did not speak and nor did Verena. As soon as she had seated herself comfortably the Duke set his horses in motion and they trotted out of Manchester Square towards the Park.

They had travelled some way in silence before the Duke said:

"I should inform you, Verena, that I have arranged for your horses to be moved to my own stables."

"Why have you done that?" Verena asked sharply. "I have no wish, Your Grace, to avail myself of your hospitality or of your stables."

"That is unfortunate," the Duke replied suavely, "because if you intend to house your bloodstock where it is at the moment, there will be no room for the pair of bays of which I spoke to you last night."

Verena, knowing that her Godmother's stables were not large, was aware that the Duke had scored a point.

"Then I would prefer," she said grandly, "to find my horses other accommodation."

"You are, of course, quite at liberty to look for it," the Duke answered. "When you find a place to your satisfaction I will have your horses moved there immediately."

"How obliging of Your Grace!" she said sarcastically.

"I am really trying to be obliging," the Duke answered with a touch of laughter in his eyes as he looked down at her. "In fact, I was so obliging as to do exactly what you commanded me last night, and since you are so interested, I slept well, thank you, and my head feels much better this morning!"

Verena gave a hastily suppressed little chuckle of laughter. She found it difficult to remain aloof when the

Duke teased her with just that particular note in his voice that had amused her when she had sat for hours at his bedside and they talked and laughed at so many things.

However, she did not intend to capitulate so easily!

"As Your Grace is so much better in health, I imagine you will soon be leaving London."

"Why should I?" he enquired in surprise.

"I had thought that you would wish to continue the series of visits which were so unfortunately interrupted on our first acquaintance," she said. "You may have by this time a slight disinclination to visit Lord and Lady Upminster, but the other two young Ladies of whom your sister spoke last night will undoubtedly still be waiting for your arrival with panting hearts."

"My sister's conversation was not intended for your ears," the Duke replied.

"It is unfortunate that I am not hard of hearing," Verena remarked.

"I might have known that you would use this ammunition against me," he said. "What female could resist the gratuitous present of a red-hot cannon-ball?"

"If I had a cannon," Verena answered, "I would certainly fire it at Your Grace, for your behaviour in this matter only confirms all that I suspected before we even met!"

"I might have known," the Duke said again, "that you are like all your sex—a nagger, a shrew, a scold!"

"That is not fair," Verena retorted angrily. "I am not a shrew and I have not the interest either to nag or scold Your Grace."

"Then if this is not nagging," the Duke said, "I can only be heartily sorry for anyone, Verena, who has your interest and must stand corrected by you!"

"I think this conversation is quite pointless," Verena said coldly. "Perhaps Your Grace would be so obliging as to tell me instead about the bays you consider I might wish to purchase."

"Certainly," the Duke replied. "Lord Manson is sending them to my stables tomorrow."

"You seem quite sure that I shall wish to own them," Verena remarked, trying to find fault.

"I have already purchased them on your behalf," the Duke answered.

He saw, as she turned to look at him, that she thought it an impertinence, and added:

"If you are not interested I should be delighted to keep them myself. In fact, I consider I am making a considerable sacrifice in allowing you to have them."

"So I have to be grateful to you, do I?"

"Not in the least," he replied. "Just be your usual disagreeable self—I am getting used to it!"

She laughed because she could not help it.

"You are impossible!"

"Good gracious!" the Duke exclaimed. "You have found a new adjective—I was beginning to think you had run out of them and that we should return to contemptible, outrageous, and of course, odious! I really feared that your vocabulary, Miss Winchcombe, was not very extensive!"

"You are not to make me laugh!" Verena said and there were dimples in both her cheeks.

"However bellicose you may be feeling, you might at least try to look pleasant," the Duke continued. "We are now approaching Rotten Row, and when the *Beau Ton* see you beside me they will be full of speculation as to who you are, how well we know each other, and if in fact I have any ulterior motive in inviting you to drive with me."

"I collect by that," Verena said in a demure voice, "that Your Grace is being so obliging as to make me fashionable and introduce me to the *Beau Ton*!"

"Most certainly," the Duke replied promptly. "You cannot really expect me to be seen driving any young female who is not of the first water?"

Verena laughed again.

"Conceited Cockscomb was right!"

"But of course!" the Duke agreed. "All wearers of strawberry leaves are conceited. They have so much consequence to be conceited about!"

"Do not make me laugh!" Verena pleaded. "You know perfectly well I should look cool and slightly bored. Any fashionable Lady of the *Ton* must show her consequence by appearing dissatisfied with her surroundings, whatever they may be!"

"Who told you that?" the Duke asked.

"I think it must have been in one of those nonsensical novels which you were so anxious for me to read," Verena retorted. "I am only sorry now that I did not make you listen to the whole thirty-eight chapters of *Love at First Sight* or *The Lost Heir*."

"You bullied me enough as it was," the Duke said. "God help any man who is at the mercy of a woman's 'tender hand'! It is as heavy, I assure you, as any artillery!"

By this time they were entering Rotten Row and Verena saw innumerable open carriages drawn by fine bloodstock; Ladies in entrancing gowns holding court under tiny lace-frilled sunshades; Gentlemen riding on spirited mounts; High Phaetons and dashing curricles each tooled by some incredibly smart and elegant Buck with an expertise which Verena admired as much as their horseflesh.

She would not admit to the Duke that this was the first time she had ever ridden in a High Perch Phaeton, and she felt an exhilaration at being so high off the ground, seated so precariously above the huge wheels and knowing that the fragility of the vehicle made it extremely vulnerable to accidents unless it was driven very competently.

There was no doubt that the Duke was a Non-pareil with the ribbons or indeed that his Phaeton, like his horses, was undoubtedly the smartest in the Park.

"What do you think of it?" the Duke asked, being aware of the wonder in Verena's wide eyes and knowing that she was thrilled by the scene before her.

"I never knew it would be so beautiful or the horses so breathtakingly magnificent," she answered rapturously, as if she had forgotten to whom she was speaking.

Then suddenly she gave a cry.

"Stop! Stop! There is Giles!"

Impetuously, forgetting everything at the sight of a familiar face, she called out:

"Giles! Giles!"

They had almost come to a standstill at that particular moment owing to a congestion of Phaetons and Curricles near the centre of the Row, and the man on a showy grey horse moving in the opposite direction was just about to pass the Duke's Phaeton when he heard Verena's cry.

He looked round in surprise, then stared at Verena without recognising her.

"Giles! It is I! Verena! Surely you remember me?"

In astonishment the Captain's hand went towards his hat.

"Verena!" he exclaimed. "I hardly expected to see you here!"

"But I am, I have just arrived in London and, Giles, I was hoping very much to find out where you were."

The Duke holding in his cattle watched Captain Winchcombe-Smythe draw his horse alongside the Phaeton. Verena bent down towards him and the Duke thought that he was good-looking of his type.

He, however, looked his age and had the heavy, paunchy figure of a self-indulgent man, and under his eyes, which were set slightly too close together, the lines of dissipation were beginning to show.

But to an undiscerning girl the Duke thought he would be prepossessing because besides his good looks he was obviously a Dandy.

The Captain's hair, painstakingly arranged in the fashion set by the King when he was Regent, had undoubtedly taken hours to achieve, and the Duke's experienced eye travelled from the over-curled brim of the tall beaver hat to the points of Captain Winchcombe-Smythe's collar, which were too high.

The large bright buttons which ornamented the exaggerated style of his riding-coat and the excessively broad white bands on his riding boots would have made Beau Brummel, who had invented the vogue, shudder at their vulgarity.

"I had not expected to find you in London, Giles," Verena was saying.

"I am stationed here," Captain Winchcombe-Smythe replied.

"I had imagined you must be in India or somewhere like that as I had not heard from you."

"I am afraid we must move," the Duke interrupted, realising his Phaeton was holding up a number of vehicles behind him.

"I will come and call on you, Verena," Captain Winchcombe-Smythe said hastily. "Where are you staying?"

"With my Godmother, Lady Bingley, in Manchester Square."

"I will be there this afternoon," he promised.

He then was forced to move or be run into by a Curricle driven by a very lovely Lady whose horses appeared to be almost beyond her control!

The Duke drove his Phaeton further down the Row. After a moment Verena said a little breathlessly:

"I had not expected to find Giles . . . here of all places, and . . . so smartly dressed!"

"A very Tulip of Fashion!" the Duke remarked drily.

"He had no money when he last came to visit Grandpapa."

Verena was talking almost to herself rather than to the Duke. As he did not answer she went on:

"Did you see the diamond in his cravat? Surely it was a little odd to wear anything so flashy in the daytime? And it must have been extremely expensive!"

The Duke had indeed noticed the diamond and thought it in the worst of bad taste. And he could not help feeling glad that Verena's discerning eye had realised that diamonds of such magnitude were not worn when riding.

"What did you think of his horse?" she asked, but still in a low, rather puzzled tone.

The Duke was too wise to say what he really thought of the animal.

"Perhaps your Cousin hired it," he suggested generously.

"Yes, he may have done that," Verena answered.

The frown between her eyes vanished.

"I would not like to think that Giles of all people should be taken in by a showy piece of horseflesh which doubtless after a few miles would be gone in the wind."

"You are being bitingly critical," the Duke smiled.

"Oh, am I?" she asked. "I hope not indeed!"

There was no doubt that her meeting with her Cousin had disturbed her. Her laughter had gone and the Duke had great difficulty in getting even a smile out of her before he drove her back to Manchester Square.

She thanked him politely and jumped down from the Phaeton without difficulty. The Duke was unable to leave his horses and in fact there was nothing he could do except to raise his hat and drive away, leaving her standing on the doorstep.

She looked, he thought, rather forlorn and a trifle apprehensive.

Lady Bingley had difficulty in discovering from Verena whether she had enjoyed her drive in the Park or not. But as Her Ladyship was slightly indisposed owing to the gaieties of the day before, she retired to rest after luncheon, saying she intended to sleep off a tiresome headache.

Verena went into the Drawing-Room and picked up a book. But after holding it in front of her eyes for nearly a quarter of an hour she realised she had not read a word. Rising, she walked about the room.

She knew she was beset by problems which she could hardly put into words but nevertheless made her restless. She was about to go into the garden and seek some fresh air when the Butler opened the door to announce:

"Captain Winchcombe-Smythe."

"Giles, I was just thinking about you!" Verena exclaimed.

"You could not say anything that would gratify me more," he replied, but with the complacency of a man who knows his worth.

He came into the room and she was dazzled by the splendour of his attire: the bright green of his coat, the golden yellow of his pantaloons and the mixture of colours in his embroidered waistcoat. The flashing fob which hung beneath it seemed almost as dazzling as the diamond he once again wore in his cravat.

"You are very dandyish, Giles!" Verena ejaculated, as usual saying the first thing which came into her head. "I did not expect you to appear as, what is the right expression? . . . a Tulip of Fashion!"

She remembered the sarcasm in the Duke's voice

when he had made the same observation in the Park, but the Captain obviously took it as a compliment.

"And you are even prettier than I remembered," he replied. "Tell me, what brings you to London?"

"I have . . . come for a . . . short holiday."

"You do not mean to tell me that crabby old Firebeard has let you off the leash?" Captain Winchcombe-Smythe asked with a low laugh.

"You must not speak of Grandpapa in such a manner," Verena said, feeling suddenly angry. "He was such a wonderful man!"

Even as she spoke she realised the mistake she had made. She saw that her Cousin Giles stiffened, and then almost incredulously he ejaculated:

"Was! You said 'was', Verena! Do you mean to tell me the General is dead?"

For a moment Verena thought to deny the truth. Then she knew it was impossible.

"Yes, Grandpapa is dead," she answered in a low voice. "But it is a secret . . . he did not wish it announced for three months."

"A secret!" Captain Winchcombe-Smythe repeated in astonishment. "But why? What was his reason?"

Verena did not reply and a crafty look came into his eyes.

"A secret, and he sent you to London," he said slowly. "You are not in mourning and I find you driving in the Park with some Buck who can afford the best horses and a slap-up High Perch Phaeton. What is the explanation, Verena?"

"Grandpapa had a great dislike of mourning and any fuss being made over his death," Verena tried to explain. "He wished me to . . . enjoy myself. I had been alone with him for so long, not entertaining, not meeting anyone . . ."

"And your Grandfather also hoped that you would

find someone else to captivate your heart," the Captain said slowly. "Have you found that person, Verena?"

"No, no of course not," she answered.

"And yet you have not tried to get in touch with me!"

"I intended to do so," she replied. "I only arrived the day before yesterday. But you left me no address, you did not write to me, Giles!"

"How could I do so?" he asked, "when I had been forbidden the house and the General so vehemently disapproved of me? Now he is dead, Verena, and I judge by your appearance that he has left you well provided!"

Verena did not answer and after a moment he continued:

"What has he left you—the house and Estate as he told me he would do, and all his money? How much did it amount to?"

Verena turned aside her head.

"Well, I have an idea it was a great deal more than most people anticipated," Captain Winchcombe-Smythe went on. "I found out what your Grandfather received in prize money and knowing him I am certain he invested wisely. Is it a hundred thousand pounds, Verena, that you have inherited?"

"No! Not as . . . much as that."

"But not far off it," the Captain remarked, his eyes on her face. "Well, that should keep you in comfort in your old age—if it is well administered by your husband."

Verena moved restlessly across the room.

"I do not think we should be talking about . . . such things."

"And of what else should we be talking," her cousin asked. "Our marriage? When do you intend to marry me, Verena? For I should like to know there was still a Winchcombe on the Estate. A Winchcombe owning the

Priory, as we have always owned it for so many centuries."

"I am not thinking of . . . marriage at the . . . moment," Verena faltered.

"That is untrue!" he contradicted. "Have I omitted to tell you how much I have been thinking of you, dreaming of your innocent eyes? Yearning of course for this day when there is no longer any obstacle in our way and we can be together."

He had an amused look on his face as he saw Verena's hands flutter as if to still a sudden nervousness.

"She has improved," he thought, "and although she is not my type she is damned well endowed!"

He was sure of himself, well aware of his physical attractiveness, and he knew that women liked to be soft-soaped in sentiment—and who could do it better than he?

"You have greatly increased in looks, little Verena," he said, "and I promise you, my pretty one, that we shall deal well together."

"No . . . no . . . !"

The Captain was pulling Verena into his arms and she was struggling frantically against him when the door opened.

"His Grace, the Duke of Selchester," old Johnson mumbled.

Verena, flushing with embarrassment, wrenched herself free of her Cousin's arms as the Duke entered the room.

He seemed for a moment overpoweringly big and broad-shouldered, and Verena thought unhappily that the expression on his face was one of disdain, almost of disgust. But his voice was calm and portrayed nothing but an indifferent courtesy as he said:

"Good afternoon, Verena. I was expecting to find Her Ladyship with you."

Verena knew there was a subtle rebuke in the words and replied hastily:

"My Godmother had a . . . headache and has retired to . . . rest. I do not think you have met my . . . cousin, Captain Giles Winchcombe-Smythe."

"How do you do," the Duke said, holding out his hand. "I believe you are in my old Regiment."

"The Life Guards," the Captain replied.

"I congratulate you," the Duke answered. "I cannot conceive a better!"

The Duke was obviously so genial that Verena felt her agitation subside.

"We had no time to meet this morning in the Park," he continued, "but Verena has spoken of you. You were previously in the 11th Foot, I believe?"

"Yes, I transferred two months ago," the Captain replied. "Now there is no fighting it is pleasant to be in London!"

"Yes, indeed," the Duke agreed.

"I am sure Your Grace finds it as devilish amusing as I do," the Captain remarked with an innuendo in his voice.

"But of course!" the Duke answered.

Verena was puzzled. She was well aware that the Duke seemed to be going out of his way to be pleasant to her Cousin, and yet she had the feeling that the two men had little in common.

It was hard not to draw a contrast between them even though she felt disloyal in doing so. The Duke's clothes were so unobtrusive, so part of himself, that one hardly noticed them. He only appeared supremely dignified and elegant, while the attire of Captain Winchcombe-Smythe seemed to scream loudly to be noticed.

The only jewellery worn by the Duke was a plain gold signet ring on a finger of his left hand. Giles, Verena perceived, had a ring on each hand and both were sparklingly bejewelled.

"That was a fine pair of bloodstock you were driving this morning," the Captain was saying in the over-hearty manner of one man of the world talking to another.

"Yes, indeed," the Duke replied, "I am pleased with them."

"Must have cost you a pretty penny. I paid a monkey for the animal I was riding and I have two others in mind. I am sure Verena will lose her heart to them, if it is not already given to someone else."

He gave Verena a knowing glance.

"She was always mad about horseflesh."

"So I understand," the Duke said quietly.

"Well, one thing I would like to do, Duke," the Captain said in an ingratiating manner, "would be to visit your stables. I am sure you would not object to Verena and me trotting along to see them one day."

"I should be delighted," the Duke answered.

Verena found she was clenching her hands together because she knew that Giles should not be talking in such a way; should not be soliciting invitations, should not be forcing himself on the Duke as if they were old friends.

Her agitation must have communicated itself to the Duke; for he turned to her and she thought that the disgust had vanished from his eyes and instead there was a kindness which unexpectedly made her heart leap.

"Verena, I came to ask you . . ." the Duke began, but at that moment the door opened again.

"Mr. Jasper Royd, Miss," Johnson announced.

Verena, who had her back to the door, turned round and then as she did so felt herself freeze into immobility!

For a moment she could neither move, speak nor think! She could only stare, unable to believe her eyes. Standing in the doorway was the Gentleman with the pointed features, the tight lips and the dark greedy eyes she had last watched from between the barrels in the cellar of the old Priory.

It was the "Evil Genius" and for a moment she felt she was unable to breathe. Then as if in a dream she heard her Cousin say:

"Jasper! I was hoping you would drop in. That was why I left a message for you at the Club. I wanted you to meet Verena. And I dare say you know the Duke of Selchester."

"I do indeed," Jasper Royd replied. "But I am surprised, Theron, to find you here."

"The surprise is mine," the Duke said. "We have not met for some time, Jasper."

"No, and you need not expect me!" Jasper Royd answered. "I shall not be calling on you as the importunate beggar! I am as it happens now quite warm in the pockets!"

His voice was taunting with an insolent note in it, but the Duke replied gravely:

"I am indeed glad to hear it."

"Jasper, you have not said 'how do you do' to Verena!" the Captain interrupted.

"How remiss of me!" Jasper Royd exclaimed. "The sight of my Cousin Theron put everything else out of my head. You must forgive me, Miss Winchcombe, for I can assure you that ever since Giles told me about you I have been eager to make your acquaintance."

He took Verena's hand in his. With a tremendous, almost superhuman effort she managed to curtsey and murmur, without stuttering:

"Thank you, Sir."

"And now if you will excuse me," the Duke said, "I

would, before I leave, ask Miss Winchcombe whether she would come to dine tonight with my Grandmother?—"

"—and my Grandmother!" Jasper Royd interposed.

"But of course," the Duke replied. "I had not forgotten that, Jasper."

"You are not proposing a very gay evening for the girl," Jasper Royd sneered. "The Duchess must be eighty if she is a day, and that dismal house the other side of Hampstead Heath is as full of ghosts as any graveyard!"

"I should still like you to meet my Grandmother, the Dowager Duchess of Selchester," the Duke said, speaking only to Verena.

Her face was very pale and there was a stricken look in her eyes which he had last seen when she had come from her Grandfather's bedroom having seen him dead.

"Not . . . tonight," Verena faltered. "I must . . . be at home . . . tonight."

"Then tomorrow night," the Duke said gently. "I will let my Grandmother know that you will accept her invitation for tomorrow. She is greatly looking forward to making your acquaintance, Verena.

"Tomorrow night . . . would be very . . . pleasant," Verena murmured.

The Duke took her hand and her fingers tightened on his. She felt she must hold on to him, she could not let him go!

Yet somehow he did not seem to understand her need of him. He released her hand and turned towards the door.

"Good-day, Captain Winchcombe-Smythe," he said politely. "Good-bye, Jasper."

The door closed behind him. Jasper Royd stood looking at it as if he could watch the Duke descending the stairs.

"Curse him!" he said aloud. "If ever a man has bedevilled my existence it is my Cousin Theron!"

"What has he done to you?" Captain Winchcombe-Smythe enquired.

"What has he not done?" Jasper Royd asked with a shrug of his shoulders. "Besides, can you be so corkbrained, my dear Giles, not to realise that he stands between me and the Dukedom."

"Good God," the Captain exclaimed with a ribald laugh, "I cannot envisage you, Jasper, as a Duke!"

"But I can," Jasper Royd said very quietly.

There was someting in his voice and a sudden narrowing of his eyes which told Verena as clearly as if the words had been shouted in her ear, that the Duke was in danger!

Danger—from the "Evil Genius!"

9

Verena found it impossible to sleep. She had longed all the evening for the moment when she could be alone in the darkness and try to sort out her thoughts.

But when the moment came she felt so agitated and in such a state of restlessness that after a while she rose from her bed to walk about the room.

It was not only the fact that the "Evil Genius" was the Duke's cousin that was perturbing her, although that was bad enough by itself! How could she go to the Duke and say:

"Your Cousin is a Bullion robber! Your Cousin is the man who has deliberately murdered the guards on the Bullion coaches!"

That seemed a problem heavy enough in itself; but there was worse! She knew now what had been troubling her at the back of her mind ever since the Duke had been struck down in the cellar of the old Priory.

It was an anxiety she would not face up to, would not

acknowledge even to herself. But now she could no longer ignore the whisperings of her conscience.

She could see all too clearly Giles sitting beside her in the Drawing-Room after her Grandfather had told him he was to leave the house never to return.

"How could the General do this to me?" he had asked angrily. "I am a Winchcombe!"

He had seen the expression on Verena's face and corrected himself:

"Half a Winchcombe at any rate! There is Winchcombe blood in my veins—blood that has been distinguished all down the centuries. How dare the General treat me in such a scurvy manner?"

He had seemed genuinely upset, and because Verena had a tenderness for him she tried to assuage the hurt.

"I think of you as a Winchcombe," she said, "and to show you that is what I truly believe, I will tell you a secret!"

It was then that she had revealed to him the secret of the cache in the cellar where the monks had hidden their keys—a secret known for many generations, her Grandfather had told her, only to each head of the family in succession and to his sons.

As she told Giles what was to her something of tremendous import, she had known that he was not really interested. Indeed, he hardly appeared to listen to her, being immersed in his own grievances: grumbling because the General had not paid all his debts; complaining bitterly that he had been insulted.

But now Verena faced the truth—she had known it, she had to admit, when she discovered the keys were missing and the cellar door locked; had known that only one person could have revealed the secret to the "Evil Genius!"

In the darkness of her room she put up her hands to her face! Then she climbed back into bed to lie ashamed that she should have betrayed her Grandfather's trust, humiliated that anyone with even one drop of Winchcombe blood should so disgrace it.

Her first impulse was to confront Giles with the truth and to tell him that she would never see him again. Then she was sensible enough to realise two things: first, that in doing so she would deliberately put her own life in danger, and second, that to break her word was to lower herself to his level.

She could hear her Grandfather years ago saying to her: "A man who breaks his promise or who is a coward is beyond contempt!"

Although Verena did not realise it, she had been brought up by a soldier with a soldier's code of chivalry. These were the ideals and standards which had inspired Wellington's Army in the Peninsula to suffer incredible hardships and yet remain men of honour.

They had believed, as Verena's father and Grandfather had believed, that a man must take on a bully and punish a cheat, be tender towards women and the helpless, and above all else, keep his parole!

"How can I marry Giles?" Verena whispered to herself. "He is a murderer, there is blood on his hands!"

And yet she had given such a man her promise—a promise that by her rules must not be broken.

There were lines beneath her eyes the following morning and she was unnaturally pale when she came down to breakfast.

Fortunately Lady Bingley was full of plans for another "At Home" that she intended to give for Verena the following week, and she was so occupied in making lists of friends who were to receive her cards of invitation that she did not notice her God-daughter was unusually silent.

Lady Bingley was later interviewing the cook and arranging the menus for the day when the Butler announced that Captain Winchcombe-Smythe had called.

He was shown into the Morning-Room and Verena tried to force a smile to her lips. He was wearing uniform and looked at his very best in his shining steel breastplate and high black boots. But as she looked at him Verena could only see weeping women, fatherless children and the guards of the Bullion coaches lying dead by the roadside.

"I am just going on guard at the Bank of England, Verena," the Captain said. "I thought you would desire to see me in my uniform."

With difficulty Verena prevented herself from screaming! The Bank of England! So it was Giles who learnt the destination of the Bullion! Giles who was the informer who told the "Evil Genius" where to ambush the coaches!

But the Captain, preening himself, was waiting for her reply.

"Yes, of course I would wish to see you," she answered with an effort. "You look very fine."

"I imagined you would think so, my pretty one," the Captain replied complacently. "What I really came to see you about is to tell you that I have other plans for you this evening. I do not wish you to accompany the Duke to dine with his Grandmother. You need not trouble to inform him so, I will do that myself later in the day."

"But I promised I would go," Verena protested.

"You will have to change your mind. Another time perhaps," Captain Winchcombe-Smythe remarked.

"I am afraid I could not do that," Verena replied slowly. "The Duke is my Guardian and if he so wished he could easily forbid me to accept another invitation."

"Your Guardian!" the Captain ejaculated in astonishment. "How does that come about?"

"The Duke's Great-Grandfather married a Miss Winchcombe," Verena answered. "He therefore considers himself a relation."

"Indeed," the Captain said reflectively. "So, of course, he is also a relative of mine. Good blood! Something of which to be proud, eh, Verena?"

As he spoke Verena heard the self-satisfaction in his voice and knew that personally he was delighted at the news—it was something to boast about, something to tell his friends.

"The Duke of Selchester is my relative."

She could almost hear him saying it!

"Nevertheless," he continued after a moment, "it would be best for you to cry off from crossing Hampstead Heath."

Even as he said the words Verena had a premonition of danger—something was being planned—planned by the "Evil Genius" and her Cousin!

"No, I must go as arranged," she answered firmly.

The Captain walked across the room and back again, his spurs jangling as he did so, his breastplate reflecting the sunshine.

After a moment he cleared his throat.

"There is something else of which I wish to speak to you, Verena. I have recently come into money—quite a fortune—and I have decided, as we are betrothed, to make a will in your favour. In fact I have already done so."

He paused as if he sought for an excuse.

"There are so many accidents on the roads these days," he continued, "that apart from the dangers of war, one should always be prepared. I would not wish my wealth, should I die, to be enjoyed by anyone but you!"

"I am quite certain you are not going to die, Giles," Verena said.

"One can never be sure," he answered with a frown between his eyes. "One should always be prepared. See how sensible your Grandfather was to make a will before he was struck down!"

"But Grandpapa was over seventy-five!" Verena said.

"Nevertheless no one should die intestate," Captain Giles insisted. "So what I suggest, Verena, is that you come with me this afternoon to your lawyer and make a will in my favour—just as I have done for you!"

Verena drew a deep breath. It was, she thought, as if she was watching a performance of a play acted so badly that the audience knew what was going to be said before the actors spoke their lines!

For a moment she felt like raging at her Cousin, telling him that she saw through his nefarious plot and driving him from the house even as her Grandfather had done.

Then she knew he would merely assert that she was deranged—and after all, what proof had she save her own intuition?

Like a flash of lightning she saw how clearly the "Evil Genius" and Giles had protected themselves from every eventuality. As the Duke had said:

"Their whole scheme is brilliantly thought out and organised."

Now this by-plot of the Captain's, obviously concocted with the assistance of the "Evil Genius," was just as clever.

Taking a deep breath to calm the agitation within her, Verena managed to say sweetly:

"But of course, Giles, I am only too willing to make a will in your favour, or anything else you wish of me, but unfortunately it is impossible for me to come with you this afternoon."

She saw he was about to protest and continued:

"I have already arranged to drive with my Godmama and call on several of her friends. She would not understand were I to refuse to accompany her, and if she heard what we were about I am certain she would wish us to discuss it first with my Guardian!"

"There is no reason for you to do that!" the Captain said quickly.

"No, indeed," Verena replied. "This is obviously something intimate which concerns only you and me. But I am afraid we must leave my will until another day."

The frown was back between the Captain's eyes and she knew that he was put out, but apparently he found her prevarication quite plausible. Finally he left the house with a promise to call on the morrow.

When he had gone Verena found herself trembling. Never, she thought, had her clairvoyant powers spoken more clearly than they had at that moment. She knew—she knew irrefutably and without question—that something would occur when they crossed Hampstead Heath that evening.

And she knew too that, while it might not be dangerous for her because she had not yet signed a will in her Cousin's favour, it would undoubtedly bring real danger to the Duke!

She put her hands to her forehead, trying to think. If she told the Duke what she feared, he would be unlikely to believe her. But even so, if he did make the journey, she was convinced that he would refuse to take her with him—that was one thing of which she was as sure as if she had heard him say it!

No, the Duke would go, but he would leave her at home. And because he would behave with decency, not firing until he was fired upon, not attacking before he was attacked, then undoubtedly the "Evil Genius" would gain his desire and become the next Duke of Selchester!

It was so clear to Verena that she could almost see it happening—the shots in the dark, the Duke falling dead, the "Evil Genius" personally taking no part in the murder, but waiting to gain the reward!

"I am a soldier's daughter," Verena told herself. "This is a campaign in which the enemy has the initiative. I must meet the attack as if I was a man! What would Grandpapa have done in the same circumstances?"

Lady Bingley found her surprisingly quiet as they drove out as arranged, leaving visiting cards on various friends and invitations to Her Ladyship's "At Home."

When they had done all they set out to do, Verena said:

"I wonder, Godmama, if you would mind if we stopped at the Duke's stables on our way back. I would like, if you would be kind enough to wait for me, to see Assaye. He is inclined to fret if we are apart for long."

"But of course, my dearest," Lady Bingley replied. "I know what an affection you have for your horse!"

On arriving at the stables, which were situated at the back of Selchester House, Verena was led by a groom to Assaye's stall. He whinnied at the sound of her voice and nuzzled her affectionately.

"I will ride you tomorrow," Verena promised him. "You must be longing for some exercise."

She patted his neck.

"Was he very tired after the journey here?" she enquired of the groom.

"If he were he showed no signs o' it, Miss! He be a plucky animal with plenty o' spirit in him!"

"That is what I have always found," Verena said with a smile, then added in a low voice:

"Would it be possible for me to speak to one of the

grooms who will be accompanying His Grace on his carriage tonight?"

The groom looked surprised but he replied:

"I be certain Fowler'll accompany His Grace, Miss."

"Then ask him to come to me," Verena said.

She stood whispering endearments into Assaye's ear and making a fuss of the animal until a man appeared. She recognised him as the groom who had helped her into the Duke's High Perch Phaeton the day before.

"Good afternoon," she smiled.

"Good afternoon, Miss," Fowler replied. "Can I be of any assistance?"

"I wish to say something to you in confidence," Verena said, "and you may think it strange."

The man did not answer but she saw he was all attention.

"I am clairvoyant—my mother was the seventh child of a seventh child—you know what that means?"

"I do indeed, Miss. I'm from th'country," Fowler told her.

"I have a very strong presentiment," Verena went on, "that when we cross Hampstead Heath tonight the Duke's carriage will be attacked by Highwaymen. I am convinced that it is not money nor jewels they will be seeking, but His Grace's life!"

"Have you spoken of this to His Grace, Miss?" Fowler enquired.

"No, I have told no one but you," Verena answered. "I must beg of you not to mention it to His Grace, because if you do, then, as you well know, His Grace is unlikely to believe it and still less likely to take proper precautions."

"That's true enough, Miss!" Fowler agreed. "If ever there was a brave man 'tis His Grace!"

"I know that," Verena answered, "and that is why I

am asking you to help me make quite sure that nothing occurs to endanger his life."

"The footman on th'box nearly always has a firearm with him," Fowler said. "But I'll take one myself as well."

"That is what I hoped you would say," Verena said, "and shoot on sight, do not wait, for I am convinced—and I promise you I am never wrong—that these men are killers!"

Fowler gave her a sharp glance but he said respectfully:

"How many do you expect, Miss?"

"Four!" Verena replied. "One will shoot at the footman on the box, another at you if you are up behind the landau. Kill them as soon as they appear."

"And the other two?" Fowler enquired.

"If what I anticipate is correct," Verena replied, "they will simultaneously open the carriage doors on each side and shoot at the Duke!"

"Surely, Miss, 'twould be wisest to tell His Grace what you fear!"

"His Grace will not believe me! I am trusting you. I am trusting you with his life and my own. But if you talk unnecessarily and the attempt is not made tonight, it will be made another time—in which case we may not be prepared!"

"I sees your point, Miss!" Fowler said reflectively. "I'll make sure th'lad up in front is handy with the blunderbuss, and I'll see the man who attacks me doesn't get off scot-free!"

"Thank you," Verena said. "Leave everything else to me! And not a word to anyone!"

"I gives you me word, Miss," Fowler promised.

Knowing by his carriage and the manner in which he spoke that he had been a soldier, Verena was satisfied.

She drove back to Manchester Square and, as soon

as her Godmother had gone upstairs to take off her driving clothes, she slipped into the room which had been Lord Bingley's Study. She had entered it before and had seen lying on the table what she required.

It was a box such as most Gentlemen possessed containing—when she opened it—a pair of fine duelling-pistols.

They were slightly old-fashioned, but when she handled them she knew they were well made and well balanced.

The bullets were beside them.

The Duke arrived at Manchester Square at seven o'clock. Lady Bingley was waiting to receive him in the Drawing-Room. He kissed her hand and smiled at her in a manner which she thought privately was quite irresistible.

Verena was ready to leave, wearing over her evening gown a cloak of strawberry-pink satin edged with swans-down. She carried a large and fashionable muff which, as it was summer, was also made of swansdown.

It would have taken a very discerning eye to realise that it was extremely heavy and contained two duelling-pistols.

"I wish, Ma'am, I could have asked you," the Duke said to Lady Bingley, "to accompany Verena to visit my Grandmother's this evening. Unfortunately, being old, she dislikes entertaining more than two people at the same time. She will not admit to being deaf, but that, I am convinced, is the reason."

"Of course, I quite understand," Lady Bingley replied. "And I shall hope, Your Grace, to meet the Duchess on another occasion."

"I would be most gratified, Ma'am," the Duke continued, "if tomorrow I could persuade you and Verena to be my guests at Selchester Castle. I have to post to the country, and it would give me great pleasure to entertain you both from tomorrow—Thursday—until Monday."

"Visit Selchester Castle!" Lady Bingley exclaimed with a lilt in her voice. "I assure Your Grace that there is nothing that would please me more. I have heard so many tales of its magnificence and its great historic interest."

"I shall have much to show you," the Duke answered, "and I thought, if you agreed, it might amuse Verena to drive down with me in my Phaeton. But I should not like you to feel yourself neglected, Ma'am, and I suggest that you travel with Lady Edith Sheraton, whom I shall also have the honour of entertaining."

"Lady Edith Sheraton!" Lady Bingley repeated, a puzzled look in her eyes.

"I believe you were girls together," the Duke said, "and Lady Edith is looking forward eagerly to renewing your acquaintance."

"Edith Sheraton! She was Edith Cecil—of course I remember her!" Lady Bingley exclaimed. "What a lovely girl she was! How does she appear today?"

"In great good looks, like yourself," the Duke answered gallantly.

Lady Bingley laughed.

"Your Grace is a flatterer and I am far too old to listen to you. Take Verena to your Grandmother and say something pleasant to her, for she has seemed to me to have been out of sorts the whole day!"

The Duke looked scrutinisingly at Verena, who said quickly:

"No indeed, there is nothing amiss and I am looking forward to meeting the Duchess."

"Then if we are not to incur her wrath by being late for dinner, we should leave now," the Duke replied.

He kissed Lady Bingley's hand and followed Verena downstairs to where his Town Landau was waiting.

She saw at a quick glance that Fowler was sitting up behind the carriage and that the footman who was holding open the door was a stalwart-looking young man with an alert expression on his face.

Verena stepped into the landau and the Duke seated himself beside her. The horses were fresh and they were soon moving swiftly away from the traffic towards Regents Park.

"What made you ask us to Selchester Castle?" Verena enquired.

"I want to show it to you," the Duke said casually, "and in case you are thinking I am enticing you away from the gaieties of the Fashionable World, I have also invited your cousin to be my guest."

"You have asked Giles to Selchester Castle?" Verena exclaimed in astonishment. "But why?"

"He expressed a desire to see my stables," the Duke replied. "I have only a few horses in London but a very large number at Selchester. I am afraid that horseflesh is a considerable extravagance where I am concerned!"

"I doubt if Giles will be able to accept," Verena said quickly.

"Perhaps you feel he would not wish to leave London," the Duke suggested. "I have no wish for him to be bored, so I have also invited his close friend, my cousin Jasper, to accompany him."

With difficulty Verena suppressed a cry of horror. How could the Duke do anything so foolish? she asked herself. And then she thought despairingly that he was doing it for her sake!

Surely, she wondered, he could not believe that she was really attracted by a man so monstrously overdressed and so ignorant of bloodstock that he would pay a ridiculous sum for the horse which they had seen him riding in the Park?

Then she remembered how warmly she had spoken of Giles when she had been nursing the Duke at her home. Of course he supposed her in love with her Cousin! Her face burnt at the thought.

Realising they must be approaching Hampstead Heath, she bent forward to look at the roadway and at the unfrequented, tree-covered land on either side of it. She saw at a glance how easy it would be for Highwaymen to hide amongst the bushes in the woodland, and without warning hold up a vehicle almost anywhere along the high road over which they were now proceeding.

At the same time she felt sure that the men the "Evil Genius" would have hired under the command of Hickson would not attack in daylight. The sun was sinking in a golden glory behind the trees and she remembered that when she had told the Duke's fortune she had seen danger in the darkness.

It was on their return journey that they must be careful!

The horses were drawing to a stop and Verena had a moment's fear that she had been mistaken. Then the Duke said:

"We have reached the Toll-gate. Do you see the Inn opposite? It is known as 'The Spaniards' and has a very bad reputation. They say it is the haunt of Highwaymen!"

"Highwaymen!" Verena repeated.

"Yes, but do not be afraid," the Duke smiled. "The groom on the box of my carriage always carries a blunderbuss at night, especially when we drive into the country."

"I have heard that Hampstead is beset with Highwaymen and footpads," Verena said.

"Most of such tales are exaggerated," the Duke answered. "And of one thing I am certain, Verena, we shall not find our Bullion robbers lurking about in these bushes!"

He spoke jokingly, but Verena felt herself shudder. It would not be for Bullion that the "Evil Genius's" men would commit murder tonight—it would be for a coronet!

How could the Duke, she asked herself, be so blind, so stupid, as not to realise that his heir presumptive, even if he did not know he was the "Evil Genius," was envious of his position?

But perhaps, she thought, he would not expect someone of his own blood to behave so despicably and would credit him with at least some attributes of a Gentleman!

"I hope when we return from Selchester Castle," the Duke was saying, "I can arrange a number of entertainments to amuse you. My sister intends to give a Ball the week after next to which you, and of course Lady Bingley, will be invited. My Aunt, who is widowed, has eight daughters, two of whom have made their debut this season and will be attending all the functions which make the Season an exhausting round of gaiety. She has already promised to chaperone you."

"It is kind of you," Verena answered, "and I know I should be very grateful. But I hope you will not think me rude if I tell you that I feel too old for such frivolities."

"Too old!" the Duke exclaimed. "Really, Verena, you are an endless source of surprise! What exactly do you mean by that?"

"As you know, I have always lived with older people: my Grandfather, my Mother, and of course when she died, Grandfather's friends. I like being with older people, I like talking seriously! I think perhaps I have forgotten or never knew how to be young and empty-headed!"

The Duke laughed.

"What a sad story! I see we must somehow coax you into throwing away the cares of old age and being as young as you appear!"

"You will not believe me if I tell you I am completely happy with older people, with my horses and my books?"

"I shall not only disbelieve you," the Duke said, "but I shall make every effort to prove you wrong."

"Then it is extremely unlikely that you will succeed," Verena said sharply.

"We shall see," the Duke answered. "In the meantime, tonight you will be in your element; for my Grandmother is over eighty and you two old people should find a lot in common!"

The Duke had spoken jestingly, but he soon realised that Verena had in fact a way with the elderly. Most of the young, when they met the Dowager Duchess, were frightened immediately into an embarrassed silence and remained completely tongue-tied in the presence of such an awe-inspiring old lady.

The Duchess, who had been a great beauty in her youth, was in fact a relic of the scandalous days of social irresponsibility in the middle of the last century which culminated in the wild gaiety and vast extravagance of the young Prince of Wales.

The Duchess, like the rest of the *Beau Ton*, bored with the respectability and the dismal gloom of the Court, had made Carlton House the focal point of amusement.

The Duchess, dressed in white and wearing no less than six ropes of pearls—and as many bracelets—and several diamond rings on her blue-veined hands, received Verena and the Duke in a grand Salon, hung with Van Dykes, which overlooked the extensive grounds of her residence.

She did not rise as they entered, but sat bolt upright in a high velvet chair, her legs covered with a stable rug. Beside her stood a small black boy wearing a turban and wielding a large fan of peacock feathers.

The Duke bent first to kiss his Grandmother's hand and then her cheek.

"Good-evening, Grandmama," he said. "I am, as you well know, delighted to see you."

"I know nothing of the sort," his Grandmother snapped. "I only know it is nigh on a century since you last condescended to visit me!"

"The last time I came," the Duke rejoined, with a hint of laughter in his voice, "you told me to stay away until I could present you with my bride. As I could find no one suitable enough to please your critical eye, I thought I was utterly in disgrace!"

"You thought nothing of the sort!" the Duchess retorted. "And as you are better looking than the rest of my tiresome Grandchildren, I prefer you to those feather-brained moon-calves your Uncle Cornelius brought into the world. I never could abide females!"

"That is unfortunate," the Duke remarked, "because tonight I have brought you both a female and a relative, Grandmama. Allow me to present Miss Verena Winchcombe."

The Duchess held out her hand and Verena, curtseying, was aware of two shrewd blue eyes in the wrinkled face which seemed to scrutinise every detail of her appearance.

"Winchcombe! Winchcombe!" she said reflectively. "I did not know we had anyone of that name in the family."

"Great-Grandpapa married Arabella Winchcombe,"

the Duke said. "But I dare say you were not told about it."

"Of course, I recall it!" the Duchess exclaimed. "A shocking scandal! No one spoke about it except in whispers. I once asked your Great-Grandfather when he was old, what the girl had been like. He said he could not remember. Such fustian! As though one would not recall the face of a wench with whom one had spent five months reaching Gretna Green!"

The Duke threw back his head and laughed.

"Is that not like you, Grandmama? Uncle Adolphus has been falling over himself these past years to keep such a disreputable story from sullying the purity of our ears. And you knew about it all the time!"

"Naturally I knew," the Duchess ejaculated. "Adolphus is an old woman! I have always thought so! You will become like him if you do not marry."

"That is a development definitely to be avoided!" the Duke replied.

The Duchess looked at Verena, who was regarding this formidable old lady with interest and amusement.

"And you, child, what are you trying to do? Catch yourself a rich and titled husband?"

"No, Ma'am," Verena replied. "I am not interested in wealth or titles!"

"Indeed! Then you are different from most pretty chits," the Duchess remarked. "What then do you seek in a husband?"

Verena felt embarrassed. She knew the Duke was watching her, his eyes on her face. But her honesty made her answer the Duchess's question truthfully.

"If I marry, Ma'am, I would wish to wed a man I loved and who loved me!"

Her words seemed to vibrate on the air. She dared not look at the Duke!

"A very unfashionable sentiment!" the Duchess snapped. "Where can you have come from?"

"From Bedfordshire," the Duke answered. "Her Grandfather, as I told you in my note, Grandmama, was General Sir Alexander Winchcombe."

"I had not forgotten," the Duchess replied. "A fine soldier. I met him once, it must have been fifty years ago. He was in love with a married woman at that time so would pay no attention to me. A pretty rattle she was too!"

Verena laughed.

"Oh, you must tell me about it, Ma'am," she said without a touch of shyness. "Grandpapa used to hint that he had been somewhat of a dasher in his youth, but I could never get him to tell me of his love affairs. I was, however, quite convinced there must have been a number of them!"

From that moment the Duke was aware that Verena and his Grandmother got on famously together. Verena, unlike the Dowager's Grandchildren, was quite unshocked at the unbridled manner in which she spoke, one which the younger generation thought shocking and unconventional.

When they took their leave immediately after dinner as the Duchess retired early to bed, she admonished her Grandson to bring Verena to see her again at the earliest opportunity.

"I should much like to come, Ma'am," Verena said, and quite obviously meant it. "And I was wondering if one day I could not ride over to visit you and show you my horse. I am sure you would be amused by many of the tricks he can do."

"He is a remarkable animal," the Duke agreed.

"Then bring him, child, and while you are about it, ginger that Grandson of mine out of his fastidious ways.

Never could stand a man myself who had not a touch of the Rake about him!"

"I will do my best, Ma'am," Verena said mischievously. "But I am convinced it would be difficult to make a leopard change his spots!"

The Duke laughed at this. Soon they were driving back down the Duchess's drive, and Verena, holding her muff in her lap, found the elation and amusement she had felt during dinner ebbing away.

She was suddenly very cold and something was constricting her breathing—something which made it almost impossible for her to speak naturally.

The landau turned out of the Drive Gates and now, Verena knew, they had only a very short distance to travel before they reached the Toll-Gate.

She knew—she could not explain how—but she was certain that the Highwaymen would be waiting somewhere near "The Spaniards." Moving uphill and slowing automatically for the Toll-Gate, the landau would be an easy target!

It was as they reached the foot of the incline that she drew a pistol from her muff and handed it to the Duke.

"When the door of the carriage opens," she said, "shoot without question—do not wait. There will be two men, and they mean to kill you!"

She rose as she spoke and blew out the candle-lantern in front of them. She was confident that the men would have instructions to spare her. Giles wanted the Priory. If she were dead, not having made a will, there would be no chance of his obtaining it.

"What the devil is all this about?" the Duke asked in astonishment.

"I will explain later," Verena replied. "Just be ready. Shoot as the door opens and do not miss!"

"And you?" he enquired, striving to see her through the darkness.

"I have a pistol and I shall shoot the man on this side," Verena said. "Be ready, for God's sake, Leopard, be ready!"

Even as she finished speaking she realised the carriage had almost come to a standstill. Two shots rang out, followed by another, as the doors of the landau were wrenched open.

As Verena had anticipated, the men, who had expected the carriage to be lit, paused for a split second. As they did so Verena shot at the figure on her side of the carriage. Almost instantaneously the Duke also fired.

Two bodies crashed to the ground, and Fowler was at the doorway asking urgently:

"Is Your Grace safe?"

"We are neither of us hurt," the Duke replied quite calmly. "They did not get a chance to shoot at us."

"I killed me man, Your Grace," Fowler answered, "but one got away an' I thinks James has been winged."

"Let me have a look," the Duke replied.

He climbed from the coach. Verena did not move, she sat still and put her head against the soft cushions. She had been right! It all had occurred exactly as she had anticipated. It was a pity, she thought, that one man should have escaped. She was quite certain it must have been Hickson.

The Duke and Fowler were lifting the injured footman down from the box, while the horses, plunging with fright at the shots, were being soothed by the Coachman. The landau moved backwards and forward, and after a moment Verena leant forward to the door and looked out.

By the light of the carriage lamps she could see that the footman had been lowered on to the side of the road and his livery coat had been pulled away from one shoulder.

His shirt already had a crimson stain on it and Verena got out and, stepping over a dead body lying on the roadway, went towards him. Before the Duke could prevent her she had knelt down beside the wounded man and drawn aside the blood-stained shirt.

"It is only a flesh wound," she said after a moment, "but the bullet will be lodged in it and must be extracted. Give me your handkerchiefs!"

Fowler dived into his pocket, the Coachman produced a square of coarse cambric. Verena pulled from her neck a soft chiffon scarf that she had worn over her pearls.

She rolled them all into a tight ball, covered them with the Duke's fine linen handkerchief, which was unused, and pressed the pad against the wound.

"Lift him into the carriage," she instructed. "He can lie flat on the back seat with his legs bent."

She knew as she spoke that Fowler looked up at the Duke as if for confirmation of such an order.

"Do as Miss Winchcombe says," he ordered.

Carefully, they lifted the man, Verena striving to keep the pad in place. When finally he had been laid on the back seat, she knelt on the floor of the landau beside him holding the pad firm.

The Duke had the candle-lantern lit again.

"Can you manage?" he asked Verena.

"Yes," she answered. "But tell the Coachman to drive slowly."

"The Duke gave the order and climbed into the landau to sit with his back to the horses. The Coachman started the horses up the hill again. They paid their dues at the Toll-gate and soon were moving at a steady pace across the Heath.

"I be sorry I lets 'im escape, Yer Grace," James murmured after a little while.

"Did you touch him?" the Duke asked.

"I thinks I may have scraped 'im," the footman answered. "But 'e kept a bit behind th'others. Didn't seem eager to approach th'carriage. That's why I waits too long,"

"It cannot be helped," the Duke answered. "You did your best."

"I thanks Yer Grace."

It had been Hickson, Verena thought, who had got away. He had been too clever to expose himself as he made the others do.

"What about the dead men?" she asked the Duke, turning her head round to look at him.

"Let someone else find them," the Duke answered. "They are not our concern."

He spoke quite indifferently and yet she knew there was something particularly searching and curious in his eyes. She realised with a sinking of her heart that later there would have to be explanations.

What could she say to him? How could she tell him the real reason why she had carried the pistols in her muff and been so certain they would be attacked?

She had, however, little time to think of anything but the wounded man. The movement of the carriage was causing him pain and she knew by the way he bit his lip and turned his head from side to side that the bullet in his shoulder was agonising.

There was, however, little she could do except try to stop the bleeding. The Duke, realising what was happening, took a flask from the pocket at the side of the landau and unscrewing the top, gave it into her hands.

"Let him drink as much as he wishes," he said. "It will help him bear the pain."

Verena held the flask to the footman's lips and he drank gratefully. It certainly made his suffering more tolerable, and after several gulps of brandy he closed his eyes as if he felt sleepy.

It seemed a long way to Selchester House. Verena's knees were aching and her right hand which held the pad in place was stiff before finally they drew up outside the front door.

The Duke stepped out and arranged for several of his flunkeys to lift the injured man carefully from the carriage and carry him indoors.

"Send for a surgeon, Matthews," he said to the Butler. "I will take Miss Winchcombe home and then see what can be done for him!"

He stepped back into the landau. This time he and Verena sat side by side on the back seat. She leant back with a sigh, moving her right arm to release the tension which was almost like a cramp.

The Duke did not speak and they drove quite a distance in silence. Verena was trying to collect her thoughts and to realise all that had happened. Had she really saved the Duke and killed a man in doing so?

She thought that she should feel horrified and guilty at having taken a life. Instead she just felt it was all a dream and that somehow her brain was not functioning clearly. All she knew was that the Duke was safe!

"For how long?" a voice asked her silently.

And she knew as her breast contracted in fear that the "Evil Genius" would hate the Duke more viciously than before because by a miracle he had escaped the trap that had been set for him!

Verena trembled at the thought. And then suddenly the Duke reached out and took her left hand in his, holding it closely.

"There are a lot of questions I want to ask you," he said in a deep voice, "but they must wait until tomorrow because I think you are tired."

"I am a . . . little," Verena admitted.

"Then I will not plague you," the Duke said. "I will only say thank you, Verena, for saving my life."

As he spoke he raised her fingers to his mouth and kissed them one by one. Then as he felt them quiver in his hold, he turned her hand over and kissed the palm, letting his lips linger on the softness of her skin.

"Thank you, Elf," he said very quietly, and she knew in that moment that she loved him!

10

Verena, who had lain awake half the night wondering what she should say to the Duke when he arrived to drive her to the country, saw with relief that, instead of the High Perch Phaeton which she had expected, he was driving his curricle.

This meant that Fowler was sitting up behind. She wondered, as she saw the Duke from the Drawing-Room window, whether he was intentionally avoiding a private conversation with her or whether, which was far more likely after the events of the night before, his good sense had persuaded him that they should be protected by a groom.

Verena's speculations, however, were forgotten when she saw the team of chestnuts which were pulling the curricle.

She had never seen them before and she had not imagined that anyone could find four such perfectly matched bloodstock. It would be, she thought, the happiest day of her life if she could ever persuade the Duke to allow her to drive them.

Having assured Lady Bingley that the landau which had gone first to fetch Lady Edith Sheraton was on its way, and that the Baggage coach in which the valets and lady's maids in addition to the luggage would travel, was only a few minutes behind, the Duke escorted Verena downstairs.

Being with him made her feel shy as she remembered the manner in which he had kissed her fingers the night before.

But any embarrassment was forgotten once they were out of London on the Dover Road, and the Duke could let his team move in a manner which made Verena turn to him with a radiant face.

"They are wonderful!" she ejaculated. "I never believed that I could travel as fast as this!"

"I will push them a little more when we are clear of the traffic," the Duke promised with a smile.

His eyes met Verena's for a moment and there was a look in them which made her turn her head away quickly, conscious that her heart was beating unaccountably fast.

Verena had learnt from Lady Bingley that Selchester Castle was only about two hours' drive from London. Situated in a wild and lovely part of Kent and lying only a mile off the swift, well-surfaced Dover Road, it was a focal point of social entertainment.

"The King was a frequent guest at Selchester Castle when he was Regent and I have often heard of the magnificent parties the Duke gave for his Royal Highness," Lady Bingley related.

"Who is hostess for the Duke as he has no wife?" Verena enquired.

"I imagine his sister or his Grandmother," Lady Bingley replied. "But I assure you, dear, that when anyone is as important and attractive as the Duke, there is no lack of lovely ladies only too willing to play hostess at his parties!"

Lady Bingley laughed.

"Indeed, a large number of them would be only too glad to oblige His Grace in such a position permanently!"

"I suppose so," Verena answered, and found the thought very depressing.

She had admitted to herself in the darkness of her bedroom that she loved the Duke overwhelmingly.

"I love him," she whispered. "I love him—I love him!"

She must have loved him, she thought, from the moment she had met him, only she had not been aware of it. She had only known that he was the most interesting man she had ever met.

Later when he had been struck down and she had sat beside his bed trying to keep him amused, striving to make him forget the pain of his wound, she had known an irrepressible happiness.

Because she was so unsophisticated she had not recognised it as love—only sometimes when his eyes met hers had she felt an unaccountable breathlessness, a sudden constriction in her throat.

"I love him!" she said aloud, and wondered why the word seemed so very different from anything she had ever said before.

"How could I have been so foolish," she asked herself, "as to think for one moment that what I felt for Giles was love?"

She knew that she had only been beguiled by his flattery, and now that her eyes were opened to his perfidy she could see all too clearly how the Captain's mind had worked when he learnt that her Grandfather intended to leave her everything he possessed.

Looking back she could remember the change in him from the moment the General had told him to leave the house and never return.

How idiotic, how childish it had been of her to credit for one moment that he was sincere in the things he said, in the manner in which he persuaded her so quickly that he desired her for his wife.

"Fool! Fool!" she whispered and felt not only anger at herself, but a humiliating shame that she had been so easily deceived.

She had been gratified by the Captain's attention, flattered by it and swept off her feet by an experienced and scheming man into promising to be his wife.

"How can I marry him?" Verena asked herself for the thousandth time.

The thought of his hands touching her, of his lips on hers, made her feel sick with disgust.

"I could not bear it! . . . I could not let him! . . . Oh, God, help me!" she prayed desperately.

And later she cried aloud:

"What can I do? What can I do?"

She had found no answer to the question when the dawn came. Now, driving with the Duke, she felt for the moment secure and unharassed.

It was a feeling which she told herself had no basis in reality, and yet just to sit beside him, to realise how big and strong he was, to watch the brilliant manner in which he tooled his horses, was to enjoy a false paradise, if only for the length of time it took to travel from London to Selchester.

They talked very little on the way; the Duke was occupied with his horses, Verena with her thoughts; and there was always the conciousness that Fowler sat behind and could hear what they said.

They had turned through the great stone-flanked gates of the Castle and were travelling down the long drive with its avenue of lime trees, when the Duke turned his head to say:

"Welcome, Verena, to my home!"

"I have wanted so much to see it," she anwered, and felt her heart turn over in her breast because his voice was so kind.

Then suddenly the lime trees ended and they saw the Castle. There was a river in front of it and a great arched bridge which carried the drive over the silver water.

The Castle—enormous and tremendously impressive—had a majesty and at the same time a beauty which to Verena was undescribable. Behind it, protecting it from the winds which blew from the North and the East, was a forest of pine trees. They encircled the grey stone of which the Castle was constructed as if it was a jewel they held protectively in their keeping.

And the Castle was well worth protecting! The great Norman tower was now enriched by the additions of many succeeding generations.

There were Elizabethan and Restoration wings, a Queen Anne annex, and the Duke's Grandfather had in the middle of the last century employed the Adam brothers to add a façade which architecturally was supreme.

It was difficult for the eye to take it all in at once. The beholder was only aware of something unique and at the same time exceedingly beautiful. An appreciation of the Corinthian pillars, the sweep of wide stone steps, the Grecian statues, the urns and decorative stonework, could only come later on closer inspection.

Now Verena gasped:

"It is magnificent! Just the sort of house you should have!"

"Thank you," the Duke answered.

They crossed the river and drove with a flourish into the gravel sweep to pull up at the steps which led to the impressive entrance. Flunkeys came hurrying from the house wearing the Duke's livery, their crested silver buttons glinting as they moved.

The Duke drew his gold watch from his waistcoat pocket.

"An hour and fifty-four minutes, Fowler!" he remarked. "Not our best, but still a good run!"

"Yes, indeed, Your Grace. The chestnuts proved their worth!"

"I am pleased with them," the Duke said in a tone of satisfaction.

He stepped from the curricle and held out his hands to Verena. Just for a moment she looked down at him, and because there was something magnetic in the firm grasp of his hands under hers and in the expression in his eyes, she could not speak. But there was no need for words . . .

The Duke helped her to the ground and she walked slowly up the steps, conscious of the sunshine, of the birds singing in the trees, and of the wonderful vista that could be seen from the castle over the parkland and beyond it to the lands undulating towards the blue horizon which she knew hid the sea.

The Major-domo bowed them through an enormous marble Hall into a Salon with large windows overlooking the rose garden.

For one moment Verena was afraid that she would be alone with the Duke and she wondered how she could answer his inevitable questions. As they entered the room she saw that a silver tray holding sandwiches and other refreshments had been placed on a sidetable.

"Would you care for a glass of wine or perhaps a cup of chocolate?" the Duke asked. "Unless you prefer,

Verena, for my Housekeeper to show you upstairs so that you can have a chance to tidy yourself?"

"I would prefer to tidy myself," Verena replied quickly.

She thought as he spoke that the wind must have ruffled her hair beneath her bonnet and she might in fact look sadly disarranged.

An elderly Housekeeper in rustling black with a silk apron and a long chatelaine of keys hanging from her waist, appeared as if by magic. Verena was escorted to a room that seemed to her beautiful but overwhelmingly impressive and which held a huge four-poster bed.

"This is one of the State Rooms, Miss," the Housekeeper explained. "His Grace asked particularly that you should be given it because it is known as the Queen's Room, and every Queen who has ever visited the Castle has always slept here."

"Have there been many of them?" Verena enquired.

"I think Queen Anne was the last, Miss, but there were many before her."

It took Verena some time to look at the treasures in the room, to stare at the view from the window, to wash, and when she had taken off her bonnet to allow a superior but very skilful-fingered housemaid to rearrange her hair.

When finally she came downstairs over half an hour later, it was to see the flunkeys hurrying to the front door and she realised that the Duke's travelling carriage, also drawn by four superb horses, was arriving with Lady Bingley and Lady Edith Sheraton.

They were not alone, as Verena had anticipated; for Lady Edith's son, Captain Sheraton, was with them.

"Delighted to meet you, Miss Winchcombe," Harry Sheraton said when they were introduced. "Been hearing astounding dramatics about you from Theron."

There was a twinkle in his eye and Verena took an instantaneous liking to the young man, who had an amusing way of shortening his sentences so that at times she had to laugh at the way he phrased them.

"I regret that the other two guests I have invited, our cousins, Verena," the Duke said, "cannot be here until later this evening. Captain Winchcombe-Symthe is, I understand, on guard today and Jasper has offered to bring him down in his own Curricle."

Verena gave a start at the words. Had the Duke any idea, she wondered, that his Cousin's curricle was very different from anyone else's? Had there been something deliberate in the way he informed her that Jasper Royd would be bringing it to Selchester Castle?

Then she knew she was being imaginative. As far as the Duke was concerned he was merely being kind to her in inviting her Cousin, with whom he could not possibly have any taste in common save that for the last two months Giles had been serving in his Regiment.

And Jasper Royd? Why was he coming to Selchester Castle? Why had he accepted an invitation from the Duke when apparently they had not met for a long time?

There could only be one reason, Verena thought, that having failed in his first attempt to destroy his Cousin, he would try again! Yet how?

There was one thing that was very obvious in everything that had occurred to date, and that was that the "Evil Genius" had an uncanny sense of self-preservation.

He was not involved ostensibly in the Bullion robberies. Had the Duke been shot by the so-called Highwaymen on Hampstead Heath there was no one except Hickson who could connect Jasper Royd with the cowardly attack of four men on a traveller they expected to be unarmed!

Only Hickson was in the position of being able to incriminate the "Evil Genius." And Verena could not help guessing that Hickson himself sometimes wondered how long he would survive once Jasper Royd had no further use for him.

It was all frightening. At the same time to Verena, here in the Castle, laughing at the things Harry Sheraton was saying, seeing the Duke standing in front of the fireplace with a smile on his lips, his broad shoulders and great height seeming to dominate the Salon for all its size, it seemed as if the "Evil Genius" and his machinations were but a figment of the imagination!

The afternoon passed most pleasantly. The house-party visited the stables where Verena went into ecstasies over the Duke's horseflesh. They saw the goldfish ponds which ornamented the formal gardens and the fountains from Italy which played into sculptured stone basins.

They were shown the covered Tennis-Court where the Duke and Harry challenged each other at the game which Henry VIII had played so often at Hampton Court and at which each successive Duke of Selchester had been an expert.

And of course the Duke took them to the long Picture Gallery with its magnificent portraits of every succeeding owner of the Castle and their families; pictures from Holland, France and Italy that had been collected over the centuries, besides those by many English Old Masters.

"It is even more marvellous than I had expected," Lady Bingley said as she and Verena went up the stairs together to change for dinner.

"You like being here?" Verena asked.

"Who would not enjoy such a place?" Lady Bingley replied. "Ever since you came to stay with me, dearest child, you seemed to have waved a magic wand over my whole existence!"

She pressed Verena's arm and continued:

"I had grown low and depressed; I was feeling lonely and in the dismals until you appeared. Now I am meeting new people—people I have always longed to know—and renewing acquaintanceship with old friends, which recalls my youth and makes me feel young again."

"Lady Edith is charming!" Verena said.

"And so is her son!" Lady Bingley answered with a glance at Verena. "He is a very eligible young bachelor!"

It was strange, Verena thought, that her Godmother had never once suggested that there was any likelihood of the Duke being interested in her. It was somehow a dispiriting thought that Lady Bingley could not contemplate His Grace having even a passing attachment for anyone so insignificant and unimportant as herself.

"Yet I love him!" Verena thought as she stood looking out of the window of her bedroom over the parklands.

She loved him not because of his possessions or because he was a Duke—that indeed was a disadvantage in her eyes—she loved him because he was a man! Because he had been a soldier, and because her Grandfather would have approved of him.

But most of all she loved him because her heart leapt when she saw him; just to be beside him made her feel as if something drew her towards him, so that it was with considerable difficulty that she refrained from putting out her hand and touching him just to confirm he was there!

She changed for dinner and dressed herself with unusual care in one of the prettiest gowns she had bought from Madame Bertin in Bond Street.

She hoped the Duke would admire her in it, knowing that the soft shell-pink of the dress and the tiny roses that trimmed it made her look very young. At the same time it also gave her a sophisticated chic which was not to be found in the unfashionable gowns she had worn when he had seen her in her own home.

"Will his eyes show a little admiration for me?" she asked her reflection in the mirror.

But when she came down to the Salon before dinner the Duke was not alone. Giles was with him and Jasper Royd. They all three had glasses in their hands and as the footman opened the door she heard the Captain's loud laugh ring out. It sounded a jarring note which put her instantly on the defensive and a little afraid.

She stood for a moment uncertainly in the doorway. The Duke saw her first.

"Ah, here you are, Verena," he remarked. "And here are our missing cousins arrived safely from London."

"Need you have expected anything else?" the Captain asked, again for no apparent reason laughing. "The road is in excellent ply and there was no chance of our being delayed by Highwaymen or the like."

"Did you expect any?" the Duke enquired.

As he spoke Verena was aware of a quick glance which passed between the "Evil Genius" and the Captain. She remembered that they were neither of them supposed to know that anything untoward had happened to the Duke and herself on their way home the previous night across Hampstead Heath. She had not seen the Captain to relate to him what had occurred and the Duke would not have seen his Cousin.

Giles had been speaking loosely, and aware that he had made a slip, almost over-hastily he said:

"No, of course. I was but bamming. Highwaymen are a thing of the past!"

"I wish that were true!" the Duke said quietly. "After dinner I will tell you two Gentlemen a very strange adventure that befell me when I visited my Grandmother last night!"

"An adventure with Grandmama!" Jasper Royd interrupted.

"She fortunately was not involved," the Duke answered. "But Verena was, and as she wishes to forget a very unpleasant episode we will not talk of it now."

Again the Captain's eyes met those of Jasper Royd's and before anyone could speak further Harry Sheraton joined them, followed almost immediately by his mother and Lady Bingley.

Dinner was a gay meal and when the Ladies withdrew to the Drawing-Room it was only a quarter of an hour before they were joined by the Gentlemen. Verena wondered what had been said, but apparently it had not in any way upset Jasper Royd or made him suspicious.

The footman brought more drinks to the Salon and soon, with what Verena thought quite considerable dexterity, the Duke had the two elderly ladies, his Cousin Jasper, and Captain Winchcombe-Smythe seated at a table playing whist.

He then insisted that Harry Sheraton should challenge Verena to a game of chess.

"You are a better player than I am, Harry," the Duke said, "but I will wager my money on Verena. She is an expert!"

"Case of champagne I beat her!" Harry Sheraton replied promptly. "If so ungentlemanly not permit female be victor."

There was a twinkle in his eye as he spoke but Verena rose to the bait.

'Do not dare insult me!" she said. "I will beat you in

a fair game. That is, if I keep my fingers crossed for luck."

"I should warn you," the Duke smiled, "Verena is not only superstitious but almost uncannily clairvoyant. It will not be a fair game, my poor Harry. She will use every magic wile she knows. A hundred years ago she would have been burnt as a witch."

"I thought you did not believe in my premonitions." Verena said, looking up at the Duke.

"I do now," he answered quietly, and she flushed as she knew to what he was referring.

The evening passed swiftly and when she was in bed Verena wondered if in fact the dangers and horrors of the night before had really happened.

One thing, however, was unquestionable: she loved the Duke more every moment she was with him. When he looked at her with a twinkle in his eyes her heart leapt in her breast!

When he touched her hand as they said goodnight she had a wild impulse to throw herself into his arms, to confess that she loved him, to tell him that his life was in danger.

Then pride made her determine that he must never know of her love. He must never guess that when he had kissed her fingers she had longed with a hopeless but inexpressible yearning for him to kiss her lips!

She tossed and turned restlessly in her bed, one moment quivering with love, the next distraught with terror lest the Duke might die at the hand of the "Evil Genius."

Verena was coming downstairs the following morning when she saw beneath her in the great Hall her Cousin and Jasper Royd standing close together.

The "Evil Genius" was holding a note which had obviously just been delivered to him by a footman who was walking away with a silver salver in his hand.

Jasper Royd opened the note and read it slowly. Verena, coming down the stairs, her soft slippers making no sound on the thick carpet, heard the Captain say:

"All right?"

"All right," the "Evil Genius" replied, and there was a note of satisfaction in his voice.

He tore the note into several small pieces, and very quietly, so that Verena could only just hear the words, he added:

"We will slip away at the first opportunity."

As he spoke he walked across the Hall to the big fire-place where although it was summer a log was glowing on a mound of ashes. He threw the fragments of the note into the fire and as he did so the Captain glanced up and saw Verena descending the stairs.

"Good-morning, Verena," he said. "You are early. I did not expect to see you until the world was well-aired."

"You forget I am a country lass," Verena replied. "Are we riding this morning?"

"I planned that for this afternoon," the Duke's voice behind her remarked.

She turned round to see him quietly and discreetly dressed in one of his favourite grey whip-cord jackets, his pantaloons the colour of pale champagne, his cravat skilfully tied and without a jewel-pin.

The Captain on the contrary was as flamboyant as a West Indian parrot, and as they went into breakfast Verena wondered how anyone could be so tasteless, so vulgar, and yet be unaware of it.

The Captain had expressed a desire to see the Duke's horses, so once again they visited the stables. Verena could hardly bear to listen to the ignorant remarks he made, or to the manner in which he boasted of his own horseflesh.

The Duke, however, treated her Cousin with a courtesy which was all the more shaming because she knew how easily he could have snubbed him. Jasper Royd, she guessed, was not listening to their conversation, being intent on mental stocktaking of what he was determined would one day be his!

It was, naturally, the "Evil Genius" who wished to visit the Estate Office so that they could see the plans and maps of the Estate. On a table in the office was a model of the Castle and its surrounding buildings, exquisitely contoured. Verena was as fascinated by it as a child would have been.

"I always wanted to play with it when I was young," the Duke told her, "but I was never allowed to do so. Perhaps it was a good thing because it would probably have been damaged. It was made a century ago and every detail is correct to scale."

Verena looked at the river, painted blue and winding through fields and marshland until it passed in front of the Castle.

"What is this?" she asked, pointing to something marked on a tiny little island in the centre of the river.

"That is a Temple," the Duke answered, "erected by my Grandfather. He bought it back from Greece and had it re-erected here. It is rather incongruous in an English landscape but at the same time very beautiful."

"And this?" she asked, pointing to a building a little further along the river and right on the edge of the water.

"That is the Old Mill," the Duke replied. "You see the river is bridged just below it and there is another drive going through the Park and up to the main road. The Mill is no longer in use, but when Jasper and I were boys we used to watch the big wheel going round and the water dripping from it."

"If this model is to be brought up-to-date you will have to enlarge the stables, Theron," his Cousin remarked.

"They look very small," the Duke answered, moving to another part of the model, "but I believe our Grandfather kept nearly two hundred horses in those buildings."

"They would not be large enough for him today!" Jasper said, "or for you!"

"No, indeed!"

His Grace turned away but Verena noticed that his Cousin's eyes followed him and she saw the almost fanatical hatred in them.

"He is dangerous—dangerous as a wild animal!" she thought.

She knew then that she would have to tell the Duke the truth. She could not let him continue in ignorance of the "Evil Genius's" intention. In saving his feelings she might be placing a noose round his neck.

"Save him, please God, save him!" she prayed soundlessly.

But even if she never was to see the Duke again she wanted him free of the menace his cousin constituted. Only God could protect him for evil always had an advantage in plotting and striking secretly and without warning.

"I have ordered the horses for two o'clock," the Duke said as they went into Luncheon. "I have a feeling, Ma'am," he added to Lady Bingley, "that you and Lady Edith may wish to enjoy a quiet siesta after Luncheon."

"Your Grace is very considerate," Lady Bingley answered, "and indeed I am sure that Lady Edith and I will find it a wise precaution if we are to challenge these experienced gamesters again tonight."

"You do not mean to tell me that you played Ladies against Gentlemen at the card-table?" the Duke asked.

"We did indeed," Lady Bingley answered, "and Lady Edith and I won by only two points—not a very big win you might say but still a famous victory as far as we are concerned."

"Tonight our luck will change!" Captain Giles prophesied, and finished his sentence with a laugh.

Verena went upstairs when Luncheon was over to change into her riding-habit. It was one she had bought in Bond Street and was exceedingly becoming. The emerald green velvet was frogged with black braid and had sparkling buttons which she thought when she chose them were extremely distinctive.

Her fashionable high hat was very different from the old tricorn she had worn for so long, and sported a green guaze veil which floated out behind her as she rode. Copying the Duke, she wore her hat at an angle, but she was too perturbed to realise that it made her look provocative.

She was waiting in the Salon for the rest of the party and the Duke, followed by Giles and Jasper Royd, had just joined her, when the Butler announced:

"His Excellency the Minister for Hungary and the Princess Zazeli Muzisescu, Your Grace."

The Duke turned round in astonishment as with a little cry of delight the most entrancing creature Verena had ever seen ran across the room to him.

She had the impression of dark flashing eyes, of an inviting red mouth, of a sinuous figure barely disguised by a pelise of crimson silk and a bonnet covered with feathers of the same hue which was so French and so outrageously smart that Verena could only stare.

"*Mon brave*, you are surprised to see me? I saw the flag flying on the Castle as Viktor and I drove past. 'He is there!' I exclaimed. 'The Duke—that adorable but elusive *gentil homme* who leaves London the very moment I arrive!'"

"This is indeed a surprise!" the Duke said when he could make himself heard.

Zazeli clung to his arm to look up into his eyes, outrageous as usual in shamelessly displaying her confidence that her partiality for the Duke must be reciprocated by him.

"How are you, Viktor?" the Duke asked her husband, who, handsome and diplomatically suave, was watching the encounter between his wife and His Grace with a faint air of amusement.

"Delighted to see you," the Minister replied. "But forgive our intrusion. Zazeli insisted that you were at home and who can deny Zazeli?"

"Who indeed?" the Duke replied. "Let me present my friends."

"But I know Harry," Zazeli cried impetuously, holding out her hand to him but still retaining her hold on the Duke's arm.

"What are you about? Wicked enchantress?" Harry asked, kissing the gloved hand she extended to him and looking into her eyes with a quizzing expression in his.

"What am I about? *Hélas!* How English! What a banal question!" Zazeli replied. "I am reminding this bad Duke of yours that his manners are excruciating! His behaviour to someone who loves him is disgraceful! If we had time, I would ask Viktor to 'call him out'. *Mais alors* we have a reception in London this evening and must not stay long."

"You must at least stay long enough for us to drink your health," the Duke answered. "And now let me try again, Zazeli, to present Miss Winchcombe, my Cousin Jasper Royd, and Captain Giles Winchcombe-Smythe."

Verena curtsied but was well aware that the Hungarian's beautiful eyes merely fluttered over and the little bow of her head was so perfunctory as to be almost insulting.

The Princess was far more effusive to Jasper Royd, and Giles received a bewitching smile which obviously cast him into an ecstasy.

Champagne was brought but no one needed any further stimulant than Zazeli's conversation. She flirted outrageously with the Duke, but at the same time she managed to keep the three other men all hanging on her words.

She made them laugh; she made the Duke apologise for a dozen things he swore he had not done; and the whole atmosphere seemed to pulsate with her beguiling, exciting personality.

After a little while Verena slipped away. She was jealous—desperately jealous! And frank enough to admit it! She could not bear to see this exciting creature, as beautiful as a Bird of Paradise, looking up into the Duke's eyes or to watch the expression in his.

Unsophisticated though she was, Verena knew instinctively that the Duke and this lovely woman had been lovers. Perhaps he still loved her. How could she know? She only knew that the pain within her breast was an agony which she had never known before in her whole life.

She wanted to run away; she wanted to hide; she wanted to cry; and yet her eyes felt dry and past tears.

Hardly realising what she was doing she walked out of the Salon and into the Ante-Room. She stood there for a little while fighting for self-control, and then because she could not bear even to think of the Duke she felt she must go outside.

She must ride Assaye; she must get away from the Castle!

The horses which had been ordered were waiting outside the front door, each with an attendant groom. Then as Verena came down the steps she saw driving across the bridge which spanned the river—a curricle!

There were two men in it, and she knew as she saw them go who they were. When she had left the Salon Jasper Royd and her Cousin Giles must have left immediately afterwards. It was the opportunity of which they had spoken, she thought. The moment for which they had been waiting!

It would have been impossible for the Duke to leave The Minister and his wife, and Harry Sheraton would remain with him.

With sudden resolution Verena hurried to Assaye. As usual he gave a little whinny at her appearance, but without stopping to pet him as she usually did, she told the groom to assist her into the saddle.

"Are you waiting for the others, Miss?" the groom enquired.

"No, I am riding in the Park," Verena answered.

Then putting Assaye into a trot she hurried up the drive, realising as she did so that the curricle was almost out of sight. But under the shade of the lime trees Assaye, in a gallop, soon began to catch up.

The curricle turned out of the main gates with Verena not so very far behind, and when she reached the main road it was to see it speeding along in a cloud of dust.

She hesitated for a moment, wondering, since there was no cover from view on the road, what they would think if they looked back and saw her. Then she saw the curricle about two hundred yards away turn right and re-enter the Park.

She guessed then where Jasper Royd was going. He

had left the main road and was instead proceeding up the other drive which had been marked on the plan they had been admiring that morning in the Estate Office—the drive which led to the Old Mill.

In that instant her gift of clairvoyance told Verena what had occurred. It told her that that very morning a Bullion coach had been held up on the Dover Road. The note which the "Evil Genius" had destroyed so carefully had been from Hickson to tell him that the loot had been hidden in a safe place.

And what place safer or more improbable as far as anyone else was concerned than the old Mill on the Selchester Estate?

It would have everything that the "Evil Genius" required: a place for hiding not far from the main road; water, in the shape of the river, into which the Bullion boxes could be thrown once their contents had been removed; and the advantage that no one would ever guess at such a hiding-place!

Verena turned Assaye round. There was no reason for her to go on to the main road. She could keep in the Park in the shelter of the trees and see if she was not right in her supposition.

She rode inside the wall and sure enough as she came to a rise in the ground she could see the curricle speeding down the other drive and in the far distance, out of sight of the Castle and hidden from it completely by a belt of pine trees, the Old Mill.

Moving under the boughs of the great trees, Verena followed. It was only as she saw the curricle crossing the bridge which led to the Mill that she wondered if she should go back to the Castle and tell the Duke what was happening.

Then she knew she could not speak to him while the Hungarian was with him. She could imagine the laughter and the innuendoes with which that exquisite creature would tease him should she go to the door of the Salon and ask to speak to him alone.

She knew also there would not now be time to fetch the Duke and return to the Mill to catch Jasper Royd and her cousin Giles red-handed.

It would not take them long to empty the Bullion boxes. Verena knew how swiftly the "Evil Genius" and Hickson had managed it. In a quarter of an hour they would be clear of the Old Mill; the boxes would have been dumped into the water; and they would drive back to the Castle with some excellent excuse for having left so precipitately.

No, she thought, she would look for herself and see if once again they had hidden the stolen bullion in the curricle. She could inform the Duke of that later; but how foolish she would look if Jasper Royd had made other plans.

It was in the curricle he had hidden the gold the first time she had seen him at work, but now he might have evolved some quite different scheme. Who could foresee how his mind worked?

She was riding nearer and nearer to the Old Mill. She saw that the bridge had been built as part of a lock which had regulated the flow of water through the Mill. Now, the water was flowing through unrestricted.

Verena drew Assaye to a standstill. She had an idea! She would send Assaye home and the Duke would, on being informed that the horse had come back riderless, come and search for her.

He would remember—surely he would remember—that he only had to tell Assaye to find her for the horse to seek her out as he had done ever since he was a foal.

If when the Duke arrived Jasper Royd and her Cousin Giles had left and there was no evidence of what they had been about, she could always say she had had a fall; that Assaye had put his foot in a rabbit-hole and then galloped home without her.

The Duke might not believe such a story, but he would not challenge her in public, and when they were alone she could tell him what she suspected. Verena slipped from Assaye's back, patting him and said in his ear:

"Go home, Assaye. Go home at once! Go home!"

Assaye put his muzzle against her cheek and obediently went on his way, the stirrup flapping at his side. Verena waited until she was quite certain he was going towards the Castle, then moving very softly in case her footsteps were heard, she crossed the bridge.

She saw a clump of bushes by the Mill and thought she could hide in them, after she had listened to what was taking place inside. Jasper Royd's curricle was standing outside an open door, the horses tied to a post. Verena had hoped to find a window through which she could look without being seen but found only a blank wall.

She drew near to the open doorway and she could hear the murmur of voices. Then, as she crept a little closer she heard the Captain say:

"Not a very big haul!"

"About five thousand pounds, I should think," the "Evil Genius" replied. "But worth having. It would have been a pity to pass it up!"

"Yes, indeed, although tomorrow's load for Dover will be double or treble this!"

"All the same I am grateful to the Bank of Canterbury," Jasper Royd answered. "I am not so wide-mouthed as you, Giles. I am thankful for small mercies!"

"So am I!" the Captain agreed—over-eagerly, Verena thought, as if he would ingratiate himself. "I was really apologising to you for the spoils not being larger!"

"You need not apologise," the "Evil Genius" said. "You deal very competently with that obliging gabster in the Bank. At the same time if he endangers our security in any way, you will have to dispose of him!"

"Hickson can see to that," the Captain replied quickly, as if he had no wish to take such action personally.

As they were talking there was a clink of coins, and Verena knew that they were putting the sovereigns into the bags as she had seen the "Evil Genius" do before. She moved a little further into the doorway.

As she did so she trod on a pebble and it made a very slight sound. She held her breath, fearful that it might have been heard! She thought that for a moment there was a pause in their conversation. Then the "Evil Genius" continued.

"No one is more efficient than Hickson at disposing of undesirables!"

"Was he perturbed at what happened on Hampstead Heath?" Giles asked.

"No, not in the slightest," the "Evil Genius" answered. "Hickson is extremely resourceful. So resourceful, my dear Giles, that we never need worry ourselves however difficult a situation might appear, or whatever we may have to . . ."

Verena gave a sudden scream. Round the corner of the doorway against which she had been leaning, listening to what was being said, a hand came out and caught her by the neck.

It was so sudden, so unexpected that she could not struggle, could not even turn to run away before the fingers, hard and biting cruelly into her soft skin, dragged her inside the Mill.

"Well, what a surprise!" the "Evil Genius" remarked. "If it is not your future wife, Giles—sweet ingenuous little Verena—spying on us!"

11

Verena was for the moment unable to speak because of the pressure of Jasper Royd's fingers on her throat. Then as he released her, Giles, jumping up from where he had been crouching behind a bullion box, exclaimed:

"Verena! What are you doing here? Why did you follow us?"

The "Evil Genius" relaxed his grip and Verena, her hands going to her bruised neck, managed to reply:

"I thought . . . you would . . . w.wish me to be . . . with y.you!"

"You thought nothing of the sort!" Jasper Royd ejaculated. "Tell the truth, you were spying on us, were you not?"

Verena looked into his face and knew that somehow she must try to extricate herself from the danger she was in.

"No . . . of course . . . not!" she managed to say.

Her words ended in a cry as he slapped her hard across the cheeks.

"You are lying!" he said accusingly. "It was you who warned Theron of the attack on Hampstead Heath. I was suspicious at the time; now I am sure! You know too much, Miss Winchcombe, and there is only one thing to be done about you!"

There was so much menace in his tone that Verena instinctively braced herself. She was a soldier's daughter! She would not show herself a coward in front of a man like this!

"What do you mean, Jasper?" the Captain questioned before she could speak.

"I mean," Jasper Royd replied, "that your Cousin is going to be most regrettably drowned. For your information, Miss Winchcombe, we will hold your head under the water until you are dead and then throw your body into the river. There will be no question of foul play!"

Verena drew in a deep breath. She knew that Jasper Royd meant exactly what he had said, that he had every intention of translating his threats into action. No amount of pleading from her or anyone else would alter his determination.

She had endangered his security and therefore must die unless the Duke could reach her in time.

"But Jasper, you cannot do that!" the Captain exclaimed. "Verena has not yet signed a will in my favour!"

Verena looked at him scornfully.

"Do you suppose, Giles," she asked, "that I did not realise you were asking me to sign my own death-warrant?"

"You blasted fool! You clumsy idiot!" Jasper Royd stormed. "I told you to be careful what you said! Can no one carry out my orders competently?"

"I want to own the Winchcombe Estate!" the Captain said sullenly, looking, Verena thought, like a small boy who has been denied some special treat on which he has set his heart.

"Then want must be your master!" the "Evil Genius" snapped.

His hand went out to take Verena's arm as he spoke and she forced herself not to wince away from him. She would at least die proudly, not cringing, not crying or pleading with a man so despicable, so utterly barbarous.

Suddenly the "Evil Genius" gave an exclamation:

"I have a better idea!" he said. "One which in fact is even safer than destroying this inquisitive chit by drowning. You will marry her, Giles! You have the Special Licence, I suppose?"

"Yes, I obtained it as you told me to do," the Captain answered, drawing it from his inner pocket as he spoke.

"At least one of my orders has been carried out," the "Evil Genius" snarled. "Very well, we will repair at once to the Church in the village. I know the old Vicar and I will tell him some yarn about your being a runaway couple!"

"I will not marry Giles," Verena ejaculated.

"You will marry him," the "Evil Genius" contradicted, "and remember that even though you live, a wife cannot give evidence against her husband. I have thought of that, you interfering jade, because there is no detail that escapes my mind!"

"That I can well believe!" she retorted, "a detail like murder, for instance!"

She glanced at him contemptuously as she spoke, half expecting him to hit her once again. But he merely grinned at her evilly, and she thought that in some horrible way he even admired her courage.

"You will marry him," he said silkily, "but it will not be for long—do not let the thought of that perturb you!"

He turned towards the Captain who was still standing by the bullion boxes, a sack of sovereigns in his hand.

"Giles, you will drive from the Church to the 'King's Head'. It is about a mile and a half down the road towards Dover. You will find Hickson there, and as you are so squeamish I know that he will oblige in getting rid of your wife!"

"How will he manage that?" the Captain asked, without apparently any regret or even surprise at the thought.

"A carriage accident would, I imagine, be the most plausible," the "Evil Genius" replied. "But I will leave you and Hickson to work out the details."

His lips curled as if he thought the idea was positively pleasurable.

"But do not let us waste time," he continued, "in case the alluring Madame Muzisescu should fail to hold my Cousin's interest. Let us throw the empty boxes into the river. You will see that Hickson, who—like myself—thinks of every detail, has left some bricks handy to weigh them down."

Turning his head towards Verena, Jasper Royd said:

"Do you wish me to tie you up? Or will you give me your word—which I have a feeling you will keep—not to run away? You would not run far in any case!"

"You have my word," Verena answered quietly.

She felt as she watched the two men put the bricks into the bullion-boxes and throw them through the aperture at the end of the mill which opened directly onto the river, that she must be living in some strange nightmare from which she could not awake.

Her cheek was burning from the violence of the "Evil Genius's" hand where he had struck her, but otherwise she felt curiously detached almost as if she was watching everything happening in a play-house.

It could not really be true that she was to die or that she was to be married to a man she loathed and despised even more than she hated the "Evil Genius."

It was like sinking into the depths of a foul degradation to recall that she had ever imagined for one moment that she could marry Giles or that he genuinely loved her.

He had only one idea and that was to obtain possession of the Estate which had belonged to the Winchcombes for generations.

Her Grandfather had been right—Giles was not a Winchcombe, he was a Smythe! And just as he had no real right to the name, none of the characteristics—the bravery or the honour—of the Winchcombes, had been transmitted to him.

It only took a few minutes for Jasper Royd and the Captain to dispose of the bullion-boxes, to pick up the sacks of coins, to carry them outside and stow them in the secret hiding-place in the curricle.

The "Evil Genius" returned to say with a mocking smile:

"Would your Ladyship condescend to honour my curricle? Pray seat yourself between us. We must not take any chances on your endeavouring to escape!"

Holding her chin high, Verena did what was asked, even though squeezed between the two men she felt disgusted by their close proximity.

"Where is your horse?" Jasper Royd asked as they crossed the bridge over the river.

Verena looked back in what she hoped was a convincing manner.

"I left him by those bushes," she answered.

The "Evil Genius" seemed satisfied with the explanation, but she was suddenly tense with fear lest her cousin should remember the tricks she had taught Assaye. He certainly must have known about them in the past.

But to her relief the Captain's thoughts were clearly concerned only with the present. For after a moment he asked in a low tone:

"Why did you have to interfere?"

"I do not wish to speak to you," Verena replied. "I am ashamed, Giles—ashamed that I ever believed that you were a trustworthy and decent man!"

"It is hard to be either without money!" he replied, "and you know how open-handed your parsimonious Grandfather was to me!"

"Do not dare to speak of him!" Verena exclaimed angrily. "I am only thankful that he is not alive to learn of your behaviour and to be aware that any relative of his, however slender the connection, should be a criminal!"

The "Evil Genius" laughed.

"High-flown words, Miss Winchcombe! Doubtless your husband may wish to punish you for them before he becomes so regrettably, so unexpectedly a widower!"

"It is you who have led Giles astray," Verena cried. "Do not put any more of your loathsome ideas into his head!"

"So you have realised that he is weak and very amenable?" the "Evil Genius" asked.

"Really, Jasper," the Captain interposed, "there is no need to be unpleasant about me!"

"Oh no, of course not!" the "Evil Genius" said with a sneer in his tone. "You are a very fine figure of a man—a credit to your Regiment, a sporting chap no one would credit for a moment with having the brains to rob a bank!"

"You pick your servants well," Verena said bitterly.

"Of course," the "Evil Genius" retorted. "As you have already recognised, I have a head for detail and can command my forces as well as any General in the field!"

As he spoke he drove the curricle out through the gates of the drive and Verena saw that directly opposite there was a small grey-stone Norman Church.

It stood a little apart from the village which lay further up the road. There was a lych-gate leading to a churchyard full of ancient tombstones, and a door into the Church was open. She saw the "Evil Genius" taking everything in with a quick glance of his dark eyes.

"It appears as if the Vicar may be here," he said, "if not, I will fetch him from the Vicarage. All you have to do, Giles, is to produce the Special Licence. I will do the talking."

He paused and looked at Verena.

"One word from you," he said menacingly, "just one word that you are being forced against your will to marry Giles, and the Vicar will have to die! Do you want that on your conscience?"

There was something in the way he spoke, so terrifying, that Verena's eyes fell before his.

"Remember what I have said, for I do not speak idly!"

As he spoke the "Evil Genius" stepped out of the curricle.

"What about the horses?" the Captain asked.

"They will stand," the "Evil Genius" replied. "But let us be sure that the moment you are wed, you can post for the 'King's Head'."

He beckoned as he spoke to a small boy kicking a stone about the road saying:

"Here, youngster, I'll give you a penny to hold my horses!"

The boy ran eagerly to the horses's heads.

"Oi'll 'old 'em, Sir!"

Jasper Royd walked away toward the Church. Verena moved across into his seat so as to be further away from her cousin.

"I am sorry about this, Verena," the Captain said in a blustering tone, which she knew was partly embarrassment.

"I do not wish to hear your apologies," Verena answered. "You disgust me!"

He shrugged his shoulders petulantly, but she knew at the same time that he was agitated and apprehensive. He kept glancing towards the Church door, looking up at the clock on the tower and drumming with his fingers against the side of the curricle.

After a few moments Verena could not help saying:

"You realise that you will be caught in the end, do you not? And even though you are a soldier, they will hang you, Giles! Hang you at Tyburn for all to see!"

"Be quiet!" he said furiously, "or I will box your ears! What the devil can Jasper be doing?"

Even as he spoke, the "Evil Genius" appeared in the porch and beckoned to them. Verena tried to be slow in stepping from the curricle. She still hoped that by some miracle the Duke would come to her rescue.

Even as she thought of it she knew how impossible it would be for the Duke to find her in time. Even if he were told that Assaye had returned to the Castle riderless, he might not at first understand what it implied. And then, if he did understand, Assaye would lead them to the Old Mill!

How could the horse lead them to the Church? It would be taxing him too high to play "hide-and-seek" in a place where he had never been before. But still she hoped and beneath her breath prayed for deliverance.

"Come on, hurry up!" the Captain said impatiently.

"My skirt is entangled in my heel," Verena answered,

stooping down and pretending to release the velvet hem of her habit.

"Never mind!" the Captain said impatiently, and clutching her by the arm he dragged her up the Church path.

She knew he was in a state of agitation. She could tell it by the tremor of his voice, by the roughness of his grasp, and by the way he was trying to pull her into a run.

They reached the porch.

"The Vicar is in his house," Jasper Royd said. "The Verger has gone to fetch him. Give me the Marriage Licence. I will talk with him and explain exactly what is required."

The Captain drew the Licence from his pocket and the "Evil Genius" took it from him.

"Go and sit in the front pew," he said, "you must keep out of sight. Anyone passing might see you and think it strange if you were outside the Church!"

He turned as he spoke and walked up the Aisle. The Captain and Verena followed him. The Church had rounded Norman arches and a beautiful stained glass window over the altar.

At the top of the aisle Verena entered a big, carved oak pew and sank on her knees.

"Help me, Oh God, help me! If it is possible, save me . . ."

She paused.

"If not, let me die bravely, without screaming, without crying, without showing that I am afraid!"

She thought of Hickson and shuddered. She had never been able to forget that smooth, sanctimonious face with its hard glittering eyes. She could remember the chuckle he had given when, before he left the cellar, he had looked down at the Duke—unconscious from the blow he had inflicted upon him.

Hickson would have absolutely no compunction in killing her, she knew. And then she was praying again.

The Church was very quiet. The only sound was that of the Captain's breathing and the disturbance he made as he fidgeted beside her. Verena felt the faith of generations was there to sustain her. It was almost like a cool hand laid comfortingly on her brow. Yet deep inside herself she was still desperately afraid—afraid not so much of dying, as of being afraid!

"How the devil can they be so long?" the Captain ejaculated.

But it was another five minutes before Jasper Royd appeared, the Vicar beside him. They approached the pew. Verena and Giles rose to their feet.

"Is this the young couple?" the Vicar quavered.

He was an old man—very old—with dead white hair and veined hands which trembled, and eyes which had difficulty in seeing.

"Mr. Royd tells me that you wish to be married," he said. "Is that right?"

"If you please, Sir," the Captain answered.

"They have very little time, Vicar, as I have already told you," the "Evil Genius" interposed. "If they are to catch the ship from Dover they must leave almost immediately!"

"Very good, my boy, it shall be as you wish," the Vicar said. "It seems only yesterday that you were but a child coming to me at the Vicarage asking me to help you with your Latin in the holidays. Ah well, we all get old!"

Muttering to himself, the old man disappeared into the Vestry.

"Damned old fool!" the "Evil Genius" whispered beneath his breath.

They all waited holding their breath, as it seemed to

Verena, until the Vicar came slowly into the Chancel wearing a surplice, a prayer-book in his hand.

"What about the ring?" the Captain asked suddenly.

The "Evil Genius" gave him a look of contemptuous disdain.

"Do you mean you had not thought of that?" he asked.

He drew his signet-ring from his finger as he spoke.

"Come along," he said sharply. "Get in front of the doddering old Clod-head!"

The Captain stepped out of the pew and Verena followed him. The "Evil Genius" stood beside them. For one moment Verena was tempted to scream out the truth—to cry that she would not marry a thief, a murderer, a felon, but she knew that Jasper Royd had not spoken idly when he had said he would kill the Vicar.

She had known as she sat next to him in the curricle that in the pocket of his driving-coat there was a pistol. She had felt it against her side.

He would not hesitate to use it, although she suspected—so that the blame would not fall on him—he would choose a better and more subtle way of killing the old man.

The Vicar was so ancient, so decrepit, that if he were merely flung violently to the ground there was every chance of it killing him!

"No," she thought, "I can say nothing!"

The Marriage Service began. The Vicar was slow but his cultured voice seemed to echo round the tiny Church as he read the prayers and the introduction to the Service. Then addressing the Captain he said:

"Say after me: 'I, Giles Rupert' "

"I, Giles Rupert," the Captain echoed.

"Take thee, Verena."

"Take thee, Verena."

"To my wedded wife."

"To my wedded wife."

Verena shut her eyes. There was no escape. She was not to be rescued; she was being married to this criminal. Even if she was murdered within a few hours of the ceremony, the idea of becoming her cousin's wife was a humiliation and a degradation beyond expression.

It seemed to her that Giles's voice speaking the words after the Vicar was very far away. Then it was her turn.

"Say after me," the old Clergyman said to her, " 'I, Verena . . .' "

For a moment Verena's voice seemed constricted in her throat. She could not speak, she could not force the words between her lips. At last, almost in a whisper she began:

"I, Verena . . ."

There were hurried footsteps in the porch then from the back of the Church a voice cried:

"Stop!"

She turned as her heart leapt and with an almost inexpressible joy she saw the Duke standing at the end of the aisle.

"Stop this mockery!" he commanded. "I will not permit it!"

"He has found us! We must get away, we must escape!" the Captain cried, his voice shrill and hysterical. "It was not my fault—Jasper made me do it!"

There was a sudden explosion of a shot with a deafening report! Verena, turning from watching the Duke advance towards them, saw Giles crumple and fall to the ground and a smoking pistol in the "Evil Genius's" hand.

For a moment she could only stare, shocked to immobility. Then she saw Jasper Royd draw another pistol from the pocket of his coat, transfer it to his right hand, and look towards the Duke.

"If I must face a trial," he said evilly, "I will be tried by my Peers."

He was bringing the pistol down on his target when Verena, realising what he was about, flung herself against him. She forced his hand upwards as he pulled the trigger and the shot passed harmlessly over the Duke's head. A second later Harry Sheraton, coming through the Vestry door, shot the "Evil Genius" dead!

He fell over Verena, who was still clutching his arm, pulling her down with him. But even as she reached the ground she felt herself caught up in a pair of strong arms and knew she was safe.

For the moment she must have lost consciousness, for when she was aware of what was happening she felt the sunshine on her face and the breeze on her hair.

Someone was holding her very tightly and because she was afraid it was but an illusion after the nightmare through which she had passed, she reached up her little hand to clutch at the lapel of the Duke's coat.

"It is all right, my brave darling," he said quietly, "you are safe."

She heard the click of the lych-gate as he pushed it open. Then something soft and warm nuzzled against her cheek.

"Assaye!" she murmured and opened her eyes.

"Yes, Assaye," the Duke said, "he led us here. Without Assaye I would never have found you!"

"We must . . . thank him," she said childishly.

"Of course we will," he answered.

The Duke stepped into the curricle waiting outside the gate and set Verena very gently on the seat. Her bonnet had fallen from her head and was caught only by its ribbons at her neck. He undid them, and let the bonnet fall on the floor of the curricle.

Then he threw the boy holding the horses a coin and looked towards the groom holding Salamanca and another horse in the shade of a pink may tree.

"Wait for Captain Sheraton," he ordered, and taking up the reins drove away from the Church.

Verena lay back against the cushions with her eyes closed. She felt as if she were still half unconscious, as if she could not realise what had happened except that she was safe and that her prayers had been answered.

Giles was dead! She did not have to marry him, she did not have to keep her promise! He was dead and she was free!

The Duke was driving the horses down the road, and now she realised as they turned that they had entered the main drive to the Castle and were in the shadow of the lime trees.

The Duke drove for a little distance, then took the horses off the drive and onto the grass verge. He drew them to a standstill and threw down the reins. The horses, not being spirited bloodstock like those he drove, immediately dropped their heads to the grass. Assaye, who had followed the curricle, did the same.

The Duke turned round in his seat and putting both his arms round Verena, drew her close to him.

"Once again, Elf, I have to thank you," he said softly, "for saving my life!"

She gave a shudder and hid her head against his shoulder.

"I . . . thought he . . . was going . . . to kill you," she murmured.

"How could you have been so crazy as to follow them?" the Duke asked. "I realised that was what you had done when Assaye came home without you. My courageous sweetheart, they might have hurt you!"

"They intended to . . . kill me," she answered. "I was to . . . marry Giles, we were to travel to the . . .

King's Head where . . . Hickson is waiting . . . I would have had what would have been called an accident and then . . . Giles could inherit the Estate."

"My God!" the Duke exclaimed, holding her so tightly she could hardly breathe. "It is my fault, Verena, you should never have been involved! Everything was planned for tomorrow. A fake consignment of bullion to Dover, soldiers hiding in the coach instead of the usual guards; and the arrest of Jasper and your cousin Giles in the Old Mill."

"You knew then?" Verena asked.

"I saw your face, my darling, when Jasper walked into the Drawing-Room," the Duke answered. "Why, my foolish little love, did you not trust me?"

"I thought . . . it might . . . embarrass you!" Verena faltered.

"Jasper's perfidy could not embarrass me," the Duke answered. "I was only desperately afraid for your safety! I knew how ruthless he would be if he guessed that you knew his secret!"

"But you asked him and . . . Giles to . . . stay at the Castle?"

"I wanted them under my eyes—and I wanted you beside me," the Duke answered. "I also had an idea that the Old Mill was too convenient a place of hiding for them to ignore it. Harry arranged everything else with his Colonel and the officials at the Bank."

The Duke paused and then he said:

"But I will never forgive myself, nor can Harry excuse himself, for overlooking the fact that a genuine movement of Bullion must have left the Bank this morning for another town. It was only when Assaye led us to the Mill that we realised what had happened."

"It was for . . . Canterbury," Verena answered.

"So through sheer stupidity I endangered your precious life," the Duke exclaimed.

"I was afraid," she said, her face still hidden in his shoulder, "afraid you would not . . . come in time to . . . save me!"

"If he had married you," the Duke said firmly, "I would have killed him before he touched you."

"He was not . . . interested in . . . me," Verena replied. "He only wanted . . . the Estate—a Winchcombe of Winchcombe—that is what he wished to be."

Forget him," the Duke commanded. "It is all over now."

His hand smoothed the silky softness of her hair.

"Why did you follow them alone?" he asked softly.

"The . . . Princess . . . is . . . so b.beautiful . . ." Verena stammered.

"I thought she might be the reason for your leaving the room," the Duke answered, "but my adorable Elf, there was no reason for you to be jealous of anyone! Do you not realise that I love you, my dearest Heart? And as far as I am concerned there is no other woman in the world!"

He drew her closer to him.

"How soon will you marry me?" he asked. "I am afraid for you to be away from me even for a moment."

Verena raised her head. He saw the wonder in her eyes, then with a little inarticulate cry she hid her face again.

"I . . . cannot," she whispered. "I cannot . . . marry you . . . I love you too . . . but you must realise . . . you must know . . . that I cannot . . . possibly be a . . . D.Duchess!"

There was an expression of tenderness in the Duke's eyes that no one had ever seen before. Then with a little smile on his lips he said:

"But of course not, and what a bad Duchess you would make! No air of consequence, no dignity, no icy manner in setting down an impertinence as you would brush a caterpillar from your salad!"

He felt Verena give a little choke of laughter, and he continued:

"The Duke, of course, agrees that such an unsuitable match would be unthinkable! But there is a simple soldier, Verena, who finds you are the only person in the world who can talk to him of elves and goblins, of sprites and dragons."

She quivered.

"Oh, Leopard," she whispered.

Then after a moment she asked hesitatingly:

"Could I not . . . just be with you . . . without having to marry . . ."

Her voice trailed away into silence.

"While deeply honoured by such a suggestion," the Duke replied, his eyes twinkling, "I would, of course, have to ask the permission of your Guardian."

"My Guardian . . .?" Verena questioned. "But that is . . . you!"

"And as your Guardian, Miss Winchcombe," the Duke said, "I must state firmly and categorically that I would never give my permission for an arrangement so certain to outrage the sensibilities of the Social World—except perhaps those of my Grandmama!"

Verena gave a strangled laugh, then murmured:

""But it is the . . . social world . . . which makes me so . . . afraid."

"I want you to answer me something truthfully," the Duke said. "If I were poverty-stricken without any prospect of bettering my circumstances—would you marry me?"

"But of course!" Verena replied instantly.

"And if I were a man of no account—a nonentity?"

"You do not suppose that would matter to me?" she asked.

The Duke sighed.

"It is very mortifying, Elf, to find that, after all we have been through together, you do not love me!"

"But I do!" Verena cried. "I do love you . . . more—much more—than I can ever . . . tell you!"

"Then, my foolish, ridiculous little goose," the Duke answered, holding her close to him, "why are we arguing about such trifles as rank and wealth, consequence and ceremony? We have, my darling, the only thing which matters!"

He felt her stir against him and very gently he put his fingers under her chin and raised her face to his.

"I cannot live without you, Elf," he said softly.

For a moment they looked into each other's eyes. He felt her tremble and knew that her heart was beating as violently as his. Then his arms tightened and very slowly, as if he must savour the moment, his lips sought hers.

It was a kiss as soft as the touch of a butterfly's wing, and yet Verena felt as if he lifted her high in the sky towards the sun. The world was forgotten.

They was one—a man and woman caught up in an ecstasy, untrammelled and free—so beautiful, so spiritual, that it was part of the divine itself . . .

"I love you!" the Duke ejaculated hoarsely. "God, how I love you!"

"I love . . . you . . . too," Verena whispered.

His lips sought hers again. He had not known a woman's lips could be so soft, so sweet, so innocent.

Then as he felt her quiver in his arms, as he knew that she responded to the pressure of his mouth, his kisses grew more insistent, possessive, passionate . . .

After a long time their lips parted but they looked again into each other's eyes and were spellbound by an enchantment so lovely that their faces were transfigured.

"My darling—my sweet—my little love—my Elf," the Duke said at length, and his voice was unsteady.

"Leopard! Leopard!" she whispered.

He held her close until at last with a sigh of utter happiness he said:

"Shall I tell you, dearest dear, what I have planned for us both?"

"Will I have to . . . talk to the Magistrates about what has . . . happened?" Verena asked.

"That is what I am determined to avoid," he answered, "and that is why, my beloved little Sweetheart, I intend that we shall be married tomorrow morning immediately a Special Licence arrives from London."

"Tomorrow . . . morning?" Verena questioned wide-eyed.

"We will be married in my private Chapel by my own Chaplain," he answered, "and then while Harry goes to London to face all the explanations and congratulations regarding the death of the Bullion robbers, you and I will leave quietly for the Coast. My yacht is waiting in Dover Harbour. We will cross the Channel and start our honeymoon in Belgium."

He knew as a tremor ran through her that she was excited at the idea.

"I thought," the Duke continued, "we would take with us not only my travelling carriage, but also Salamanca and Assaye. I would like to ride with you over the field of Waterloo. You could see where your Grandfather, your father and I fought."

"Could we . . . really . . . do that?" Verena asked.

"We can and we will," the Duke replied. "And then, my sweet dream, I intend to take you to Venice—a town devoted to love and lovers. When we return the nine-day wonder which will follow the discovery and death of the Bullion robbers will have been forgotten."

"It sounds wonderful!" Verena said. "So wonderful,

that I feel I must be dreaming! But you are sure . . . quite sure . . ."

She hesitated before she added in a very small voice:

"Perhaps if you helped me . . . I could . . . pretend to be . . . a good Duchess!"

"We will pretend together," the Duke answered. "I am not interested in Duchesses—only in an incorrigible, unpredictable but very adorable little Elf."

"You do not . . . think you will find it . . . dull being married to . . . me?" Verena asked anxiously as she thought again of the fascinating Madam Muzisescu.

"Dull!" the Duke exclaimed, and his eyes were dancing with laughter. "When I think what you have done already to my quiet, well-ordered, perfectly organised life, I am appalled at what the future will hold! I am quite certain that you will contrive that we will be attacked by pirates crossing the Channel; we shall be set upon by robbers in France and Belgium; and undoubtedly you will involve me in a Vendetta in Italy—you attract criminals!"

"It is not my fault," Verena said indignantly. "How can you be so unfair . . . so . . . ?"

"Odious is the right word," the Duke interposed. "But all the same I adore you, my irresistible Elf."

His lips were very close to hers. Verena slipped her arm round his neck.

"You are magnificent . . . Leopard," she whispered. "I know . . . you will . . . kill all the dragons."

She could say no more because the Duke's lips, compelling and demanding, held hers utterly and completely captive.

Barbara Cartland, the world's most famous romantic novelist, who is also an historian, playwright, lecturer, political speaker and television personality, has now written over 300 books and sold 200 million books over the world.

She has also had many historical works published and has written four autobiographies as well as the biographies of her mother and that of her brother, Ronald Cartland, who was the first Member of Parliament to be killed in the last war. This book has a preface by Sir Winston Churchill and has just been republished with an introduction by Sir Arthur Bryant.

Love at the Helm, a novel written with the help and inspiration of the late Admiral of the Fleet, the Earl Mountbatten of Burma, is being sold for the Mountbatten Memorial Trust.

Miss Cartland in 1978 sang an Album of Love Songs with the Royal Philharmonic Orchestra.

In 1976 by writing twenty-one books, she broke the world record and has continued for the following four years with twenty-four, twenty, twenty-three and twenty-four. She is in the *Guinness Book of Records* as the best selling author alive.

She is unique in that she was one and two in the Dalton List of Best Sellers, and one week had four books in the top twenty.

In private life Barbara Cartland, who is a Dame of the Order of St. John of Jerusalem, Chairman of the St. John Council in Hertfordshire and Deputy President of the St. John Ambulance Brigade, has also fought for better conditions and salaries for Midwives and Nurses.

Barbara Cartland is deeply interested in Vitamin Therapy and is President of the British National Association for Health. Her book *The Magic of Honey* has sold throughout the world and is translated into many languages. She has a magazine, *Barbara Cartland's World of Romance,* now being published in the U.S.A. The World of Oz travel bureau is doing Barbara Cartland's Romantic Tours in conjunction with British Airways.

EXCLUSIVELY FROM JOVE

All-new, never-before-published stories of romance by the internationally popular Barbara Cartland!

05444-5	A SONG OF LOVE	$1.75
05565-4	MONEY, MAGIC AND MARRIAGE	$1.75
05569-7	THE HORIZONS OF LOVE	$1.75
05860-2	COUNT THE STARS	$1.75

And, don't forget Barbara Cartland's other novels of romance from Jove:

05566-2	THE CAPTIVE HEART	$1.75
05560-3	THE COIN OF LOVE	$1.75
05568-9	THE COMPLACENT WIFE	$1.75
05497-6	DESIRE OF THE HEART	$1.75
05509-3	THE GOLDEN GONDOLA	$1.75
05859-9	THE UNKNOWN HEART	$1.75
05567-0	THE UNPREDICTABLE BRIDE	$1.75

Available at your local bookstore or return this form to:

JOVE PUBLICATIONS, INC.
BOOK MAILING SERVICE
P.O. Box 690, Rockville Centre
New York 11570

Please enclose 75¢ for postage and handling if one book is ordered; 25¢ for each additional book. $1.50 maximum postage and handling charge. No cash, CODs or stamps. Send check or money order.
Total amount enclosed: $

NAME

ADDRESS

CITY   STATE/ZIP

Allow three weeks for delivery.

SK-31